DEADLY DECEPTION

Jack Engelhard

GOLLEHON BOOKS™
GRAND RAPIDS, MICHIGAN

— m - 4/98 $ 24.00

FIRST EDITION

Library of Congress Catalog Card Number 97-73567

ISBN 0-914839-43-8
(International Standard Book Number)

GOLLEHON is an exclusive trademark of Gollehon Press, Inc.

GOLLEHON BOOKS are published by: Gollehon Press, Inc.,
6157 28th St. SE, Grand Rapids, MI 49546.

GOLLEHON BOOKS are available in quantity purchases; contact Special Sales.
Gollehon does not accept unsolicited manuscripts. Brief book proposals are
reviewed.

Printed in Canada

Books By
Jack Engelhard

Deadly Deception
Indecent Proposal
The Horsemen

Plays By
Jack Engelhard

Clark Street
No Visitors, Please
The Laughing Man

In writing this novel, I was very fortunate
to have so many good friends to count on
for information and counsel.

In gratitude (and in alphabetical order), I salute:

John Alcamo
Sid Ascher
Leo Flasch
Al Glasgow
John Gollehon
Rabbi Howard Kahn
Marvin Karlins
Glenn Lillie
Steven Miller
Larry Rubenstein
Sonny Schwartz
Steven Sless
Louis Yank

If the single man plant himself indomitably on his instincts, and there abide, the huge world will come round to him.

— Ralph Waldo Emerson

*This novel is dedicated, happily, and once again,
to Leslie, David, and Rachel; also to Sarah in Jerusalem,
and to the loving memory of my parents, Noah and Ida,
who added Eleazar to my name.*

CHAPTER 1

Dewey stood there at the craps table, sucking on a cigar a mile long, eyes narrowed in deadly concentration as the dice made the rounds. He was alert to the ebb and flow of the action, but he showed no emotion, inscrutable, taming the gambling tiger that raged in his gut. He was coiled, but he'd never let on. The cigar wasn't lit. He'd light it up when his turn came, if, that is, he decided to shoot at all. First, he needed that feeling in his bones—that telling rush. If it felt right he'd play, and play big.

Dewey was a big man and he did everything big. He had big connections here and abroad and when he had troubles, he had big troubles. Very big. Dewey was on the brink, in dire need of half a million—never mind what for. But he needed the cash like yesterday. He'd never been so desperate, on the edge of despair. He used to go to church to get himself saved. Now he came to the casinos, just like the rest of America that had caught the fever and found religion in Our Lady of Slots.

He had already traded in five thousand in cash for greens and blacks—$25 and $100 chips—which were neatly lined up in cascades in front of him, like an army poised to march upon his command. No symbolism intended. To Dewey Smith, this was war. Life and death.

This was always the case when Dewey gambled, but especially so today. Every player had his reasons for pursuing the American jackpot, beyond the obvious inclination for riches, and round this table surely each man had his own yearnings, dreams, and secrets, but Dewey had a secret, his reason for being here, that he was ashamed to whisper even to himself. But it had to be done. The girl had to go down. She had asked for it, and in this life you get what you ask for, if it's trouble you want. Trouble you want, trouble you get, mess with Dewey.

This was a black-chip table here at the famous Versailles Hotel/Casino in Atlantic City—a hundred dollars MINIMUM—and when the action was good, there was enough money spread out to buy a heart transplant or two, but nobody thought of it directly in those terms since those were chips on the layout and chips were chips—made you lose all contact with reason.

Right now the action was *not good,* not good at all, Dewey was thinking, as he watched the dice thump lifelessly from end to end, from shooter to shooter, without a pass in sight. The table was ice cold, void of the magic that happens when one man, a dice messiah who happens along only now and then, sets the table ablaze and those red and white cubes come to life and streak across like shooting stars. *That's something,* Dewey was thinking, *but it sure ain't now.*

Right now the action was so slow and predictable that the dealers—in fact, the entire crew—practically forgot the players and started yawning and swapping shoptalk as if they were already off the clock. The stickman, distracted by boredom and snoozing on his feet, kept forgetting who was next.

"Yo, Stick, it's my shoot!"

"Sorry, pal."

Poker-faced, aloof, seemingly detached, Dewey assumed the attitude of an observer as the flirtatious dice kept changing partners to the sound of groans and hisses as the call *seven-out, line away* resounded and the dealers swiftly and pitilessly scooped up the chips and gathered in the remains of a thousand shattered dreams.

"Let's see us a shooter," was the refrain, with the addendum, "for shit's sake."

That could be me, thought Dewey, *if I so decide.* But he still wasn't in the mood and kept abstaining when his turn came—seeing that the table was still cursed and wanting no part of the blame.

How bad can it get? he was thinking, when along came a wild-eyed, spike-haired cowboy dashing up from out of nowhere, breathing fire and set to make a one-roll killing, betting five hundred on a hard 10, odds eight to one. "Hard 10, asshole, the lady's friend," he sneered at the stickman who in his apathy mistakenly placed the man's five black chips on a hard 8. "What the hell is this, some kinda clip joint?" the cowboy persisted.

The boxman gave the man a reproachful stare: "Watch your manners, son."

"I'm nobody's son and the name's Rodney, asshole."

"Okay, Rodney, we'll teach you some manners."

"Like hell you will. Who the hell is shooting? Let's go."

Some guy down the other end was shooting and immediately rolled a 6-4, 10 the easy way.

"Too bad," said the boxman shaking his head in mock sympathy. "This is so-o-o sad."

"Goodbye, Rodney," taunted the crew as the cowboy fled, fairly tripping over the tail between his legs.

Dewey kept taking it all in—and he almost smiled. *So many punks and losers in this world,* he was thinking.

Things were no better for the squat curly-haired lady playing the field. She kept getting wiped out as hardly any field numbers were rolling. Mostly 7s were still happening and almost always at the wrong time. So only the guy playing wrong—the *don't* pass-line—had anything to crow about and he sure didn't do much crowing because he was betting against the shooter, against the *table*. So it wasn't exactly safe for him to cheer and wake up the angry dead.

Dewey, the unlit cigar still planted defiantly in his mouth—Dewey wasn't angry. Nothing to get angry about, being the innocent bystander that he was, though as time went on, restraint was becoming less and less of a virtue for him. He was getting ready to *pounce*. The only question was *when*.

"Innocent" was hardly the term for Dewey and he'd be the first to admit as much.

Neither, however, would he concede that he was bad. He sure didn't think of himself that way. Instead, being his own judge, he saw himself as a good man who had to do bad things every so often in order to survive, which, he figured, made him no different from the rest of humanity. We're all just trying to survive: it's in the genes, and we do what it takes. No such thing as good and evil. We're all good. We just do bad things, that's all. Plain old human nature, and not just human. Think of the beasts, they hunt; for what? For food. They hunt and kill for food and this is no different. It's all about food and the hunting and the killing for it, and craps, craps is the hunt!

For the moment, Dewey was merely stalking.

He wasn't a regular here at the Versailles, so *caution* was the word.

Dewey was still impassive when the dice made their way to the guy next to him, who had stepped up only moments before, politely asking if there was room for another couple of elbows, Dewey just shrugging as if to say, "It's your funeral, sucker." At a cold table, when it wasn't being abandoned altogether in unanimous disgust, the traffic was a series of comings and goings, so here was another lamb ready for slaughter. This new guy, as Dewey had him measured, wasn't much. Dewey never played another man's roll anyway. Make that *usually* never. Oh, once in a while he spotted a slicker and took a ride with him. This individual, though, would have to be something special, preferably a cigar-man like himself, never a cigarette smoker with fright in his eyes. Never *anybody* with quick, nervous motions or that hang-dog look to the face. The face was not only a mirror to the soul, at the craps table it was a reflection of mastery or subjugation—and a man's conduct at craps was the entire man in a nutshell, which was why the game was no game but the measure of life itself, individual by individual, vulnerable, fully exposed against the caprice of the dice, and the dice representing nothing more, nothing less than the whim of existence.

Occasionally Dewey put some money down—not much, say a couple of greens on the line, if it was a woman shooting for the first time. He believed in beginner's luck. He also believed that some women have something of the witch in them. He once did very well at the Tropicana when a black guy from Haiti was blowing voodoo on the dice and sweeping the box numbers, 4, 5, 6, 8, 9, and 10, for 50 magical minutes. Dewey had liked black people ever since, though he'd never really been bigoted against any particular group since he hated practically everybody anyway, especially nowadays with the entire world on his neck. But all that was rare, so far as playing on another's shoot. Dewey only trusted Dewey.

That's because, now in his 50s and been around, he had a sixth sense that split the winners from the losers. He read it in the face, the eyes, the gestures. The *attitude*. Winners had an attitude. A boldness. A command. A presence. Losers were meek and maybe someday the meek would inherit the earth, but no, never the craps tables.

So losers, meaning the majority at any craps table and even the majority of any given population, were to be shunned lest they contaminate—like husbands who let their wives interfere during a game. Guy's shooting the eyes out of the dice, everybody around him cleaning up. Along comes the wife after tapping out at the machines: "Hi, honey, how ya doin'?"—the kiss of death. Guaranteed the guy throws a 7. Never fails. Wives, always bad luck. Hell, even randomness, supposed to be the name of the game—even randomness had rules, predictable moments, like when the shooter tosses one over the table, dice come back and you can bet your firstborn that the jerk immediately rolls a killer 7. Same deal if the dice hit someone's hand on their way to the wall—and usually it's the hand of a first-timer that does the damage. That's why you hated having them around.

This creampuff next to Dewey belonged to the majority. A loser, in other words. Or so it seemed. He was just a kid. Maybe 30; young for a rich table or any kind of table. Craps was a game for men 50 and up, men who knew combat, men who still referred to women as gals, men who knew no movie stars beyond John Wayne and thought music ended with Frank Sinatra.

This kid, the product of another age, was dressed in blue jeans and blue polo shirt. A bit casual for a black-chip game. Actually downright disrespectful.

Dewey was insulted by the mockery of an apparent chippy and kept crowding the kid, who took no notice. Dewey expected severity and reverence at the craps table, so much money at stake, money and pride and power. Mostly money, as money encompassed all the rest. Money was everything to Dewey, especially now that he was so down-and-out, practically broke, broke and broken, so full of urgency despite his cool demeanor. So today he was here for keeps and he was not here for the FUN of it, for shit's sake, and how he hated people who played for *fun*. You want *fun?* Shoot marbles. Not dice.

Talk about cool. This shooter next to him now shaking the dice for his first toss from the second-base side of the table was the epitome of it, if *cool* was the word instead of clueless, but he sure was noticeable for some reason, as eyes all around the casino seemed to be focusing on him.

He was sort of good looking, Dewey had to admit, brown hair with reddish highlights, slim, trim, delicate features, poetic eyes, hair long in the back but no pony tail, and no earring, for crissake (take the '90s and shove it!), but the expression on his face was that of boredom, blank, like any minute he'd break into a yawn—like he'd seen it all or seen nothing.

There was something altogether too passive and too serene about him, as if he didn't care, as if he were Alan Ladd in *Shane*—Dewey's favorite movie. He always wept when the boy cried "Shaaaane, Shaaaane."

They didn't make movies like that anymore, and what was so great about *Shane* was that there wasn't much killing in it. Only one guy got killed, so far as Dewey could remember, and that was Jack Palance. One killing. Now, that's real violence, and that's real justice. Sometimes justice had to be done even if it wasn't Jack Palance, even if it was just a girl of 16.

But about this clown next to him, this kid, he simply did not have the face for war. The kid lacked gravitas. Actually, the kid lacked just about everything. He had no attitude at all. Not of a winner, not of a loser. Probably—it figured—just a day-tripper, a greenie who lost his way from the video poker machines; the usual stray from the slot pits. A refugee.

On the come-out the kid rolled a couple of naturals—first a 7, then an 11, winners, then tossed an 8, his point, and a couple of tosses later nailed it the easy way, which caused the players to rejoice with high-fives and fists in the air and shouts of "Yeah!" FINALLY. Jeez.

"We got us a shootTAH," bellowed the stickman, but maybe just for the whammy.

Dewey saw it, of course, but Dewey was not impressed and still demurred, on the proposition that everybody gets lucky once in a while, even losers get a moment, like broken clocks that still get it right twice a day.

The kid, now with some character to his features, and in fact beginning to take on a Christlike appearance with those blazing eyes and that comely bloodless complexion, then came out on a 6, the dice turning up 4-2, and damned if he didn't come right back with it 3-3 after zipping those galloping dominoes in a sublime, fluid motion. Couple of boys had it the hardway, at a nine-to-one payoff.

Hmmm, thought Dewey. Just *hmmm.* Nothing more. Still tracking.

But from the boys, more cheering and backslapping, and now believers, they started pressing their bets. Maybe this was the long-awaited redeemer, the messiah, except that this particular messiah didn't appear to have too much confidence in his own powers, increasing his own bets just lightly—other than the 5, on which he kept telling the dealer to keep on pressing, as if waiting for the 5 to erupt and wanting to be there to pick up the spoils.

"Please try to hit the wall, Mr. R.," cautioned the boxman between numbers, which the kid kept nailing.

"No problem."

So it's Mr. R., thought Dewey.

The boys followed Mr. R. on the 5 and upon all his other place-bets and were rewarded toss after toss. Now the game turned wide open, the table red hot and bloated with greens and blacks, the players exulting with victory fists and shouts of "Yeah" following each triumphant toss, cries of "press my 9," "press my 6," "press my 5" clamoring across the casino floor, as this was that sublime moment, the dream of every craps player, to stand on such hallowed ground when a table heaves and rocks to the rhythm of a sharpshooter *on his game.*

There was nothing like it, not even sex, when those dice were sizzling—and when those dice were sizzling life was good, you were under a spell, you forgot home and family, wife and kids, bills and mortgages, taxes and death; you had nothing but bliss, the Lord as thy shepherd.

The kid himself—growing taller and more masterful by the minute—was impervious to it all, remaining all-business, tranquilly going about his work, tossing those bones smoothly and cleanly in a motion as graceful and as poetic as a Ted Williams swing, and still pressing rather lightly, risking conservatively, except for the 5, upon which he must have had ten blacks, and also the hard 8, on which he had two blacks, Dewey noticed—Dewey still in reserve, especially now that a 7 was bound to show. It was time, well past the time.

The kid was shooting up a storm, defying the percentages, and it was time to seven-out, for sure, for Dewey had seen these morning glories before, busting the boys just when the table was brimming with blacks and the going was good, too good, tempting fate, wicked fate lurking deceitfully in those dice, though meanwhile this kid, this Mr. R., had already put most of the boys in velvet. As for Dewey, it would have been smart for him to jump in when the moment was right—in the middle of the hot action—only now it was too late, the 7 was coming, had to come, unless something funny was going on, and so far, Dewey, he of the sharp eye, had seen nothing to suggest trickery.

Until the moment another cowboy started kicking up another fuss down at the other end, the crew momentarily diverted, and the kid—well, now the kid cupped the dice a bit differently, this time locking them in his grip, giving them the Marine twist and tossing them high in the air so that they spun like helicopter blades and landed sliding up against the wall.

The boys roared in approval even before the stickman announced, "Eight hard."

Dewey was awestruck.

So was the boxman.

"Next time, please, be sure you hit the wall, Mr. R.," said the boxman after the tumult.

"As always."

"I'm being nice, Mr. R."

Dewey, of course, knew that the dice had to hit the wall for a random tumble and he likewise knew that strangeness had just transpired as the kid—this ho-hum, I'm only-a-hayseed kinda guy—had just thrown a damned spinner, a helicopter, a toss beyond the means of anyone but a genuine sharpshooter, and a move Dewey hadn't seen since his days in the Army.

Was it possible? This kid a shark? Dewey, always ready to imagine a scam anyway, could only think *maybe,* but without a doubt on that last shot the kid had displayed that rare thing, *control of the dice,* and if that was so, WOW—and notice how the kid, Mr. R. all right, used his skill sparingly and timed it to coincide with a commotion so as not to draw attention from the crew and disqualify himself from the action, although sure, they suspected; the boxman had his eye on him, all right.

But that last toss was a show-stopper, very impressive, and right there Dewey knew he'd be dreaming about it all night, first for the marvel of it, and second for the fact that he, Dewey, had *not been in on the action.* Dream? How about a nightmare! Why the kid shook them bones all right, or so it seemed, and they spun all right, or so it seemed, and hit the wall all right, or so it seemed, but bottom line was this: The stirring of the dice was merely *cackling,* the cubes artfully framed so that the spots in the kid's fists showed 4-4 upright and weren't really rattled but rather, held in control by the pinky, forefinger, and thumb; the spinning was a perfectly balanced horizontal rotation, hence the helicopter effect, and as for hitting the wall—well, they did *touch* the wall but not hard enough to spoil the result.

Meaning, to Dewey (still hedging because one toss doesn't a sharpshooter make) that possibly some very legit action was going on, or some grand deception was at work if the kid had The Method, something like the Greek Shot that Dewey had seen in Barracks 29 when dice were sometimes known as G.I. Marbles and cheating was as widespread as the clap, and Private Buzz McCormick kept raking it in until he was blown and had his fingers broken.

Randomness was supposed to be the name of the game. God was in the percentages unless a sharpshooter came along with a system, a system to control the dice. This kid, maybe he had the system, maybe he didn't. Maybe he was just lucky. Or maybe his system was so good, right there in that gray area between legal and unlawful, that the House couldn't touch him. Just yet.

If it turned out that the kid really was a mechanic with a spinner as his trade, he had to be admired, really admired, because to toss the spinner took months, actually years of practice; and even that wasn't enough. You had to be *gifted,* near-genius, terrifically skilled.

Dewey, easily charmed by any man who could beat the House, straight or crooked, was gradually becoming a believer, but he'd certainly be no finger-man against the kid, as he had been against Buzz, because the House was the *enemy.* The House was fate, and fate was always something to be beaten, by whatever means. There was no cheating when it came to fate, because fate itself was a cheat.

The real charm was this: The kid used the gaff only once, mostly rolling the dice according to regulation but with the same triumphant effect—and play it straight he had to because he was being clocked by his second-base dealer and the boxman; the boxman, name-tag Teddy Blake, a short, swarthy man posting a permanent shit-eating grin, repeatedly smirking: "Shoot 'em kosher, Mr. R."

"No problem."

"Keep 'em low. We don't want to take people's eyes out, do we, Mr. R.?"

True, flying dice were known to cause eye injuries to crew and spectators, but the real reason for the warning was something else—a caution against being nabbed with a gimmick.

"They're low, Mr. B."

"I know. Just some fatherly advice, Mr. R. No need to take offense."

"No offense taken."

"Attaboy."

Dewey decided that he'd had enough of patience. He wanted *in,* and preparing to lay two blacks on the come, he spotted a WIFE!—a giggly wife running up to her husband with a bucketful of coin, the husband, standing to the third-base side of the boxman, flinching and trying to give her the cold shoulder, but too late, though just in time for Dewey to change his mind.

Impervious to the superstition, the kid made another pass with no more than light action on the line, and Dewey, outfoxed again, remained out in the cold and was resolved to stay there because now he was absolutely sure that fate had detained him when the table was sweet, just so it could trick him into playing when the table went bitter.

That's how things were going for him lately, and not that he was a superstitious man, but when things started going rotten you trusted nothing and nobody and became a believer in everything, everything bad, omens all over the place.

Like why, with his apparent skill, the kid wasn't pressing big—what was that if not an omen, a sure sign that the kid himself was of little faith. Except for the fact that he kept loading up on the 5, which was now brimming with maybe two grand in chips. Why?

The answer came when the crew was diverted again, this time by a blonde with big tits who was settling in down at the other end, giving the kid the moment to lock-grip the dice a second time and send them spinning up in the air to land *3-2* and produce one fine payday for all the boys, including the kid, of course, who got a rousing ovation, though not from Teddy the boxman, who, smiling wickedly, said: "Wouldn't be like you to be using a gaff, now would it?" sarcasm dripping like spit.

"Like I always say, prove it," said the kid.

"Someday, Mr. R. Someday..."

But not today.

The kid had had enough. He finally did seven-out but only *after* he took down all his place-bets. In fact, being the shrewd judge of character that he was, Dewey was willing to bet the mortgage that the kid had sevened-out on purpose, now convinced absolutely, what with that second *big toss* on top of the first, that the kid had the *control,* by hook or by crook, whatever... he had the power to make those dice come *alive.*

But when the kid rested, as if it were Sabbath after a hard week, Dewey bristled as he listened to the final round of applause, the kid getting a big send-off from the boys. Just what Dewey had to hear—he, Dewey, the one man who hadn't scored, so busy waiting his own turn and not believing until the very end, when it was too late, and never wagering so much as a single white chip. Never getting to light up his cigar. Same cigar still clenched between his teeth, unlit but soggy now, soggy and flaccid, as Dewey had begun to chew away at the thing.

In a flash the game emptied and everybody was gone, gone straight for the cages to collect and not waiting around for another shooter who was sure to be the *anti-shark,* as these things could seldom be counted on to repeat the same day, the same table.

So everybody left. Including Dewey. No cash for Dewey. He felt very stupid. The kid had duped him. Standing around watching everybody else win while you're abstaining was worse than losing, in Dewey's eyes—and it was all the kid's fault, coming on like a creampuff, so casual, so nonchalant, revealing nothing, until much later, too late for Dewey, a man who wasn't used to being faked out. Even though he seldom played another man's shoot, he was good at spotting a corker. Not this time. Talk about a missed opportunity. Talk about being played for a patsy. Talk about coming up *empty* when everybody else's cup runneth *over*.

Did this really happen? he asked himself.

Hell, yes!

"Who was that masked man?" Dewey kept muttering, even as traces of a plan began to take shape in his mind while he muscled his way through the casino floor, already hatching a scheme to *make use* of this kid, forget today.

Just maybe he had found him. The messiah!

CHAPTER 2

The kid, whose full name was Julian Rothschild (no relation, he had to keep reminding people), had rented a van from Hertz on Arctic Avenue, near the new convention center, where the jackhammers were still going full blast. After a horrible mile of traffic streaming in from the expressway, bottling up near Caesars, finally, circling for what seemed like an hour, he locked into a space in front of his destination, A to Z Furniture on Atlantic Avenue and Martin Luther King Boulevard, a few parking meters up from the bustling news shop. This was two blocks from the Boardwalk and the ocean, right by the Claridge and Sands. Atlantic Avenue was mostly retail, dresses and shoes, an occasional strip joint here, peep show there, still shabby with so many shops boarded up, rummies, pimps, and whores among the civilians, all of it so close to the action that you could practically hear the money sing, but still far from the gambling crowd.

15

Along the side streets you could exchange your gold wedding band for cash if you were tapped out and the habit was that bad. The glittering casinos lining the Boardwalk were like the false fronts on the Paramount lot.

Julian was exhausted from the rigors of table action—action that never failed to deplete him of energy when it was all over. That was work, there at the tables, adrenalin pumping, mind and body animated to keep up with the swift pace of the game, a game that offered so many ways to win, and lose.

But weary as he was, he had promises to keep.

A to Z no longer sold furniture. The owner, Marvin Jones, decided years ago that long after people stopped buying sofas and lounge chairs, they'd never stop buying TVs, so that's what he sold exclusively, and sold them to Julian at cost, since Julian had helped him out with $26,000 (winnings, of course) when the going got pretty rough two years back, April 15.

"Where's Marv?" Julian asked Pete, the sullen white man behind the counter reading *Penthouse* vertically and wearing biker boots and a T-shirt that promoted Ahab the Wrestling Giant.

"Your nigger-friend's gone home," said Pete.

Julian gulped and let it register but showed nothing and said nothing to reveal his outrage—and amazement. Pete had been working here, for Marv, for about a year and never let on. He sure had Julian fooled (certainly Marv), though Julian never had the pleasure of being alone with him in the shop. Now he was, and now he knew.

"I got 20 TVs to pick up," Julian said.

"So I've been told. They're in the back."

"You gonna help me load?"

"Dream on."

Okay, so he'd load them himself, and mail Marv the check, and load them he did, one box at a time, 20 in all, feeling his muscles harden and his anger rising. Done, he locked the van and remembering, returned to the shop, Pete facing him with a smirk and the words, "Forget something?"

"Yeah."

Grabbing him by the ears, Julian, a black belt, dragged him over the counter and down to the floor, ready to do no serious damage, just enough to send a message, but the man was big and put up a fight, taking a fighter's stance and landing some blows with professional rights and lefts, Julian mostly adopting a defensive strategy, arms crossed to entice the man overhead, Julian now connecting with those whipping blows—karate chops—the man ducking and coming up with a roundhouse, which left him wide open, Julian finishing him off with a kick to the balls—Pete now on the ground, howling in pain.

"That was for Marv," Julian said, so that there would be no mistake.

Marv deserved better. To Julian he was the best of AC. Sometimes in deep summer they'd pull up a chair outside and coaxed on by Julian, Marv would start remembering, wistfully naming all the splendid oceanfront palaces that were gone now, the Breakers, the Ritz, the Dennis, the Traymore, the Shelbourne, the Ambassador, the President, the Chelsea, the Marlborough Blenheim, Chalfonte Haddon Hall, all gone, along with those hazy, lazy days of summer when the big bands played the Steel Pier before crowds in tuxes and gowns, and Clark Gable and Lana Turner strolled the boards, and Joe DiMaggio took on Ted Williams in a homerun-hitting contest to see who could break the most windows from the beach, when all the hotels were taken over by the military during World War II. "Camp Boardwalk" it became, and there'd been nothing like it since. *Enjoy,* was the word back then. *Win,* is the word today. Naw, Marv would say, today it's all about money. There's nothin' like yesterday.

Back in traffic, this time on Pacific and dodging the jitneys, Julian headed to Ventnor and The Alliance Care Center For The Military, a federally-funded nursing home where old soldiers and their wives or widows came to fade away. Except for the fact that the federal funds never fully materialized—one TV in the rec room for men and women in their 80s, most of whom were too stricken with age to leave their chambers.

Used to be a ten-minute trip from here to there but now more like half an hour with all the construction going on. Atlantic City was changing, new casinos buying in, though so far, the same old casinos were merely changing names, like the Tropicana, now to Julian's left as he ducked another bull-dozer, which started off as the Tropicana and then changed to Trop World and was now back to the Tropicana; five blocks later, here was the Hilton that began life as the Golden Nugget, changed into Bally's Grand, then simply the Grand, and now it was the Hilton, finally, until another corporation decided to play Monopoly.

The traffic alone wasn't the cause of Julian's irritableness. No, traffic he knew, Pete he didn't, and it bugged him that such trash was still around, and vexed him even more that he, Julian, had resorted to violence. The guy probably had a wife and kids, all bigots, no doubt, since bigots don't fall far from the tree, but *who am I,* thought Julian, *to mete out justice?*

But this was personal, Julian reflected, *and once in a while somebody has to do the work of Phinehas,* and thinking that he felt better until he remembered this latest session at the Versailles, where things had gotten testy, the crew wising onto him, even though he had thrown the spinner twice, only two times during those disruptions, and they weren't even spinners.

Not in Julian's mind. He simply had a way of shooting, well-taught, well-practiced, that *worked,* when he held the dice a certain way, and tossed them a certain way, thought to be a spinner, known to be taboo—but he didn't think so, since he was a winner even without the gimmick, and it wasn't even a gimmick, simply skill, but suppose it was, well, even if it was, even if he was cheating, he'd still do it because hungry people needed food, homeless people needed shelter, and the dying needed a reason to live.

To all those he gave, week by week, month by month. He thought himself righteous, Robin Hood; no, not a cheat, and it gave him the willies just to hear the word, simply to think the word, but a word that kept lighting up a 24-point headline in his mind as he passed the once-upon-a-time Knife and Fork Inn and headed down Atlantic into Ventnor, leaving behind the traffic, the bulldozers, the casinos, but not the stigma.

I am not a cheat, he told his conscience, his conscience saying *Yeah, like Nixon was not a crook.*

So it went with Julian, back and forth, today and many other days, waging the constant battle to overcome guilt and to face up to the question of whether the thing he had was craft or craftiness. Big difference. He had still to resolve the issue except, for the time being, to conclude that even if he was cheating he'd still do it because it's a jungle out there, Jane, and somebody has to come to the rescue.

So he'd continue until they stopped him, and man, it sure was getting close, that boxman giving him the evil eye and saying "someday." This wasn't even the first or only time he had felt the heat. Someday what? Someday you're gonna gate a guy just because he *wins?* That's against the law? Winning?

No, cheating, that's against the law. Yeah, well, what you call cheating, I call skill.

It was all quite confusing and ambiguous to Julian, the line that divided the straight from the crooked. Of this much he was sure; deceitfulness for a greater good was good, like Jacob's stealing Esau's birthright and then in turn being deceived by Laban, meaning that what goes around comes around. There's always a tax.

So maybe it's not so good, deceitfulness, but we all do what we have to do because we're all so frail and have nothing but our wits to keep us from perishing. "Remember," Slim Sam Belmont—his dice mentor—had told him, on the topic of craps, and life, "it's you against *them*. It's always war and they're always the enemy."

So that's it, thought Julian, *I'm just using my wits, and let them prove otherwise, and anyway, the whole thing's rigged in their favor to begin with. They own the percentages, and what's that if not a scam?*

But is it still kosher to use a gimmick if it is a gimmick that I'm using?

No, he had to concede. No.

To get his mind off the subject, he turned on the radio and picked up a Philadelphia talk show, 96.5 FM, Howard Stern the point of discussion, Julian now chiming in that Howard Stern wasn't the question, it was our culture in general that was in chaos; namely, that we didn't have one anymore. The radical fringe had moved in and wiped out the mainstream in music, comedy, entertainment in general, manners in particular—no more Jack Benny or Frank Sinatra to hold up the center, and woe unto us that Howard Stern and alternative rock had captured the middle ground. TV nowadays didn't even count for low culture, it was so weightless. Not that there wasn't room for the fringe—but on the fringes.

He was talking to himself, of course, as he frequently did, imagining himself on radio or TV, slamdunking the world with his indignation and wisdom, taking on everybody, the racists, the anti-Semites, the bleeding-heart liberals, the heartless conservatives, child molesters, wife beaters, the networks and their insipid sitcoms and biased anchormen, newspapers and their slanted Middle East coverage, technology, beer commercials.... He had so much to say and said so little, except with the dice. His dice—that's what did the talking for him.

CHAPTER 3

Manny Rubin, who had been there with Patton, was wheeled out onto the porch facing Ventnor Avenue, the nurse covering his legs with a blanket despite the near-90-degree heat, Manny settling in between Rose Torbino, whose husband, Artie, had gone down flying the Hump, and Fay Proctor, whose husband, Warren, a hero in the Pacific, had died just three months ago right here on the same porch. ("We're dropping like flies," she'd begun to say.) There was no sign announcing the pink dwelling as The Alliance Care Center For The Military. Just another cottage in the quaint seaside town of Ventnor.

"He keeps his word, that much I can tell you," said Manny, who, at 84, was the oldest and most afflicted of the group, which had named itself the Rothschild Reception Committee ever since Julian made it a habit to visit the home at least once every couple of weeks, bearing gifts, one among many such stops throughout South Jersey.

"Who needs television, anyway?" said Rose, who hated to use the one in the rec room and be among the snorters.

"Something to do," sighed Fay.

"I hear he's connected," Rose whispered.

Which gave Manny a good laugh. "You don't even know what it means, Rose."

"I sure do."

"Mafia," Fay said in a hush.

"Ridiculous," said Manny.

"So where does he get all that money?" asked Rose.

"Gambles. He's a gambler."

"I'll never believe such a thing," said Fay.

"So what's wrong with gambling?" said Manny, humoring the ladies.

"Nothing," said Fay, "except it corrupts, and he's such a nice young man."

"Handsome," Rose agreed.

"Why, Rose!" Fay laughed. "At *your* age!"

"Well, he is. He's like a prince, the way he carries himself."

"He must be one of *those* Rothschilds," Fay said with authority.

"Nope," said Manny. "I asked him."

"I say he is," Fay insisted. "They just don't want you to know, those that have all that money."

"He is or he isn't," said Manny. "What's the difference? What counts is he's *a gutteh neshumeh*. A good soul. His winnings go to a hundred different charities. I know."

Manny had two Purple Hearts, one of them from Normandy, a Silver Star, plus a Legion of Merit that was accompanied by a letter of commendation signed by Patton himself for distinction in battle far beyond the call of duty. Manny had been taken prisoner later during the campaign in Belgium, was handed over to the Gestapo when they found out he was Jewish, and spent the remaining days of the war in Auschwitz.

When Manny, among the handful of men to survive both combat and death camp, came home to Atlantic City, he joined the Jewish War Veterans, and one sunny day when they were out soliciting contributions on the Boardwalk for the wounded and the handicapped, he heard one woman say to another, "Jewish war veterans. That's a laugh."

That was many years ago, but he never forgot that, never forgot all the Gentile, and, yes, Jewish boys who fought and died to his left and to his right. So, five years ago, now that he had the time, nothing but time, he put it all down on paper until he had 500 pages, but nobody in New York was buying, so he was afraid it would all go down to the grave with him— all those stories of heroism and sacrifice, the sum of his life and the lives of so many others, the memories, the precious remains of all those boys who had fought for their country and for each other. They were the best. But it was a lost cause; nobody wanted to know.

Today he was waiting for Julian with a special urgency. Never mind the televisions. That was nice, very nice of Julian to be offering them for free, as he gave everything for free.

More important, Julian, who had read and loved the manuscript and had promised to do something, had gone ahead and done it, or so it appeared from his last phone call, in which Julian had said "good news," details upon his next visit with the TVs. *So maybe,* Manny was thinking, *he got me a publisher, and if so, I can die in peace,* because more important than all the rest—it was getting late for Manny.

Yesterday he had a fainting spell again, and today wasn't so terrific, either. Minor strokes, according to the house doctor (a young Puerto Rican who spoke no English but made no difference to Manny who wasn't listening anyway), and one day there'd be a big one if he didn't go in for the operation. Not for Manny. No going under the knife for Manny, who swore off surgery ever since he saw what happened to healthy patients there in the camp. All doctors were Mengele to him.

Though now, this minute, he felt the numbness again, and he knew what was coming.

"Whatever he is," Rose was saying, speaking to Manny about Julian, "God bless him."

Manny couldn't hear her.

"Is he sleeping?" asked Rose.

"I don't think so," said Fay.

CHAPTER 4

Buzzy Sullivan, who owned the tobacco shop on Ventnor Avenue and Somerset, was wrapping up a box of cigars for a guy when Julian stopped in for his weekly refill of Captain Black Light. Julian was a regular here at Buzzy's place, which came up three blocks before the nursing home. Buzzy said, "We were just talking about you, Champ."

"No wonder my ears were burning."

"Man here says you're the greatest craps shooter from here to Vegas," the guy quipped.

The guy had one of those ear-to-ear confrontation smiles, smelled of rich cologne, and had a cream Mercedes parked outside taking up two spaces, almost three. Another dude on the make for an uncle. They came onto Julian like sailors to a whorehouse, always ready to bankroll him money-no-object if only he'd shoot for them, which he'd do, yes, he would, if it was for a good cause, then and only then. Never money for the sake of money.

"Only speaking the truth," Buzzy said, nodding pleasantly.

Julian shrugged, always uncomfortable when faced with such praise.

"I get by."

"Luck?"

"No such thing," said Julian, wondering if he should continue to dislike the man.

"You a hustler, one of them sharks?"

"Gotta run," said Julian, now that he had his tobacco and the answer.

"Hey," said the guy. "Maybe we can get together some day."

"Don't think so," said Julian making his escape.

Back in the van and approaching the nursing home, Julian kept shaking his head for all the things they suspected but did not know. It wasn't luck and it wasn't even skill and it wasn't even the spinner, though, yes, it was all those things, partly; mostly it was the blessing.

No, he wasn't one of *those* Rothschilds—which would have been too much good fortune for any one man—but God's grace did shine upon him, ever since that day in the Sinai, finding himself there among the group of journalists when he still had the job with the *AC Record*.

Going off alone into the depths of the mystical desert, the rest of them already boarded on the bus, he gazed out into the dunes of infinity in quest of a Biblical moment, inspired by Judah Halevi's splendid imagery, "When I go forth to seek Thee, I find Thee seeking me." Which aptly described Julian, a man in search of a destiny.

Always the dreamer, as in Solomon's "I sleep, but my heart waketh," Julian sought refuge from the banality of the present and the technological sameness and horrors of the future by inventing his own very secret life, a life of glory and splendor not here, not today, but there in Ur of the Chaldees with Abraham, on Mount Moriah with Isaac, in Beth El with Jacob, in Egypt with Joseph, in Jerusalem with David, in the Sinai with Moses, with all these he traversed side by side and saw them not as Biblical figures only, but as kin, sharing with them kinship and kingship, travails and triumphs; all of them very much alive and calling on him to draw near. *Lech Lecha,* they whispered through the blood of his generations. Go forth.

So Julian was seldom *here,* mostly *there,* and he was there by virtue of his grandfather, a man steeped in Biblical and Rabbinical lore. Nestled in his grandfather's lap, Julian drank it all in, those stories of Abraham, Isaac and Jacob—Abraham, the father of monotheism; Isaac, the exemplar of spiritual submission; and Jacob, father of the 12 Tribes of Israel. Jacob, moreover, so dutiful in his love of Rachel. Seven years he labored to win the hand of Laban's daughter. Beat that for a love story.

But it was the events in Sinai that stirred Julian's soul; the Sinai where the Israelites wandered in the midst of their Exodus, the Sinai that contained the Mount upon which God handed down the Torah and the Ten Commandments, and at that moment (it is written)... not a bird chirped, not a fowl flew, not an ox lowed, not an angel ascended, not a seraph proclaimed Kadosh... the sea did not roll and no creature made a sound... all of the vast universe was silent and mute... it was then that the Voice went forth and proclaimed I Am The Lord Thy God.

Was it true that every soul—even of the departed and even of the unborn—was there to witness the Revelation?

Yes, it was true, for Julian. So he too had been there, only he was still there, in spirit, in his dreams.

He never left.

Julian took his cue from Judah Halevi, the great Jewish/ Spanish poet and thinker of the Middle Ages, who declared that the Revelation at Sinai was the defining event in world history. Julian accepted this as fact, also as fact that the Revelation kept repeating itself as all events of the past continually repeat and revolve, like earth itself, according to the mystical *Zohar,* and this day Julian wanted to be there to catch sight of the Great Moment when it came around, came around again. He was obsessed with a desire to connect emotionally, spiritually, and at last *tangibly* with his forefathers, to overarch the past with the present, to trade in the worldly for the divine.

He had taken the trip on the pretext of journalism, but that wasn't it at all. No, Julian sought transfiguration. At the very least he sought to retrace the paths taken by Moses and the Israelites as they trekked to the Promised Land from their bondage in Egypt, and if that was too much, then it would be enough to find but one of the 42 recorded stops they made along the way, those landmarks erased by the sands of time but still echoing the test of wills between God and His Children, a God quick to anger and quick to forgive and His Children, so quick to complain, murmuring about their lack of food and comforts in the wilderness, so much so that one such station was named *Dafka,* which even today identifies an individual as *contrary.*

But for the moment such evidence of Moses and the Children of Israel was not to be for Julian. Meanwhile he was awed to be standing on such sacred ground. Here it was, the Sinai, and the Mount? No one knew where it was, so all of it, all of Sinai was holy. This, he knew, was where it all began, and this was where it will all end. *If only,* he thought, *I could catch a glimpse...*

They were hollering for him to get back on the bus, these journalists who were his colleagues and who had come to Israel not necessarily to praise her. They were in a hurry to get back to the King's Hotel in Jerusalem to file their copy and then party. File and party, that was the cry. They were on a "Fact-Finding Mission to the Holy Land," pay your own expenses, and were assembled from print and broadcast, men and women from the big cities and the heartland, none however, with

much feeling for the land or its people. Nice to get away from
the newsroom, take a vacation, and perhaps be at the right
place at the right time when war breaks out.

That was about it, so, while Julian was a popular member
of the group, they were a bit puzzled by his lapses into silence
and his need to go wandering off. They had parties to keep.

Julian ignored them (but how perfect, he thought; they're
actually *murmuring,* these Dafka Children of the Media) and
walked even deeper into the desert, eyes readied to meet Moses,
ears alert for the unanimous declaration of acceptance by the
Children of Israel as they stood at the foot of Mount Sinai,
saying the words of the angels, *Na'a se Veneeshma,* We Will
Do and We Will Listen.

Nothing. Nothing but silence for Julian. As he made his
way back to the highway, dejected, his momentum was halted
by the sight of a caravan moving phantom-like in the distance.
This was a tribe of Bedouin on camel—or a mirage. Whatever
the case, Julian stopped to admire the spectacle, a marvel to
behold for its footprints leading to the past.

He decided to pursue. He had to find out what this was. But
as he began his march up and over the dunes, a sandstorm
kicked up and halted him in his tracks, the wind so powerful
that it knocked him down, down flat, and there he remained,
covering his eyes against the million particles of sand whirling
overhead.

Then it stopped, and he got up and brushed himself off.
The desert was back to its silence, and as he gazed around,
the caravan was no more. But he felt something at his feet,
fluttering as if it had wings, a thing or a message obviously,
apparently, maybe, sent by the wind. He bent down to pick it
up, held it, and it wasn't a handful of sand, as he had feared.
It felt like paper, but it wasn't mere paper, either.

In fact, it was parchment, parchment so scorched and faded
that it nearly melted at his touch. Arms trembling, he studied
it and could hardly believe what he was seeing. Was there

actually writing on it, and was this writing the script of ancient Hebrew? Maybe.

But impossible to decipher. For the time being.

Still, he was thrilled by his discovery—what a moment!— and he knew he had something, something, perhaps, so age-less and precious that it wouldn't be safe to show it or men-tion it to anybody. So he didn't. When he brought it back, he began reading up on antiquities and even took a course on Biblical Hebrew at Stockton State College. Each day, using tweezers, he'd study the parchment, which, blurred as it was, seemed to consist of one word, but what word?

The first letter was no doubt an *aleph*. Next, probably a *nun*. Which produced *An... An* what?

Then, after months of examination, it came to him in a spine-tingling rush of exultation. The word was *Anochi. I am.* From the opening passage of the Ten Commandments. I AM THE LORD THY GOD. Which did not necessarily mean that this was the *original,* from the very finger of God, but close enough for Julian; original or copy, whatever, it was holy, and from that moment onward he considered himself chosen and blessed, as when the Ark rested in Shiloh and blessed everything within and around.

Today he still walked with the angels, among the 22,000 that accompanied God when He descended upon Sinai, and it did not matter to Julian whether he derived his specialness from truth or power of suggestion—of course he retained some skepticism—it was enough to believe, simply to believe to make him a man apart. To do that he adhered to his spiritual heart rather than to his mocking, rational brain, in order to feel blessed. And blessed he was.

Through the dice. Which performed miracles for him. The bounty of which he shared generously. All that was some six years ago when he became quickened to his spiritual side, and now the craps table was his tabernacle. So much so that he abruptly abstained from sex at least 48 hours prior to a session at the tables so as to be purified like Moses before entering the Tent of Meeting.

That's how seriously he took it, to the point of fanaticism. He worried about that, that inclination toward zealotry when it came to craps, though this much was fact: Approaching the craps table, he often began to quiver and shake and sense the onset of an epileptic fit, much like the ecstatic convulsions that beset the prophets when the Holy Spirit was about to address them. Maybe it was all false. Maybe he brought it all on by the frenzy of expectation—nothing new about that in a casino, the joint jumping, the table rowdy in anticipation of the next shoot—but there was no denying that it happened. He went limp, followed by a surge of ineffable power.

So, if only in his mind, the Shekhina, God's Presence, was with him when he tossed those dice, and that was enough to make him *sui generis*. Of course, it helped that through hundreds of hours of practice he had minimized the law of randomness by way of the spinner, but that wasn't the secret; he only tossed it occasionally anyway, otherwise they'd have nabbed him years ago. No, the secret was the Sinai, the blessing. God's gift to him. Pavarotti had it in the lungs, Julian had it in the fingertips, and neither of them was cheating.

So call him what you will, but don't call him a *mechanic*. A mechanic's shelf-life was fleeting, anyway. Whip shot, twist shot, slide shot, scoot shot, skid shot, whatever the gimmick, they always got caught and usually sooner than later. Not Julian, knock on wood. He was smart enough to keep switching tables and casinos to keep them guessing. Keep hitting those numbers and making passes without an ugly 7 popping up, those 7s destined to show up one out of every six tosses, more often than the rest of the 30 combinations, and the crew will stop guessing. They'll know and nail your ass. So he had to be nimble and quick and remain conservative with the spinner.

The spinner, compliments of Slim Sam Belmont out in Vegas, had arrived just in time. Julian, now 34, was in a rut before it all changed for him and craps became his genius, his calling. Throughout most of his 20s he had struggled as a writer. Got so bad, despite a newspaper job here and there, that his wife left him for another man. Another writer, actually, a man (no mutual admiration society between Julian and his ex-wife's new and improved husband) who wrote bestsellers, bestselling books and screenplays and, in fact, sometimes used Julian as a source of inspiration, Julian being the keeper of a Midas touch, and Julian being so saintly, in the attempt anyway, Julian probably thinking himself one of the 36 Just Men upon whom the entire world reposed.

Maybe he did think of himself that nobly. It certainly did not escape Julian, the legend of the *Lamed-Vov,* the 36 Just Men in every generation who hold up the world by virtue of their righteousness, *and,* 36 being the extent of all the possible outcomes on the craps table, not to mention that in Hebrew, where the alphabet is used for numbers, *lamed vov* amounts to 36, *lamed* being 30, *vov,* 6. Coincidence?

Julian did not think so. Everything came with two layers, according to his reasoning—the obvious and the hidden. Everything was by design. Even the most mundane, the most frivolous endeavors, had the spark of holiness. Like craps.

So never would he shoot those dice for anything evil and ungodly. For sure, then, his blessing would be turned into a curse.

CHAPTER 5

Julian knew something was wrong as soon as he pulled up and saw no reception committee on the porch. He knew but he didn't want to know, so he started unloading the van even before checking in. Had to be something bad. Never failed. Somebody always died. Figured, for people that age. Expected, but always tragic.

Rose came out, unsmiling, kissed him and thanked him for being so thoughtful, bringing all those TVs.

Julian embraced her, and she wept.

"Manny," she said.

Fay came out and just stood there nodding, then saying: "You missed him by a matter of minutes."

Minutes, thought Julian, *and just when I had the good news for him. Minutes. If only I hadn't tarried... if only I'd been quicker here, hadn't stopped there, to hell with Pete, to hell with the tobacco, Manny could have died smiling.*

"I found him a publisher, you know."

"Hmm," said Rose.

"Hmm," said Fay.

Then, after a pause—"He'll never know," said Fay, ever the pessimist.

"Oh, yes, he will, he'll know," said Rose, ever the optimist.

"Life sure is funny," said Fay.

Julian saw it in different terms. Seven-out, line away. Just when the table was going sweet, so sweet.

CHAPTER 6

Dewey proceeded calmly to the gilded elevators that took him up to his suite on the 28th floor, damned if he'd show his true face to the eye in the sky, those surveillance cameras up there in the ceiling beyond the mirrors that followed your every move and gesture around the casino floor even, for all he knew, into the elevators, into the hallways, into the rooms and probably watched you piss.

The suite—comped—came with a valet, a cook, a chauffeur, a bidet, sunken bathtub, and French windows for a panoramic view of the Atlantic, which nobody, certainly not Dewey, ever bothered to notice, since the business of winning claimed full diligence. Everything else was just commentary. Inside the suite practically everything was golden, including Denise, who had been waiting with a book on her lap. She gazed up and said, "You look like you just died."

"I did," he snapped, stomping to the refrigerator for his York mints, compliments of management.

Denise hated him when he was like this, but lately he was always like this, and she, she was still here, which nobody could figure out, least of all, Denise, who kept on loving him, sort of, purely on memory, on rewind.

As he had it figured, he lost maybe 50 grand not playing with the kid. Holding himself in reserve.

Fifty grand. Maybe more.

"Shit!" he said, slamming the refrigerator door, giving her a start.

Must have been a bad one downstairs, she thought—but without fear. She was used to him by now.

She wasn't afraid of him. Maybe just a little bit.

"You ate all the mints?"

"No," she drawled bitchily, "you took them all down with you."

"I did, huh?" Fifty grand.

"I'm trying to read," she said.

"Yeah, you read. Lotta good it's done you." Fifty grand. Out the window. Who was that kid?

"Please," she said, calling for silence and biting her lip against his scathing accuracy, his talent for uttering the most hurtful thing possible, because no longer did she read for pleasure or advancement; no, that was before, in another life. Now she read to distract herself, to numb the pain.

He lit up a cigar.

"I thought we agreed," she snapped.

"When're you broads gonna be happy?" he said. "When you finally turn us all into women?"

"It's coming," she laughed—but he did snuff out the stogie.

"When are *you* coming?"

"I'm not in the mood," she said, catching on, resisting, but her tone betraying a hint of compliance.

"Yeah, you're reading."

"That's right, I'm reading."

"Well, I'm in the mood."

Dewey was always in the mood when he was ticked, like-wise when he wasn't ticked. Though Denise was his particular turn-on, sex, to Dewey, was not about lovemaking; it was about getting even, with all of them. Women, especially *today's* women in their new insolence (New York women, he called them) deserved to get fucked to pay for their yuppie petulance and arrogance. Dewey was of the opinion that women shouldn't be allowed to drive—and look what's happened since they've been given the vote!

He laughed when he saw that thing on TV, one of those *60 Minutes*-type shows, where they were making the (bleeding-heart liberal) case for female Marines, how well they stood up to the rigors of basic training, finally putting to rest *all doubt* during the segment that showed them excelling in hand-to-hand combat. Except for this, which wasn't mentioned of course: They were going at it *female to female*. "So that in case of real war," Dewey snickered, "we'll have to make sure the enemy sends out its own broads to keep it fair."

"Don't think you can let it out on me just because you had a losing session at the tables, Dewey. I'm not..."

"Who says I lost? I didn't *lose*. Not the way you think."

"You won?"

"No."

"But you didn't lose, either."

"Right."

"You came out even because you needed the money."

"Wrong."

"Should I be confused?"

"This kid..."

"What kid?"

"This kid at the table..."

"Okay, this kid at the table, what? What about him?"

"He..."

But Dewey couldn't go on, couldn't reveal to her the sap he'd been. So, instead, he flung down her book and bypassing the political correctness of foreplay lifted up her skirt, pulled down her panties, and plunged into her, jackhammer style— and without resistance. No, it was consensual as always. She loved it, this was the part she loved, this full measure of raw, unrefined, unmitigated, undiluted virility, and was the reason—one of the reasons she stayed.

This time, though, he wasn't even thinking about her. He still had that kid on the brain.

CHAPTER 7

Roy Stavros, head guy at the Versailles Hotel/Casino, had been another keen observer of Julian's play at the tables, besides Dewey—Stavros watching him from the monitors up beyond the rafters in the eye in the sky, which was where 32 surveillance experts sat before their TV screens scanning the action, panning from table to table, often training their suspicious sights on one particular section, even the slots, where only yesterday a gang of Venezuelans was nabbed using slugs on the dollar machines.

So everything, every inch of the place, was taped for later review. Another five House detectives roamed the catwalk up above with binoculars, the old-fashioned way of doing it but still doing it since they were union. Stavros' attention was taken up at table 5.

"He's at it again," Stavros said to Mike Milligan, VP of casino operations, "and he's cleaning up again, that

sonofabitch. You know this has got to stop you know. What
are we doing about this guy?"

"Can't toss him."

"I know the story," said Stavros, tapping the video screen
that was filming Julian's action, and then putting his fist through
it so that the glass shattered and drew blood from his hand, on
which he wrapped a hankie but otherwise ignored. Stavros
took it all in stride. But it frightened Milligan, as did practically everything about Stavros.

"He's a damn mechanic, but," Milligan said, toughening
up to match Stavros, who kept pacing, fists clenched, not
babying the damaged one, and even enjoying the pain. He
wanted to hurt.

Stavros, who came from a family of Greek restaurateurs
based in Chicago, was once described (by Milligan among
others) as Attila the Hun without the charm. Dark complexion
but clean-shaven, lithe and athletic, competitive to a fault, he
withered both friends and foes by his blazing eyes and booming baritone of a voice. Six-foot standing, and he was almost
always standing, and pacing, seldom seated, seldom calm, he
was sometimes mistaken for Telly Savalas, a flattery much
welcomed by Stavros, even though he still had a rather full
head of hair and was somewhat burlier than the late TV-and-
movie star, and whereas Savalas was known to smile now and
then, not so Stavros. Stavros never smiled. A smile was a sign
of weakness. When he did show his teeth it was the grin of a
cheetah before a kill.

"Yeah," Stavros seethed. "Who needs the stink, right? Yeah,
I've heard it all. It's tough to prove and all that shit. He can
sue our ass or get the Commission on our case or go to the
press and beef that customers ain't gettin' no fair shake here.
Right, tossing him is not the answer. I got the picture."

"I'm open for suggestions."

"First, I want him shadowed. One false move even at another joint and we nail his ass."

"We're already doing that, Roy. Remember?"

"Guy's got me so pissed I can't think straight."

"If it makes you feel any better, you're not alone. But he's also got friends."

"Yeah, I know. He's the guy who believes in all that supernatural horseshit. Supernatural, my ass. The guy shoots spinners. Go prove it, though, right?" Even the close-ups and slow-motions failed to prove it conclusively. "God's in the dice and all that. Maybe it's time to show him there's a devil in them, too."

"Hmm," said Milligan, who had a college education and whose secondary job was to smooth over Stavros' rough edges. Like his habit of terrorizing the surveillance boys, accusing them of being blind (even in cahoots), and now going at it face-to-face with the guy whose monitor he had just busted, the guy who failed to deliver the killer close-up, again.

So Stavros was letting him have it, again, and not only in words. He had the guy up against the wall, grabbing him by the knot of the tie and shoving it up against his nose, the guy turning purple, Stavros barking, "All I ask is people do their job. That too much? Huh?"

Stavros was not the official president of the Versailles. That title belonged to a most respected gentleman, Hayden Booker. That was the man whose name appeared in all the letterheads, and Booker was the man who regularly stood before the Commission when it was time to get the casino's license renewed.

Stavros' name was seldom mentioned. When it was, it was usually whispered. In fact, he had no title. He was brought in from Chicago with a reputation within the underground nightclub circuit of being a gorilla, a hitman for hire. He was selected by Booker to clean up the joint, as the Versailles had become infested with counterfeiters, money launderers, slug operators, card counters, mechanics, name it and they were here, swarming like ants. Stavros had a budget of several hundred thousand to do with as he pleased as long as he kept order. Booker didn't want to know the details, as long as the shit didn't hit the fan.

So Stavros had to watch his step. He'd barely got his own license approved, falling between the cracks of the Division of Gaming Enforcement, which did the investigating, and the Casino Control Commission, which made the judgments—what with his Chicago background and all. Except that they couldn't pin a damned thing on him. He'd never been convicted, of anything. Never even been fingered for a traffic violation.

They couldn't even prove that he had mob ties, that he had a mob bankroll, virtually unlimited, if he wanted a head-to-head showdown with a particular shark who'd gotten on his shit list, sometimes hit list. Not that Stavros liked to kill people. He only liked to win. That's all that counted.

Losing, even if it was only the casino's money—well, he took it personal. So far as he was concerned, it *was* his money and they were all cheats, even the honest ones, simply for being down there on the casino floor.

That was enough to make them all his adversaries, since they were taking *his* money, *his* food, *his* water, *his* home, *his* children. That was *war* out there on the casino floor, them against us, and that's how you kill them, really kill them, by beating them at the tables. If that didn't work, well, yes, then there was the other alternative.

But nothing gladdened him more than steering a scam artist to a clip joint, like the one behind Sammy's Candy Shop on Morris Avenue down from the Trop, and make him cry uncle. Clean him bone dry. Clean him of all that he'd won unlawfully at the Versailles, plus double, triple, quadruple that amount. Now that's what Stavros called gambling, and fun. More fun than killing a guy, which really wasn't fun, only necessary sometimes.

The bigger the shark, the bigger the fun, and this kid Julian had it over everybody, even the Steubenville boys. He was king of the sharks, and a king you do not kill, not so fast. A king you depose, dethrone, uncrown. You humble the arrogant sharpie, you *humiliate* the motherfucker, bring him to his knees, make him beg, that's what you do. Now that's bleeding and that's murder in gambling parlance. What's more, it's the only decent and fun way to get rid of him, teach him a lesson he'll never forget.

He needed teaching, too, because Stavros had a personal bet going with Teddy the Stickman, also connected, that today, this day, the House would take him, or prove decisively by crew downstairs or video upstairs that the kid was using a spinner.

Which he was, but only twice, and so artfully that it couldn't be proven decisively—not downstairs, not upstairs, the blind leading the blind. So Stavros was out ten grand, which put him in a foul mood. How he hated the kid, so princely in his actions, but a *cheat*. He hated him even more than the Mendoza brothers, more than all of Steubenville, because the kid didn't even need the gimmick, most times. That made it real infuriating. The kid kept winning, no matter what, and that was against the law, Stavros' law. Spinner or no spinner—no wonder the kid was famed for being spiritual.

Fame, that's what Marketing kept saying. Can't bust the kid because he *brings in customers*, the drop practically doubling when he's around. No satisfaction even from Booker who kept saying can't touch him because Marketing loves him, and besides, he plays fair most of the time.

"Most of the time?" Stavros had said, incredulously, during his last go-around with Booker.

"Well, show me the proof. Something that'll stick."

"The kid's got juice," Stavros was now saying to Milligan.

Stavros loved it up in the Eye, where, even before the surveillance experts, experts my foot, he could usually and gleefully spot maybe half a dozen instances of cheating in any given day, from dealers in cahoots with a player, the dealer hiding black chips under what should have been a single green payout, to guys working as a team to count at blackjack or to distract at craps—but most of all, he liked to make the nab, personally, escorting the protesting cheats upstairs to the frisk room so they could view themselves on tape, even in slow motion. Yeah, even backward and forward, head to toe if they needed further proof that they'd been nabbed and were now cooked.

Usually that was all it took. A trip upstairs to the frisk room. When it came to repeat offenders, then it got nasty. When it came to triple repeats, then it got very nasty.

Stavros had spent two years with the Chicago police force—before he got himself sacked—and he still had the nightstick.

Julian was a repeater a hundred times over, if not more. The Versailles was his favorite casino.

Stavros usually gave repeat cheats a choice—like the right arm or the left arm, Vegas style, when Vegas was still Vegas. Fatal accidents were also known to happen to multiple repeaters, usually by mysterious drownings in Lake Calico somewhere in the Jersey Pinelands.

The Mendoza brothers from Steubenville—well, there were no more Mendoza brothers. One of them, Tony, washed up dead. But there was still Steubenville, where scam artists kept breeding like racehorses in Kentucky.

Except that the Steubenville boys used the switch ploy, switching loaders for House dice right there at the table, palm to palm, which was really a neat trick but crude, as opposed to the shark Julian, who was too slick for that and possessed *real* skill, beating the pants off the House using the House's legit ivories. Beating the House *at its own game*. Which just can't be. Cannot be. Like going against nature. The kid lost now and then but Stavros was convinced it was only part of the set-up. Marketing had told him that just the other day the kid took a bath at the Taj. "Sure does make it look good," Stavros replied.

In either case, Stavros had his eye out for anybody from Steubenville, or crossroaders from anywhere. Like Julian, the untouchable shark. But every shark has his day, his day of justice. Only a matter of time.

"The man's forcing my hand," Stavros thinking of the ten grand he was minus, thanks to the kid, who had come in and done it again. Thinking he could come in and do it again and again. "He wants to play games, we'll play games."

"Got something in mind?" Milligan said, as the two men now strolled the catwalk next to the monitor room.

"How can you tell?"

"I know you, Roy. No rough stuff. Booker's getting nervous. It's starting to get back."

"Did I say 'rough stuff'?"

"No, you didn't."

"That's right. What I am saying, *however,* is the next time that guy plays here he's playing for his *life.*"

"Please, Roy..."

"Showdown. THE ULTIMATE GAME. I'm gonna give the guy a choice. Him against the House, head-to-head. Hardly ever rolls a 7, huh? Let's see him do it with his stinking life on the line. Sevens come up one out of every six times—supposed to anyway. Okay, so for him it's one out of 20, 30, 40 times. We set a limit. You know, something like a dice duel. Hey, a dice duel to the death. Catchy?"

"Part of the tournament?" Milligan said innocently and sarcastically.

"I'm thinking more along the lines of opening a private game," Stavros said, ignoring the rebuke. Private games were rare, reserved for the highest of the high rollers, like the time about six months ago when this cowboy from Toronto came in and took the Versailles for $600,000 at craps one day, then $300,000 the next day, another $400,000 the following day, all in the heat of a busy table. Stavros, confident that in the end the percentages always favor the House, invited the bloated

can't-lose sucker to a private, legit game, where he promptly
lost all his winnings, plus $200,000 more of his own gelt.
"We've had private games before," Stavros said.

"Yes, but never for a guy's *life,* Roy."

No, it had never been that clear with the others. With the
others it had always been for money, violence only implied.
But such a game, life and death, might appeal to the kid,
being the pure gambler that he was, and so sure of himself, so
proud of his skills, his supremacy, his mastery over the dice.
If he was a real gambler, if he really had the fever in his
blood, if he really wanted to be champ and stay champ, he'd
go for such a deal. Had to.

"Yeah, well, there's always a first time. Him against us.
We say, here, shoot. You get 20 chances—we'll make it fair—
you get 20 chances *not* to roll a 7. But if you do, if a 7 gets
anywhere in there before 20, your ass is *ours.* Your ass belongs to the House. Your ass belongs to me!"

This was Chicago stuff, the kind of business Booker was
beginning to fret about—as was Milligan. "You mean..."

"I mean we take him for a ride to Lake Calico."

Milligan had heard about Lake Calico, but he didn't believe
it, or didn't want to believe it, even though some boys were
here one day and gone the next, never to be seen again. Stavros
brought the name up every now and then, talked about doing
people in, but Milligan chose to believe that it was only talk.

"You forgot to think of something," Milligan said.

"I did?"

"What's in it for him? What if he beats us?"

"Oh, I've thought of that all right. I've been thinking about
it for a while. He beats us, we lose."

"We lose? That's it?"

"No. We lose, we pay him one million bucks."

"Come again?"

"It's a fair deal. I think it's fair. Nobody can say it ain't
fair. One million bucks if he wins. He's dead if he loses.

Yeah, that's fair. Sonofabitch's gotten on my nerves. Hate guys who come in here thinking they can wipe us out any time they want. Fuck that shit, you know?"

Milligan cleared his throat. "Roy? Quick question. Why would any sane man go for such a deal?"

"Did you say 'sane'? The man's a gambler!"

Milligan was thinking it over. He had to think fast. "You're just talking hypothetically," he said, sweating.

Stavros nodded and put a fatherly arm around Milligan.

"Of course," he said, soothingly. "Now would I really hold such a game right here at the Versailles? Huh?"

Of course he wouldn't. He'd hold it at that steer joint on Morris Avenue.

CHAPTER 8

Dewey had summoned two of his friends to discuss the situation, and they were all seated in the living room of Dewey's golden suite at the Versailles. About these friends: in some quarters they might be called thugs or goons, but to Dewey they were friends. Denise was also a friend. She was not Dewey's wife, although he had a wife back in Manhattan, a wife he saw but once a year, for a couple of days, an arrangement that was fine with her and fine with him. They would never divorce since they were both Catholics, token but Catholics nonetheless, though, as we all know, religion means different things to different people, and people who are devout about one thing may not be so devout about another thing. Dewey, for example, despite his piety about divorce, was altogether more pliant about murder.

"Let me make a suggestion," he said to his two friends.

Dewey had once paid a big price for being careless with his words, so now he was forever on the alert against wiretappers and eavesdroppers. He imagined bugs everywhere—often with good reason.

Thus obsessed, and feeling constantly under surveillance by the FBI, his deportment, even in private, and there was no longer such a thing as private in this day and age—anyway, his deportment was now practically faultless except for an occasional expletive, which he sometimes used gratuitously just to throw them off, to make them think he's not on to them. Ho hum.

So Dewey no longer gave orders to his friends. He made suggestions.

"I suggest," he said, "that you find me this... this young man. Locate him for me. Please."

"We will do our best," said Fats, he with the boxer's nose, winking to show his awareness of wiretaps.

"Shall we present him to you?" asked Skinny with the long scar. Neither Fats nor Skinny belonged to MENSA.

"That would be a pleasure," said Dewey.

Denise chuckled, as she usually did when Dewey and his friends assumed wooden salon-diction to fake out the ears on the walls. (Never mind that more than half the time Dewey was as vulgar and forthright as ever.) Earlier, Denise had gotten herself a bit of a tongue-lashing when she had asked Dewey why he hadn't pursued the kid right then and there, downstairs in the casino. "All you had to do," she said, "was ask him himself." "Shut up," he explained without apologies to Ring Lardner. More to the point, what he said was: "I would never speak directly to a man the moment after he had insulted me. I'd kill the sonofabitch first."

Yes, sometimes he forgot that there might be bugs all over the place. Or got so mad that he didn't give a damn.

"You are a very troubled man," Denise told him.

Denise was right. Dewey was a troubled man. His troubles began when the famous movie star Zee Zee Sampson began making the news. The feds started going after all of Dewey's manufacturing plants—that's what he called his sweatshops—after Sampson, who had given his name to a clothing line, was accused of fronting for underaged, underpaid, overworked, legal and illegal immigrants.

None of which applied directly to Dewey, but Sampson had opened the door to a crackdown aimed at eliminating sweatshops once and for all. Dewey had 42 sweatshops in operation within Brooklyn and Manhattan, 40 more in Trenton, 36 more in Hudson and Passaic counties, 22 more in south central L.A., four more in Tucson, plus nine in Montreal, three in Wilmington, all in the manufacture of ladies' outerwear, like coats, mostly expensive, mostly vicuna. He served as a subcontractor to a very famous label, a company that claimed to know nothing about the dubious source of its product.

The feds had yet to nail him completely, but they had him on the run. No charges had yet been filed, but he was being investigated, and almost half of his operation was already shut down through new Seizure laws, known as the Hot Goods provision. The business, when it was going full blast, netted him some $5 million a year. Now, mostly he had to keep shadow boxing in and out of new locations, even so far as new *countries,* to fake out the Law, all of which was proving quite costly.

The worst of it—and there was even worse than that—was his reputation, now in tatters. He once counted movie stars, studio heads, and politicians among his friends. Now his name was associated with *child abuse.* His name was Mudd. There were charges that his workers, some as young as 12, most of them girls, were forced to labor 16-hour days. There were accusations that he had these youngsters whipped with cattle prods, that he had them drugged, that he had even brought them over illegally from such places as Nicaragua, Chile, Haiti, El Salvador, Mexico, the Dominican Republic, Venezuela, even Russia, mostly Russia as of late—and then there was this, the imputation that he imported them by kidnapping. Slave labor, in other words.

It was said that he had a private little army at his command.

Then, to top it all off, there was the Sasha Spivak matter. This little 16-year-old Russian immigrant, formerly an employee of his who started to work for him when she was allegedly 13, was set to testify before Congress about him, and if that ever happened, never mind if she told the truth or lied, he'd be finished and staring at maybe 20 years in the slammer.

The papers reported all that, using reliable sources. What even the papers didn't know was The Rest Of The Story in regard to Sasha Spivak, a prodigy who, at age 9, was hailed as Moscow's answer to Paganini. Her range and repertoire with the violin was vast. She was photographed with her parents in dress and hairstyle resembling the fabled Shirley Temple of long ago, still an icon in many parts of Russia. Sasha was dimpled, gorgeous, and immensely talented. Then in the upheaval that followed the fall of communism, her father somehow ran afoul of certain gangland members who had begun chewing up Russian territory slice by slice.

There is nothing clear about how he crossed men of such influence. According to one version, he was a surgeon who refused to operate on a dying gangland chieftain. A more plausible version, perhaps, directly concerns his daughter, Sasha, whom the warlords were bent on manipulating for their own materialistic gain. Apparently, the parents declined the kindness of strangers and were punished. Both died in a mysterious car bombing.

Sasha was placed in a foster home, where, afflicted by grief, she became incorrigible. Next stop was an orphanage for the criminally insane, where she was kept under heavy sedation. At this time a black market for orphans was flourishing. At the age of 13, two weeks after her birthday, she was among 142 children from Moscow's Petrovski Nursing Home For

Girls who were shipped to the United States as part of an underground flesh trade.

She was kept on drugs throughout most of her years of laboring in New York sweatshops. Or so it was alleged. She was now in the hands of some security organization associated with the FBI, being kept in Washington's L'Enfant Plaza under loose watch in consideration of her claustrophobia.

Altogether a tragic story, with no end in sight.

But even though the papers had scant knowledge of those details, they still had no trouble proclaiming Dewey Smith The Sweatshop King. Other banners weren't so kind, branding him "Slave Master." He became tagged with the phrase, "The love of evil is the root of all money."

Through the New York PR firm that represented him, Feld, Henley, Dawson and Associates, he denied everything, and in his innermost heart he truly believed himself a victim, the victim of a smear campaign. In fact, he was a hero, in his own eyes. He was employing the unemployable. He should get a medal. "I turn statistics into people," he liked to say. His only sin was that he didn't ask questions. That's a crime? What!

That army he was supposed to have... well, they were merely supervisors seeing that the work got done, or who facilitated the import of legitimate foreign labor. Could he help it if regular Americans were too *dainty* to do sewing machine work? That business of employing child labor... well, could he help it if people lied about their age? Drugs in the workplace? Who didn't use drugs these days?

Was he supposed to have doctors on the premises to give drug tests day after day? As for bringing them in by force—slave labor—nobody was *forcing* them, okay? They were recruits, for crying out loud! *Recruits.*

As for closing up his shops—lot of good that did the people now out on the street, hungry and naked.

Sasha Spivak? Let's see what happens. She hasn't testified yet, and there's always *my* side to the story.

That, in a nutshell, was how he explained himself to the authorities, who were still trying to separate truth from fiction, but meanwhile had him on the lam—and this was where he came to escape, to the casinos. He had always been a big gambler, a "Quality Player" in casino parlance, specifically at the craps tables. That's where the action was and Dewey loved nothing better than action, unless it was money; but then, action and money were the same thing, after all. He was a student of the game, known to drop or occasionally profit as much as $200,000 at a single session, only now it was no game, it was his life.

Lawyers, his wife, old debts, payroll, bad investments, bribes, diminishing income from the domino-like closures of his sweat shops, they all had him in the hole, actually, pretty near broke. He was desperate, for cash, respectability, love. Yes, love.

CHAPTER 9

Dewey loved Denise. People wondered how she could love him back, and in fact she did love him despite his ruthlessness, though it was a strange, debauched kind of love, based primarily on sex. She liked it rough. He gave it rough. No man but Dewey gave her those multiple orgasms and for that alone he was her master. Which was quite a turnaround for a feminist who had once declared that she hated men.

So maybe that was it; she actually hated him. As we know, love and hate are closely related, and between Dewey and Denise it was surely half of each overlapping. She was so insatiable in bed that he accused her of trying to drive him to impotency, and that may have been the truth. She chided him relentlessly that one time when he indeed couldn't get it up for a period of three months. "Big man, huh?" she liked to say.

They had met in Philadelphia some five years earlier when she had been a high-flying reporter for the *Philadelphia Star* while he, though a New Yorker, absentee-owned a nightclub on Philadelphia's Broad Street, near Temple University.

Complaints arose from the university that the club was actually a hangout for mobsters; not good for a neighborhood of students. (About here was where the feds began to take an interest in him.)

When he arrived in Philadelphia to defend himself for the first of a series of City Council meetings, Denise Barker, on assignment from the *Star* to root out blight, was there to greet him at the Bellevue, idealistic fire in her eyes. Here, before her, stood the stereotypical male. He was everything she despised. He was 46, meaning the age when men had come in too early and were now too late for *sensitivity*.

He was big, six-feet-two, meaning that he was most likely a brute; he was sort of handsome in an Orson Welles-kind-of-way, meaning that whatever he couldn't take by force he seduced. He was vulgar, referring to her for openers as "that feminazi bitch writing all those lies about me," meaning that he was surely a Limbaugh ditto-head.

Perfect.

As for Dewey, he likewise saw perfection. The perfect backstabbing, man-hating, Citadel-crashing, whining, grasping, bleeding-heart liberal. Oh, he knew the type. These were women who had gained *liberation* for all the wrong reasons.

They were women, so many of them in the news business for one reason or another, who had embraced feminism not to free themselves but to get even—and get even they did, by becoming jerks; jerkdom being a preserve once solely inhabited by men.

So here she was in the flesh—Denise Barker, reporter for the *Philadelphia Star,* no doubt the recipient of her job through a quota system that insisted on minorities and women only, no dead or living white males need apply; here she stood, the perfect example, in his eyes, of how it could all go wrong.

Of course, he was attracted to her, as he was attracted to all green-eyed dames with those sensational legs, who came across oh-so-serious and well-spoken and Vassar-educated and smart-alecky and overconfident and arrogant, altogether the kind of know-it-all abrasiveness that would be a demerit if it didn't make them even more fuckworthy. That's what Dewey saw in Denise. (In fact it was Bryn Mawr, not Vassar.)

The loathing between them was instant. Which was why—exactly why—when his business in Philadelphia was over, when he lost the license to operate his club, and she had roasted him to smithereens in the pages of the *Star,* he challenged her to go to bed with him. She took the dare because... because he was putty waiting to be molded... and because it was all so *wrong.* It was all so funny, so ridiculous, so outrageous! What a match! Really!

A woman in the prime of her career, a woman who personified feminism, with a man so utterly *primitive.* That's why she said yes, for the plain contrariness of it all. Her mom, her dad, her sister colleagues at the *Star,* they would all be so mortified. That's why she said yes.

She cleaved to him, for months, in secret, for the ecstasy of sinfulness, and she paid the first price by getting fired from the *Star,* and the second price was even more costly, in that she was stuck with him, seemingly to the end of her days. Against her upbringing, her conscience, her better judgment, against everything she believed in, she had fallen in love with him. Yes, she saw the evil in him all right. She knew what he did to others, she knew what he did to her, but love, especially when it is based on indignation—actually hatred—such love is purely irrational.

Plus this. He was not totally evil. There were definitely two sides to the man, as there were two sides to every man. Dewey was a lover of Beethoven. (Though Beethoven needed Dewey as much as Beethoven needed Napoleon.) Dewey was sentimental. (He was quick with flowers and regrets.) Dewey was generous. (He gave away hundreds of thousands year after year, back when he had the money.)

Dewey, in his quest for refinement and *culture,* so as to be a player in the big leagues, was a reader, self-taught, a man who could converse on books and literature—he could quote Shakespeare and Twain and even Rousseau, had read all the volumes of Will and Ariel Durant's series on Civilization— which was surely a magnet for someone as literate as Denise, if for nothing more than the effort.

So he was a bit crude. Nobody's perfect.

There was also a new wrinkle in Dewey's personality, somewhat endearing, actually, his inclination to weep, sometimes for a reason, sometimes for no reason, no reason she, or even he, could fathom. But he wept. It was a source of shame to him and was most probably something medical, but he'd never look into it as that would be much too embarrassing, confronting a doctor about so delicate a problem. All of which fastened her attraction to him (offset by so much revulsion) on the premise that he was a most misunderstood man, a man worthy of her efforts to redeem.

So they were not the standard picture of the gangster and the moll, but still, all in all, they were of different worlds. There was no reason why she had to abide him night and day, except for the fact that she knew too much about him. He would kill her if she left him. He had suggested as much. Never said so directly, but it was there.

CHAPTER 10

Skinny and Fats managed, without much trouble, merely an inquiry or two at the Versailles casino, to trace Julian Rothschild to Margate, down by the seashore in New Jersey, where they were headed right now—after first getting a flat tire on the expressway, then running out of gas on the causeway, which eventually took them into Margate, where they beheld the splendors of the ocean and the seabreeze. Fats was a city boy, a street-wise New Yorker, brought up on asphalt with no leisure-time for the beach. He had seldom seen water. Skinny was originally from Asbury Park, New Jersey, home of the Boss, the Bruce man, so water and boats were nothing new to him, though now concrete was more his style.

As they approached the bridge, they saw the sign that said WELCOME TO MARGATE, followed by signs that announced the presence of eight different synagogues. *Beth* this and *Beth* that.

"This Julian," said Fats, driving. "You think he's a Jew?"

"A what?" asked Skinny, distracted by the sights and memories of pleasure boats to his right and left.

"A fucking Jew."

"I wouldn't know," said Skinny.

"I know you wouldn't know. I was just wondering. Is that a problem?"

"Yeah," said Skinny, who was the tougher of the two. "It's a problem."

"What's gotten into you?"

"Shut up, Fats."

"Jesus Christ."

"What's the difference?" said Skinny, going nonchalant.

"No difference. Who cares."

"That's right," said Skinny. "Who cares."

"Just curious, that's all."

"You know what curiosity did to the cat."

"Well, I ain't no cat," said Fats.

"Well, I'm a Jew," said Skinny.

Fats laughed. Then he stopped laughing.

"Go on."

"I'm a Jew, all right, and damned proud of it, all right?"

"I swear I didn't know," said Fats, shaking his head. "I swear I didn't know. Jesus Christ. Go figure."

"I wasn't *Bar Mitzvahed* or nothin' like that, but I'm a Jew."

"Yeah, but your name is McDonald or something."

"Father was Irish. It's the mother that counts. Anyway, you know Cohen? He's fuckin' Methodist."

"Yeah," said Fats, "and I know an Armstrong. He's a Jew. You never know about people. Dewey, you think he's a Jew?"

"Dewey's a Catholic."

"But he's got all that money."

"That make him a Jew?"

"Sort of."

"But he ain't got no horns on his head nor hook nose on his face. Ain't that right, you fucking anti-Semite?"

"In my neighborhood we called all Jews 'Goldberg,' that's all. That make me an anti-Semite?"

"I also know a Goldberg who ain't no Jew," said Skinny, shifting in his seat.

"You know I meant no harm," said Fats.

"Just shut up and drive. Jesus Christ."

"How would you like it if I said 'Holy Moses'?"

"I wouldn't give a shit."

They pulled up to the address on Rumson and Atlantic and parked in front of a green, freshly painted, two-story cottage whose porch faced the sea. They spotted three men there in the back, on the veranda, sipping drinks and talking under the hot July sun.

"Sevens are bad." Julian Rothschild was in his year-round Margate home, explaining it patiently if a bit irritably to the writer and the director who had come in from Hollywood: "Sure you want a 7 or an 11 on the first roll, the come-out roll. That's called a natural because it's a winner. But after you make your point, a 4, 5, 6, 8, 9, or 10—those are the point numbers—well, after you roll one of those numbers you've got to roll it again and the last thing you want is a 7. That means you lose all your money.

"You've sevened-out; and by the way, just to show you the odds of shooting a 7, the opposite sides of any legal die always total 7. I'm only giving you the basics. It's amazing how many people don't even know that much."

By people, he meant the people in the movies, but he refrained from saying so directly, as he did not want to be tactless and totally insulting to his visitors, who had come from so far to seek his wisdom. Since Julian wouldn't go to Hollywood, Hollywood came to Julian, he was so much the final authority on craps.

He'd been out there twice as a technical advisor and *even then* they got it all wrong. So much so that they trifled and profaned the sacred game of craps. So he quit going out there. He was even in one of their movies as one of the crowd around the table in *The Nevada Kid,* a movie he kept watching over and over again for the sheer wonder of his claim to immortality. (What made movie stars gods? The fact that they could be in two places at once.)

Other than that, though, he winced at movies like *Viva Las Vegas* which had Elvis cupping the dice to his ear. Right. Sure. Just try that in real life. The dice have to be visible at all times, OVER THE TABLE!

They couldn't even get baseball right. Why do all their actors throw like girls? Or swing like sissies?

John Goodman playing Babe Ruth. Oh paw-leeze!

The director, Clive Edwards, and the writer, Donald Oaks, were in pre-production for something called *Scared Money* and what a small world this was. Donald Oaks was related to Julian through marriage. Don, the bestselling author, was married to Julian's ex-wife Debra, to be exact, and that's how it goes, life goes on; meaning that the bad blood between the two men would never interfere with business.

Debra certainly nursed no grudge against Julian; in fact, she'd been hot for Julian to become part of the project. She still had a soft spot for her ex. It was just too bad for him that he never made it as a writer during their marriage and too bad, for her, that he found his calling in craps after the marriage. She always knew he had talent. Who figured on the dice? Who figured he'd become a success? A living legend, in some parts.

She always knew he was a bit off the wall. His stories—the ones that never sold—were mostly Bible-related, so who was to know that his fatal Scripture fixation, as a thousand editors and producers called it, would one day pay off—at the casinos, of all places.

As for Julian, he was still very much in love with Debra. She had been the reason for his ambition and was now the cause of his sorrow, which he kept hidden as best he could against the world and certainly against Debra, who was confident that he was well over her. Which was not nearly the case, not at all. He dreamed of a reconciliation with the girl who had helped him build castles on the sands of Margate when they were just kids, she—the girl from down the beach, the girl with the luminous dark hair whose ponytail he used to pull in Tighe Elementary and later even at AC High. He had been in love with her since he was 8, a love still undiminished by the decades or even by the marriage to another man.

She was something special, the ballerina of his reveries, and as for her, Julian had been her hero lifeguard, there on the beach summer after summer down from Casel's, where they all used to gather for swimming by day and sand-dancing by night. He was the champion rower of the seas, the muscular striker on the beach. The girls swooned for him, but he only had eyes for Debra.

They were the perfect seashore twosome, biking the AC Boardwalk together and finally losing their virginity in typical Jersey seashore fashion, together under the Boardwalk in Atlantic City—the way virginity was meant to be lost for a couple of Margaters.

Debra had dated a few others, but Julian was the big catch. So she caught him, and threw him back. He had no winter skills to match his summertime excellence. Except, perhaps, as a writer. (He had majored in English at Rutgers.)

But, always unsure of what he really wanted to be when he grew up, his struggles as a writer had been motivated almost entirely to impress her. His failure in that department was still a mark of disgrace. Even as the rejection slips piled up higher and higher, he imagined himself a great success, the great writer who owed it all to the woman of his life. They would travel together in the best of circles—Newport, Saratoga, East Hampton—and she would glitter for the both of them.

Now, once in a while he'd run into her here and there—she glittered all right, so happy about how things had turned out, "for the best," she'd say, "don't you think?"—and he'd wonder how he'd squandered it all. Their infant had died in its crib, and that had been a crusher, especially for Debra, since there had been whispers about neglect on her part, neglect and things even worse—but all that need not have been the end of it all. No, the end was his failure, as a writer and as a man.

How strange that now he was a success, without his beloved at his side. The dice had come just a bit too late.

Edwards, the director, British, fortyish, excitable, two thriller hits to his credit, leaned over to Julian, perspiring from the heat of the sun and the rigors of creativity, wanting to know what Julian meant by mysticism, as connected to the dice. "Exactly what is it you mean? I mean dice—they're just dice."

Julian sat back and smiled. "If I explained the mysticism it would not be mystical anymore, now would it, Clive?"

"Excellent!" said Edwards, laughing too hard.

"But when you say dice are just dice, that offends me, Clive."

"Oops," said Don, speaking for Clive Edwards and himself and perhaps for his wife Debra as well.

"What's life if not a crap shoot?" said Julian. "The roll of the dice represents all our aspirations, all our hopes and dreams, our successes, our failures, but most of all—most of all, our fate. Our fate being in the hands of chance. That's dice, Mr. Edwards."

"But you... I thought you call it God."

"Oh, I do. He decides what comes up. Which is saying He decides fate."

"God is in the dice?" said Don.

"Come on, don't make me out to be a kook. But yes, I do have an edge. Everybody is subject to the whim of the roll, the law of randomness; me, I just have something more to say about it, that's all. I can determine my fate, not always, of course, but more often than the rest. That's all a man can ask for in life or in the casino. An edge. It's a matter of faith that comes from total concentration."

Julian wasn't nuts about explaining the inner workings of his gift—but he *was* trying to be helpful to these two. They seemed so sincere and they caught him in a good moment. So he went on, expounding about the combustion that takes place when a man begins to live and love the dice. Sparks fly. Chemistry happens. Some call it mystical, but it's likewise chemical. Combustion also sometimes happens at a table when for no apparent reason, it gets hot, the heat generated by the players influencing the numbers.

In either case, it's all about being utterly focused and absolutely fixated. "Look, Bobby Fischer, no matter what you think of him, he dreams chess moves. Ted Williams *lived* with his baseball bat so that he and the bat were *one*. That's me and the dice."

"Incredible," said Clive. "Absolutely incredible."

"If you want to know human nature, the human condition, just take a gander around the craps table, any casino, any craps table, and study the faces. The entire world is right there in microcosm. Delight, despair, hope, fear, success, failure, weakness, strength, love, hate, all there in one session. One table."

"That's what we'd like to convey in our film," said Clive, with Don nodding his assent.

"Well, you might also want to convey why we've become a nation of gamblers," Julian said about his favorite topic.

"You've pretty much said why. I mean the idea of testing your fate..."

"Yeah," said Julian, speaking through his thoughts, "but let's be clear. The most important thing about gambling is this—and it's something most people, even most gamblers, don't even realize. What we're doing, see, is trying to find out if God is really on our side! We're testing Him—call it God, call it fate, call it what you will, but it's always the same thing, the individual challenging God to answer prayer by way of the slot machine. A losing session means God hates you. The jackpot means God loves you.

"Money? That's our sacrificial offering. That's what gambling's really all about, gentlemen, both an act of faith and a challenge to the highest power, and it's why we've become a nation of gamblers. It's religion, man. It's our new religion, and billion-dollar temples are going up practically every day to accommodate the growing multitude of worshipers—though you may call them casinos, if you will."

Julian smiled, just to be sure that they took him seriously, but not too seriously (as being too serious was a no-no in Hollywood). He was humoring them because he knew that once they got back to Hollywood, they'd forget everything he said and go ahead and do it their way, showing no respect for the details. He had already been there, done that, and wasn't afraid of them anymore.

He had trouble respecting them as individuals and yet there was this paradox, that with all the mediocrity out there, all the backbiting and doubledealing, all the bad judgment, all the lousy scripts accepted and all the good scripts rejected, all the jerks and assholes—despite all that, they still made so many marvelous movies. It did not add up, but there it was.

At about the point when Clive was trying to persuade Julian to come out to Hollywood, just to be there, to see that everything was done right, Fats and Skinny approached, Skinny saying, "Sorry for the interruption, gentlemen." Fats then explaining to Julian that a certain Dewey Smith, staying over at the Versailles, was eager to make his acquaintance insofar as a certain charity needed help.

CHAPTER 11

Dewey was walking the Atlantic City boards with Denise, explaining all about loyalty, here amid the crowds promenading back and forth, bathers out on the beach, the sun beating down—but no walls. No walls, no ears. So about loyalty, he was saying, take baseball. Please. Anyway, there's no crying in baseball, and no loyalty, either. Players go to the highest bidder. To hell with the team, damn the fans. You have to *buy* loyalty these days.

"It's a new time," he was saying. "A new generation."

"The point being?" she asked nervously, for she knew something was coming.

She did not much care for these walks with Dewey as they usually meant the announcement of some unspeakable decision. She knew him too well; much better than she knew herself. She had started off as a brunette and was now a blonde, and that explained everything to her, about herself.

Her parents, in their late 60s but still very healthy and very much alive, both of them society reporters at the *Philadelphia Post,* were no longer on speaking terms with her, mainly on account of her liaison with Dewey but also for a lifetime of wrong choices—like running away from home at age 17 with some guitar-strumming loser, then getting herself pregnant, followed by an abortion, finally getting herself straightened out, going to college, finishing college, graduating in journalism, Dad pulling strings to land her that job across the street at the *Star* to come to THIS?

Her weak spot had always been men, the wrong kind, choices she made seemingly for one reason, to *show* them. They were so upright and respectable. Half the time they were in tuxes and gowns at the Academy of Music, mixing with Philadelphia's upper crust, that stuffy gang of hypocrites Denise thoroughly despised.

Her parents had warned her that her contrariness would one day cost her, and it sure enough did, and she'd be damned if she'd go crying to them for help or forgiveness. She was well-aware that her bullheadedness was the cause of her undoing. Irony? The irony being that her very willfulness—ordinarily a desirable characteristic for women of her generation—was precisely what landed her on her ass. Her independent spirit had made her a slave. Every day she sought to make her escape, and Dewey, being alert to her every mood because he was in love with her, and people in love need no words, had no trouble assessing her subversive thoughts, which he quelled by making oblique references to her safety, and the safety of her loved ones.

That alone did not detain her. No, there were emotions involved as well—this crazy thing called love. There was always the chance that she might reform him. She had been working at it and now, with his life going to pieces, his business in disarray, his name in disrepute, would be a perfect time to start over again—this time legit.

Somehow, start over. He had good qualities. There was stuff to work with. If somehow she could succeed, make him a better man, make herself a better woman, that would be her laurel.

"The point being," he said, eyeing the Boardwalk strollers for signs of authority, "that there's no loyalty anymore, even in my business. I have no friends left. No friends."

"That's not true," she said, overtaken by a moment's pity.

"None that count, anyway," he was saying conversationally.

"Oh, stop it," she said, in a motherly tone. "This is the best thing that could have happened to you. It's awakened you."

"They've all gone south," he continued, not paying her much heed. "Shit hits the fan, everybody goes. I need a guy, see, to do a job. Used to be I could count on 50 different people, for the right price, of course. But still, there was loyalty. I say it's all about this Generation X. Or the stinking Boomers. Me included.

"No loyalty except to ourselves. You realize one day soon we'll be left with nothing but Boomers and Generation Xers? What kind of world's that gonna be?"

"I don't know what you're talking about, Dewey."

They were now seated inside the Celebrity Corner, between the Trop and the Hilton on the Boardwalk and the favorite eatery and hangout among the locals, and here Dewey ordered his heaping hot pastrami, the yummiest cuts this side of Manhattan's Stage Deli, Denise going for the Burger Special and enjoying the respite, until Dewey opened his mouth again to continue his spiel.

"I'm talking about this girl, this Sasha Spivak that's got my ass in a wringer."

"What about her?"

"You don't know?"

"Of course, I know."

"So you know she's about to turn on me. I mean she's got all those lies to tell those congressmen. They're keeping her under wraps. Prepping her. Just to hang me out to dry. It's all lies, you know."

"Oh?"

"Says she was 13 when she came to work for me. Like I asked. Like I was even there when my guys hired her. I'm supposed to know what's going on in a hundred different operations? Says she was forced to work 12-hour days. Says we beat her. Says she was brought over as a slave laborer, by the Russian mob—that I'm connected to those guys."

"All lies?" she asked carefully.

"Mostly."

"Mostly?"

"That's not the point."

"That is the point."

"The point is, we can't let her talk."

"We? Who's we?"

"You're not with me?"

"Not when you're saying what I think you're saying."

"Oh, I'm saying it all right. You're with me."

"Like hell I am. I'm with you when you're good, not when you're bad."

"The deal is supposed to be good *and* bad."

"We're not married."

"Says who?"

"The law."

"Yeah, well, between you and me, we're married. You love me, don't you?"

"Sometimes."

He chuckled softly and put an arm around her. She circled away, pouting.

"I think you love me always, for better or worse."

"Oh, yeah? When does the better part begin?"

This time he laughed heartily, as we laugh at the unintended wisdom of a child, and she couldn't help but laugh, too. His confidence, his masculine vigor, these attributes still had her charmed.

"There's magic between us," he now said, seriously.

"Let's not forget fear."

"It's true. I am afraid of you," he said with a wink.

"Let's not get into that," she said, feeling a chill.

No, this was bad territory.

"So. What to do. What to do."

"Do I have to hear this? I thought we were talking about loyalty."

They were back to strolling the boards to walk off the meal and into his troubles, soon to be hers as well.

"I'm coming to that, my dear. It's coming. Used to be, see, that I could get a good hitman for say ten thous..."

"No," she said, stopping in her tracks near Caesars. "Include me out, Dewey. I don't want to hear this."

"The girl has got to be stopped, Denise. For the sake not of me, not of you, but of two thousand people she's going to put out of work. If they close me down completely, that's how many people end up on the street. These people, they can't speak the language, and yeah, all right, most of them are here illegally. But they're people. They're human beings."

"How high-minded of you."

"Exactly."

"Please."

"Honest, this is for the greater good. Believe me when I say those people who've already lost their jobs on account of the government—they're begging me to take them back. Same wages, same conditions. I'm even bringing them back whenever I can find new locations. That's how it is. Hey, this isn't college. This isn't philosophy. This isn't something *abstract*. You want idealism? Isn't that why you went into journalism? Okay, I'm giving you idealism. Eating and having a roof over your head. That's idealism, and that's life. Yeah, for the greater good. That's what I'm talking about."

"Still sounds like murder to me."

"No, its a sacrifice. One person for the good of thousands. Try to think about it that way."

"This has gone too far."

He shook his head. "You and your kind, you think you're so righteous. But you're only selfish."

"Selfish?" She was outraged by the accusation.

"Yes, selfish. You're only thinking of yourself. Typical of your fucking generation, and your fucking gender. Saving your own skin, that's your game. You're not thinking of the people. The *people*."

"Oh, the huddled masses," she chided as they stopped momentarily in front of the Claridge, Dewey checking the urge to pop in and try the tables there—there where he'd once had some terrific action and liked the place for its congenial atmosphere besides.

"Exactly, the huddled masses."

"You're their deliverer."

"Believe it or not, I am."

"God help us."

"The job by the sewing machines is lousy. But it's a job. It's a living. Barely, but..."

"I've heard enough," she said, stomping off in the direction of the Hilton and then for no reason turning to the inlet. He caught up to her, a bit out of breath, as it was the best of summer or the worst of summer, depending on your point of view, when the needle hit 90 degrees, downright hell for Dewey when not in his room or on his yacht—so he managed to catch up to her when she reached the Taj and went on to explain that big men had to make big decisions.

Like, say, generals in the field of battle. For the sake of a lousy hill they sometimes sacrificed ten thousand men. Big decisions were tough to make, but big men had to make them

and let the chips fall where they may. Big men were motivated by a different code of ethics. They had to see the big
picture. Little people saw only the little picture.

"Okay," she said, having gone almost completely stiff, "so
consider me a little person, okay?

"Nothing of me has rubbed off?"

"Thank goodness, no. Not along that vein."

"That's too bad."

"No, that young girl, that's too bad."

"She's made a choice. She's gonna have to live with it."

"You mean die for it, isn't that what you mean?"

"That's the problem. I can't get anybody to do the job."

"Oh," her voice gravelly in sarcasm. "So that's what this
loyalty business is all about?"

"Can't get anybody for less than, get this, five hundred
thousand dollars. Half a million this guy wants. I don't have
that kind of cash, not with them freezing me out all over the
place. Half a million. It's all about money anymore."

"Price is that high to kill sweet sixteens? My, my. What's
the world coming to?"

"Sweet, huh? Taking the food out of people's mouths. Some
sweet. I thought you would understand. Really I did."

"I understand nothing, Dewey." She was near tears now.
"Nothing. Nothing at all. I never knew the details of what you
did. Never wanted to know. Now this? Now you tell me this?
I'm supposed to love you?"

He walked her over to the benches where groups of bus
people were doing paperbag lunch. He stared out at the ocean
and began to chuckle. She asked what was so funny, what
could possibly be so funny, and he told her. He said he'd only
been pulling her leg. "Me? Kill?" he said. "No, no, no."
What he really had in mind, what he really needed the money
for, was a bribe.

"For whom?" she said, still horrified—but not as much.

"The girl, silly."

"I thought she was being hidden."

"There are ways of finding people."

"How do you know she'd even accept?"

He said not to worry. He had intermediaries. "I was kidding," he said, which was partly true, given his skill of presenting a case at its worst to set up a denouement at its best. "This was just a test."

"Well, you flunked," she said, but relief evident in the softening of her features.

"No, I was testing *you,* Denise."

"I still say it's wrong."

"A bribe never hurt anybody. Besides, I call it a gift."

"Why so much money?"

"That's *my* business."

"Seems like an awful lot for a little girl."

"Never mind that," he said. "Look, I'm in a fix. I found a solution. I need your... *support.*"

She was mulling it over, beginning to come to terms with it, a bribe, after all, being so much the lesser evil than murder, a proposition that had had her so alarmed. A bribe to save himself. To save the others. Their jobs. It was wrong, but maybe he had a point about the greater good, the big picture. Maybe this was the precise juncture where idealism left off and real life began.

Still, though, questions.

"If you silence her, how do you know others won't come along?"

He sighed. "It's a risk, but one I have to take. You know I'm a gambler."

Lips slightly trembling, she said, "I wish you hadn't scared me like that with what you said before."

"Oh, come on. You thought I was serious?"

"*Yes.*"

"Kill a 16-year-old orphan?"

"I don't know what you do. I don't know the insides of your business."

"I do a lot of things, but l don't do that, I can tell you that."

Though relieved, she was not entirely placated and not even entirely sure that the question of murder was completely out of the picture. Why had he brought it up in the first place? To make the other thing easier to go down? Well, it *was* easier, but why even bring it up, that other thing? She knew that he was *connected* to people the newspapers and TV always prefaced with the term *reputed*. Words like *reputed* and *alleged* seemed to be stuck to him. Alleged what? she often wondered, and whenever she asked, she always got a shrug.

"You still scared the daylights out of me—and I'm still not too sure about your real plan."

Chastened and feeling contrite, he said, "Let me make a suggestion."

"Uh-oh."

"No, really. Here's the deal." There was no mistaking the sincerity of his words. She knew when he meant what he said, and this was one of those times. "You come up with a better way to save those jobs, to save those people, and you're on. I'll do anything you say. Just come up with a plan. Anything."

She was receptive. "How much time do I have?"

"Depends when that Senator McLellan starts his hearings. I don't know. But don't take too long."

CHAPTER 12

Julian Rothschild took a dip in the ocean after his guests departed, the two from Hollywood back to Hollywood, the two from Dewey Smith back to Dewey Smith. He was glad to be alone again. He was a loner, not lonely, but a loner, and too much company usually frazzled him. It wasn't people that he usually minded so much, it was talk, so much talk, so little substance. Talk was talk, but action was action, and Julian craved action, mostly the kind to be found on the casino floor. He lived in his own world, apart, jealous of anyone or anything that might separate him from his dice and divert him from his dreams of grandeur, though he was never absolutely clear about that dream except that he was running toward something as abstract as glory, whatever the hell that was!

But whatever it was, he was chasing it and the chase itself was exhilarating and the beginning of wisdom. He had made craps his life, and he was as consumed by craps as Beethoven was consumed by music, an obsession that had Julian rehearsing the art of the toss when he rose up and when he lay down, all in the pursuit of something noble, if not perfection itself.

Even if he was no Beethoven and even if music was a much higher art form than dice, still, any man who pursued the sublime, from the whittler to the sculptor, deserved to be counted among the luminaries.

The compulsion made Julian so absentminded that occasionally he drove south on a one-way street going north, and sometimes he walked into a store forgetting what he'd come in to buy. He left credit cards behind and once drove off from a gas station the nozzle still in the tank, nearly taking an entire pump with him.

His eccentricities were chalked up with knowing smiles on account of his fame. He ran red lights all over town, red lights and yellow lights and sometimes stopped for green lights. A minute after he ate, he forgot what he had eaten and when Monica wasn't around, his socks seldom matched. Before Monica came along, he bought fresh socks and shorts by the day just so he wouldn't have to do a wash. On an overnight stay in New York he forgot what hotel he'd checked into. (It was the Hilton on Sixth, and they're still waiting for him.)

From his favorite reading retreat, the Margate library, he was starting to get gentle reminders about his being overdue a year on three books, one on Salinger (J.D., not Lucky Pierre), another by the brilliant Leo Lieberman, the third by the equally brilliant, and heroic, Bernie Friedenberg.

He was overdue on many things because outside of craps and charity work, Julian didn't give much of a damn about anything. Life was too short. Only at the craps table was he alive and orderly and fiercely focused. Only at the craps table was he in love with life and in love with people, like that day at the Taj, ahead 20 grand, and toking the cocktail girl 16 of it, 16 thousand dollars, after she'd said she'd just gotten married and they were saving up for a dream-house in Avalon.

"Dream no more," he said, and declined her many invitations.

By nature, in fact, Julian was a recluse, except that his livelihood, unfortunately, took him public. Seclusion, as he saw it, was the straightest line to purification. He took his cue from the two Cabbalists, Simeon ben Yohai and his son, who fled the repression of Roman justice in Jerusalem by hiding in a cave for 12 years, out in Meron, in the Galilee, where they immersed themselves in study and prayer, only to come forth so steeped in ruthless sanctity that they burned up everything they set their eyes upon. A heavenly Voice ordered them back to the cave lest they destroy the world. That, except for the latter part, maybe, was Julian's idea of fulfillment.

Like Proust locked up in his room to do nothing but write, so Julian wanted nothing but to shoot dice, not for the sake of dice but for the advancement of another step up Jacob's Ladder.

In a word, *transcendence.* Dice, to Julian, was Proust's writing, Astaire's dancing, Williams' swing, Ali's rope-a-dope, Michaelangelo's *Pieta,* but mostly, though, Beethoven's music.

Julian had no desire to excel in anything but craps. His passion would have to be singular for it to be pure. He did not identify with people who were versatile—people who could paint, write, compose, and chew gum at the same time—and he did not admire them, either. No, the true artist is singleminded. The singlemindedness is the power, undiluted.

Back in the house he towelled himself off, fed the dog, fed the cat, heard the phone, didn't pick it up, saw the TV, didn't turn it on, showered, checked himself in the mirror, needed a haircut, never mind, needed a shave, was growing a beard, then made himself some toast—that and butter, plus Decaf, one cream, one sugar, amounted to his dinner.

He was not on a diet, didn't believe in diets, didn't believe in exercise, didn't believe in anything that improved the body through heavy lifting; the mind, yes, always the mind, the soul, the spirit, absolutely yes, but not the body, though through no fault of his own he was lean, tall, trim, and rather good-looking. He did not know that he was good-looking, and he did not care. Once upon a time he had cared. But now physical vanity was more of a bother than anything else.

Half-dressed, in cut-off jeans and wearing a Yankees baseball cap, he lay down on the couch, the living room windows wide open to welcome the evening breeze (no air conditioner—too artificial) to meditate and maybe catch a quick nap, as the opening movement to Beethoven's *Ninth Symphony* came blasting from the stereo. No CD for him. CDs lacked authenticity. Clenched in his right fist was a pair of dice. Six years ago he had palmed a pair of dice for the first time, and had never let go.

Constantly broke—his ex-wife Debra more accurately referred to their condition as *poverty*—and nothing to show but rejection slips for his writing, he began paying visits next door to AC to see if he could get lucky. This was soon after his trip to Sinai when he returned with the holy parchment, feeling himself blessed, but for what?

He lived no more than six miles away in Margate, a quiet upper-middle-class resort by the sea, was born and raised there—both parents were doctors, now deceased—but AC was where the action was. The casinos, their neons promising wondrous jackpots and dreams-come-true, beckoned. He was among the millions who joined the gold rush, that stampede of daytrippers sifting through the tables and the slots to scoop up ineffable treasures. All of this practically next door!

The only game he knew was blackjack, and blackjack wasn't good to him.

The big noise kept coming from the craps tables, where the big boys played, fat with cigars and jewelry. But there was something entirely too intimidating and mysterious about craps, a game steeped in Egyptian folklore, Greek paganism, Roman witchcraft, played with bones thought to contain spirits. The outcome of a roll could sometimes determine war and peace and, on occasion, in the hands of a seer, decide life or death of an accused.

Dice used to be all about life and death, back in the good ol' days. Now, more civilized, it was all about money.

But there was so much to know about the game, so much to lose. So fast. So kind-of disreputable, even in a casino setting. Craps was a man's game. A soldier's game. World War II. Korea. Real men did not play blackjack, and real men would not be caught dead at the slots. Nothing but craps really defined gambling, gambling in its purest state, since it was there, at the tables, that a man could risk his entire fortune on one roll of the dice.

So, one day Julian had but two white chips left after another losing stint at blackjack and for no reason at all stepped up and played a chip each on a high-low. That was about all he knew; a 2 (aces) or a 12 (boxcars) had to come up on the very next toss. Which it did, aces, payoff 30 to one. Whoa! Where had this been all his life? But it was a cold table, shooters sevening-out left and right. When the dice came around to him, he declined, out of timidity, but when they came around again he accepted, the stickman saying he couldn't do much worse than the others.

The moment he grasped those two cubes, he soared. He became radiant. The very feel of those dice intoxicated him, filled him with a surge of magic. He felt powerful, risen by a world of unleashed potential in the palm of his hands. Anything was possible by a mere flick of the wrist, a single toss, the white spots covering the two red cubes representing infinity, and the haphazard pell-mell helter-skelter manner in which they landed representing life itself, the randomness of existence.

Julian, ever the spiritualist, saw the toss as symbolizing chaos—those dice twirling aimlessly in the air as they did— and how they rested he saw as characteristic of creation. The eternal clash of order and chaos resolved when a number showed, to the delight of some and the anguish of others. A snapshot of life itself—especially when they were still in the air carrying with them the cargo of expectation and dreams.

The dice seemed to have a pulse—they throbbed in Julian's grip. They were living things that snapped, crackled, and popped. Responding to the call of ancient reflexes, he tossed. He was unsure of the rules, except that on the come-out he wanted a 7 or 11 and that when he made his point—4, 5, 6, 8, 9, or 10—he'd better get it before a 7 showed up. (He would learn from that day onward to hate the number 7.) Meantime, before he had a chance to figure things out, he rolled and repeatedly nailed those point numbers, upon which the boys had place-bets.

The boys roared in approval when the table came to life, chips flying across the layout at a dizzying pace, voices from all directions hollering *"press my 5," "press my 6," "press my 8," "press my 9," "gimme the inside," "gimme the outside," "horn," "world," "yo," "buy the 10"*... they had them a shooter, a man who kept making numbers and passes, and Julian, lit up by a sense of his own might—Julian suddenly had himself a career, finally a destiny, a resting place for his blessing, which had wandered with him from Sinai.

But, this godsend was not to be frittered; this he knew almost instantly, that he'd been chosen not to enrich himself but rather, to enrich others, the downtrodden, the needy, and never mind tithing the required ten percent, but in his case, since he'd been singled out, more like 60 to 70 percent. This was his real epiphany—that from here on in he was to conduct himself like Elijah to the Jews and like Jesus to the Christians.

This, he also knew, put him in the category of a saint, or a nut, but then all saints were thought to be nuts at first, and he was willing to take the chance. In fact, he had no choice. Life had given him no intersection, only this road, this road alone.

That night he informed Debra, not yet his ex-wife, that he was giving up writing and teaching—he taught an adult course on the Art Of The Essay at Rutgers—to devote his life to craps. She thought he was nuts all right, he couldn't blame her, and soon thereafter she became his ex-wife, for that among other reasons. Lose a wife, gain a career, almost an even trade.

But from that first day forward Julian and the dice were one. He took a course on craps at Atlantic Community College, read all the books, talked to the people, learned to shoot from that master mechanic in Vegas, Slim Sam Belmont. But mostly it was not about that, not about skill, which was limited; it was about everything unlimited, the infinite, the unknown.

Slim Sam taught him the spinner and cautioned him to use it sparingly lest he be revealed, but Slim Sam taught him much more, about walking boldly and talking softly, never to surrender to vanity but to hold his head high, always to feel like a champion from a resource deep inside and never to rely on luck, which was as treacherous as Delilah. No such thing as luck, except bad luck. Luck is the refuge of a loser.

Always think of yourself as a winner and never let it show when you lose. Never let it show even when you win. Don't give 'em anything except a blank face. Be passive and princely in appearance but a lion in your heart and soul. This is serious business. You're playing against the House, against the percentages, against fate, so don't go thinking of it as a game. No, everything's *on the line,* money yes, but most of all, your character.

Out in Vegas, Slim Sam took him around and introduced him to Chilly the Whip Shot, Fatty the Greek Shot, Benny the Slide Shot, Jackie the Twist Shot, Tony the Switch, mechanics all, cheats every one of them, and they sickened Julian—dismayed to think he was in the same company.

But Slim Sam had his reasons for exposing Julian to this rogues' gallery. They were all out of business! Slim Sam explained, sitting around the pool at the Luxor, the both of them admiring the pyramid up above and the practically topless and bottomless real-live Cleopatras down below, poolside.

Out-of-business those guys were because cheating was all they did. Tony the Switch was the latest to get caught, red-handed with a fix machine outside the Mirage that duplicated the House originals. But they all had their special schemes, and they were all bagged.

The lesson being that the spinner—the most artistic and most difficult shot of all—was merely a tool to be used in emergencies, when talent failed. To Julian that meant when his blessing failed.

Still today, Julian was disgusted to think that he was in any way connected to those sharpies. He thought himself a poet who used dice instead of words. Dice were holy instruments. Monica Travers, his girlfriend of the moment, had asked only several days ago whether he held the dice even while making love to her. He said no, he didn't, but didn't tell her that such a thing would be perverse—to the dice.

Reclined and breathing in the salty air, he was thinking of Beethoven, wondering what the man had been reaching for with all that sublime cacophony, particularly in the first movement of the *Ninth*.

Julian knew the myth, or perhaps it was no myth but truth, that upon Creation God himself had trouble containing the elements, as earth, air, fire, and water competed and raged to dominate and claim singular sovereignty.

That void and fury at The Beginning—that was Beethoven's *Ninth,* and it was also the dice spinning up in the air in chaos before they rolled over, the storm before the calm.

Julian had this personal credo: Anything that doesn't elevate doesn't count. Most of his heroes, then, were dead.

His living heroes were athletes but retired sports figures like Williams, DiMaggio and Ali, which was saying something about the latter part of the century, which lost an Einstein but gained an O.J. Simpson—and wasn't it Einstein who said that God doesn't play dice with the universe?

When he awoke from his nap, it was dark inside and out and Julian stayed like that, reclined and reflective, remembering now his visit from Hollywood, that business taken care of, remembering then his visit from the two messengers, Skinny and Fats, Fats and Skinny, that business not taken care of.

He had not been altogether surprised at that particular intrusion. At the craps table in the Versailles he had felt the heat of evil, namely in the man standing next to him, the big man who refused to play, thank goodness, because he, Julian, went off his game when evil was about. The blessing vanished. Certainly he could not vouch for every man and woman at every single craps table, but when he divined evil he lost his touch.

When it started going bad, he knew that someone at the table was throwing him off, was the bearer of something reprehensible. This big man, Dewey Smith, now that he had a name; true, he wasn't playing, but evil was in the air. Bad vibes.

What did he want? He wants my action, Julian was thinking. *They all want my action.*

Yeah, but only the impoverished need apply.

For sure, this Dewey Smith was not among the needy, but Julian, after some reflection, decided to accept the invitation anyway. He was curious. He was vain enough to be curious.

CHAPTER 13

The first invitation was to go yachting, and yachting they went, around the bay, beginning from Harrah's marina, where Dewey had his craft docked, the craft being a 42-foot Austin Mariner, built in 1973 and showing its years. Dewey was still trying to sell it and $50,000 was as high as anybody would go, and that was no answer to his problems, so to hell with them. He was keeping the yacht and, while at it, keeping up appearances, which was important for a big man, especially when he wasn't so big anymore. Dewey had read that book by Mike Todd, how Todd was up a million one day, down a million the next day—and became positively extravagant when he was down to his last penny. Now here was a man after Dewey's heart. Or take Clark Gable, in *The Hucksters,* down-and-out and heading for the big interview and in a surge of damn-everything self-confidence blowing everything he had on a *necktie.* No more Clark Gables, no more Mike Todds, no more entrepreneurs. Dewey—as he saw himself—the last of a kind. A kind that had made this country great. By whatever means. The oil barons, the steel barons, the railroad barons— they hadn't used slave labor?

Come on! The money they paid, the hours they made those people work? Today, nobody remembered that; today they were remembered as benevolent *philanthropists!*

On the yacht here was Denise, bikini-clad, as were other guests, mostly young women who'd fit right in if this were an old Hugh Hefner party, Dewey making a big show of introducing Julian as the greatest craps shooter of all time, Julian flinching but holding his tongue. The girls kept giving Julian their best smiles, and Julian enjoyed the attention, for about a minute.

Dewey, busy keeping his company entertained, kept sidling up to Julian, saying, "We'll talk."

Whatever, thought Julian.

Denise didn't say much to Julian or to anybody, busy being cool, distant and altogether quite sullen, body language suggesting she'd been dragged here in chains—but not a bad-looking woman, filling out the bikini quite nicely, ample up top and tanned legs shimmering in the sunlight. But never a smile.

Troubled, too troubled for a lady so endowed. She was here under protest, no doubt, maybe, judging from that chiseled jaw of hers, so squared off, almost mannishly, a comment of her life entirely, a life endured under protest.

Only when she removed her sunglasses now and then to squint up at the sun—only then did she reveal a touch of softness and innocence. Julian was intrigued.

But he figured that she didn't like him, or maybe she did. Some women liked you so much they could only show it by hating you. Either way, she kept averting her eyes, as though she had something on her mind, keeping a million secrets. What she was doing with Dewey was the big question.

This was no match made in heaven. She was no broad, no dingbat, no bimbo, even with all that blonde hair. There was real intelligence in that gaze. She kept herself mostly on the deck, away from everybody, reading Kafka. When she'd look up occasionally, her look said, Buzz off. That included everybody, even Dewey.

Julian had read Kafka and thought maybe he should say something and then thought *nah.*

"We'll talk," Dewey said for the 12th time, which was about when they collided with a speedboat, bow to bow.

Nothing serious, just a scrape. The boaters, two college kids, boy and girl wearing Princeton T-shirts, frantically apologized and promised to pay damages, of which there practically were none.

"We should notify the Coast Guard," said the young woman in the boat.

Dewey snapped, his face turning dark red like a tick swelling up on fresh blood. "No Coast Guard. No nobody. Okay?"

"But it's regulation," said the young man.

"Nothing happened," Dewey said. "Goodbye."

"I think you hit us," said the girl, changing her mind.

"I hit *you?* Fuck outta here."

"Hey," said the guy.

"Hey, nothin'."

"We don't wanna report you."

"*Report* me? You gonna tell Daddy?"

"You're nuts, mister."

"Let's just call it quits. Peace," said Dewey holding up the peace sign as if this were the '60s.

The kid answered by flipping him the bird.

"You crazy?" said the kid—this right after Dewey, a certain look in his eye, took the helm from the skipper and began ramming them, from stem to stern. The kids began to panic and scream, Dewey delighting in it and persisting until it looked like they might capsize.

"Enough," said Julian—Julian had been below deck listening to an aspiring actress's sob story—when he finally caught up to Dewey and pulled him away from the helm with a gentle but firm hand.

Later, Dewey came to his senses and apologized and even thanked Julian for stepping in, sheepishly admitting that he'd lost control of himself, mainly on account of the arrogance displayed by those kids, college kids who had it all, thought they knew everything, no respect, everything handed to them, not knowing what it was like to make it in the real world, naked and alone, like himself. What really set him off, he said, was that fucking Princeton logo. Told you everything you needed to know, about them, about Princeton, about this new generation coming up, conditioned by sloth, MTV, sitcoms and the luxury of idleness to have the world handed to them—the worst of it being that they were right! All the fighting had already been done for them. They had nothing to do but reap.

The incident abruptly ended the partying mood on the boat, and they headed back to base cheerlessly, despite Dewey's attempts to shrug it all off and pretend it had never happened. Denise slid Julian a worrisome sideglance, a shared secret, as if to say now you know, but, Julian reflected, *there were points in Dewey's favor.* He *had* offered peace and the boy did turn on him, did flip him the finger. So Julian was ready to call it even, and as for Dewey's prognosis about the upcoming generation, well...

Which didn't mean he liked the man.

Later, back at Harrah's, Dewey was collected again, and again said, "We'll talk."

Julian agreed to listen, though he didn't know why. Maybe it was Denise.

CHAPTER 14

They agreed on a second meeting at Tony's Baltimore Grille, an Italian restaurant at Iowa and Atlantic, down a couple of blocks from the Tropicana. Julian had eaten there many times before, as had Dewey, as had just about everybody who knew anything about AC.

Dewey liked it there because it was noisy and crowded; small chance, therefore, of being bugged or snooped. Julian liked it because the service was fast and the food was usually good.

"You shoot like a mechanic," Dewey said for openers, over pizza, intending humor but getting the trace of a grimace in response, Julian flatly explaining that it was all about randomness, no such thing as skill—Julian not liking the man now any more than he did before, and therefore playing it close to the vest.

Sensing the friction, Dewey talked sports, politics, and the weather, but still failed to get a rise out of Julian, who was not asking what this meeting was all about but was clearly impatient to get on with the heart of the matter.

So be it, thought Dewey. *Fuck it,* thought Dewey.

"Listen, pal," he said, half-serious, half-joking, a talent of his that put the other person in the position of having to decide. "You owe me fifty thousand dollars," then going into how it happened, there at the Versailles. "So fair is fair and least you can do is get me even, being the *expert* that you are. So you're not a mechanic. My mistake."

"You want my action." Julian was studying the man with a fierce gaze, concluding that he, Julian, was being romanced for some distasteful score. This wouldn't be the first time he'd been called upon to perform an act of deception.

As always under these circumstances, he felt the urge to cut and run as the mere discussion of something conspiratorial soiled the purity of his work, tarnished the dice. Julian believed that every word, every thought, was recorded ("an eye sees, an ear hears"), to be played back in the next life, your friends, enemies, and relatives in rapt attendance. The world-to-come would probably be like that old TV show, *This Is Your Life,* where they trotted out people from your past. Except that up there or down there they'd trot out your enemies, too, and play back all your misdeeds and mistakes. Like talking to a man named Dewey.

"Exactly. I want your action, and I know you give action to all those charities. I know. I asked around."

Dewey still wasn't sure how to play the man, good cop or bad cop. Still hadn't figured him out, first thinking, from all he'd heard, that he was some kind of a mystic, living up in the clouds, very touchy, very sensitive, a poetic sort. Yeah, well— but the guy, the guy had balls. Dewey sensed that right away, the way the guy looked: impassive, eyelids droopy, Robert Mitchum style. Style. Yeah, the guy had style, hard to define what, but style. A cool customer. We'll see. We shall see. We shall fucking see.

"So you think I can win at will?" Julian said, cat-and-mouse.

"I know you can."

Julian kept nodding, as he usually did in order to restrain his indignation. "You think it's all about money."

"Come on. We're kids?"

"It's got nothing to do with money."

"Right, I heard that, too, about you. Like it's some kind of religious experience. Spare me."

"Listen, Mr. Smith."

"My friends call me Dewey."

"Listen, Mr. Smith," Julian began, then paused, and then reminded Dewey that the singular for dice is *die*.

Dewey chuckled. "Is this that mystical stuff coming up?"

"Yeah, it's mystical all right when people's fortunes are at stake."

Which was exactly the opening Dewey had been waiting for as he began and then went on and on about his business, the garment business, the two thousand people dependent on him for food and shelter, the government threatening to take it all away, all on some trumped-up charges, so that before you knew it, these people, maybe more than two thousand, the two thousand he still had left, would be out on the street, jobless, homeless.

"So what I need," Dewey said, "is half a million bucks, to save my operation, to rescue these people." Forgetting to mention, of course, that one detail, what the half million was really for. Buying the silence of one Sasha Spivak.

Dewey had no doubt that the word *bribe* would be something too hard to swallow for a guy so fucking righteous, so fucking religious about dice. The word *murder* was doubly out of the question, of course. Not that Dewey was even thinking in those terms. Necessarily.

"So this really is charity," Dewey said, finishing up his pizza and his discourse by adding that he needed the money to meet payroll for these poor people, the government having practically wiped him out.

Julian, unaware of the missing detail, was not wholly unsympathetic. This was not a bad cause, if true.

"I thought it was only fifty thousand you were after," Julian said.

"That, too," Dewey said with a chuckle. "That's for me personally. The rest..."

"So you think I can just step up to any table and come out winners?"

"So I hear. So I saw."

"Nobody can be a winner all the time, Mr. Smith. I *do* lose."

That was true. Sometimes Julian did lose.

"Yeah, but I'm a gambler, Mr. Rothschild. I'm gambling on you."

"Half a million dollars is a lot of money."

"But look at the purpose," said Dewey, almost believing in the goodness of his cause. "It's for people. Underdogs."

That came as an inspiration to Dewey. Underdogs. A perfect lure for a man like Julian.

"I hear you," Julian said pensively.

So he was nodding again, but not necessarily from indignation. This wasn't so easy to decline, being for people and all, jobs, food, rent. That's what he, Julian, was all about, after all. Craps in the service of redemption. But there had to be a catch here someplace, given the man. The man never referred to his operation as sweatshops, never would, but Julian wasn't that stupid—and so what if they were sweatshops? It was still about people. Should his disdain for one man cloud his responsibility to thousands? A hazy area, to be sure, but few things in life were clear-cut, black and white, good and bad.

Most of life reposed in the blurred region between the extremes, and most decisions rested on ambiguities. Such as this.

"You never played for that much?" Dewey said.

"Never."

"That makes it all the more exciting, wouldn't you say? Quite a challenge."

"I'll have to think about it," Julian said, meaning he'd check around.

Dewey, sensing rejection, brought up Beethoven. Dewey had done his homework.

"What a coincidence," Dewey said. "Both of us lovers of Beethoven."

"The whole world loves Beethoven, Mr. Smith. Now *that's* a coincidence."

"What do you think he was trying to say?" Dewey asked.

"Personally, I prefer Brahms."

Which ended that discussion, and ended the meeting altogether, but not before Dewey had the final say, which was: "Just remember, Mr. Rothschild, a decision of life and death rests on your head."

CHAPTER 15

Julian was up in a plane, destination L.A. He had sworn off Hollywood but, spooked by the decision he had already made, he wanted to get away, chart some distance, and then came the plea from Clive Edwards, the director, to please come and help out with *Scared Money,* which was now in principal photography and in trouble. They wanted to get it right, authentic, Julian's way. Promise.

For reading material on the flight he had André Schwarz Bart's *The Last of the Just,* his favorite novel. This would be his fifth reading. The novel had come at precisely the right time when Julian had just begun to relate craps with the cosmos.

Julian had already made up his mind. Maybe not completely, but he was leaning toward Dewey's request and had already told Dewey as much, to Dewey's delight; only to wait until he, Julian, got back from other business, at which time they'd finalize. Dewey, who was still waiting for Denise to come up with a better plan, that is, a plan to substitute for hush-money to silence a 16-year-old, said, "This is a great day, Julian."

Julian, sipping TWA coffee, chewed on those words and wondered why everything the man said sounded so damned counterfeit. He had made inquiries and, as expected, Dewey was a louse—but a louse who employed people by the thousands, yes, in sweatshops, yes, under-age, yes, below minimum age, yes to all that and yet what else was there for these people? They were the refuse, the remnants, Persons Without Papers, just as his grandparents had been.

They, too, had once been immigrants, who saw their kids through medical school by washing floors—his grandmother even did windows—and toiling in sweatshops, his grandfather working doubleshifts in Trenton's Jersey Suit and Coat Factory. His grandfather, the Pop-Pop with whom Julian had a very special relationship, had once said: "Never turn from your own flesh." To Julian that meant just about anybody who needed him.

That, more than anything, was what inclined him to win for the people, in this case, Dewey's people.

Julian was well-aware that these workers were being used and abused, and in a perfect world there'd be no sweatshops, there'd be no Deweys, and yes, there'd be no illness, there'd be no war, strife, or famine. But, the world was not perfect, and most things were wrong, anyway, and this was just another thing that was wrong, and to make it right—that is, to send them out on the street, or back to the countries where they'd be arrested or tortured—would make it even more wrong.

For Dewey the man, the individual, Julian had nothing but contempt. Julian would have been happier never to have met the man, and even happier to see him pay for his cruelties. But to refuse him would only cause so much more suffering to the innocents.

That was Julian's reasoning—without the Sasha Spivak detail.

Until he turned to the *Times,* courtesy of TWA, and there it was, front page, all about Zee Zee Sampson, the sweatshops, the crackdowns, the new laws, Dewey Smith mentioned most prominently, along with someone named Sasha Spivak, 16, from Russia, a girl once employed by Dewey Smith and now ready to testify against him before a Senate subcommittee headed by Senator Clarence McLellan.

Apparently, as the article had it, Sasha Spivak was a golden find for the authorities as she was the first sweatshop employee or former employee willing to talk, the others mute for fear of their jobs or fear of deportation, never mind their lack of English, in most cases.

Spivak was prepared to tell tales of Russian mobsters, kidnappings, workplace abuse, and slave labor. An opening date for the hearings was still to be determined, but McLellan was eager to hear her story, a version of which had youngsters shanghaied by the multitudes for sweatshop bondage, Sasha Spivak inclusive.

Terrific, thought Julian, rubbing his eyes, and then reading a bit more, how since the demise of communism, Russia had replaced Romania as the world's largest exporter of orphans, these doe-eyed victims supplied for illicit labor across the world by Russia's fastest growing industry: mobsterism.

Julian wondered if Dewey knew about this, about Sasha Spivak. Somehow, the subject never came up. One thing he did know. McLellan said if her story proved true, there'd be a nationwide sweep to rid the nation entirely of sweatshops, "beginning and ending with the worst offender of them all, Dewey Smith."

Which left Julian where? He did not know. Things were different now, there was a face, a name, a young girl with a direct accusation—but how different was it, really, when this young girl told a story that could spell doom for thousands? Not so fast, not so easy.

Especially as the article very briefly mentioned yet another young girl, nameless, who said conditions at the sweatshop were not all that bad, and that even if they were, she didn't care, nobody cared, they preferred the work over the alternative, starvation or deportation. Miss Anonymous was quoted as saying this Sasha Spivak was doing more harm than good and that many people like herself were wishing she would just shut up.

So there was that side, too, even if it was buried in the last three paragraphs of the jump page.

But the obvious thing, Julian was thinking, *was to take sides with the Sasha girl, stand against the bully, say to hell with you, Dewey Smith, sink or swim without me, Dewey Smith, preferably sink,* the very thoughts going through Julian's mind at the moment—and yet, was anything in life really obvious?

Even the best of things, the holiest of things, don't they often come from murky origins? Beethoven came from the humblest of beginnings, his father a most ordinary man. David was conceived from sin (said so himself in a *Psalm*), going way back with Judah and Tamar.

What today we call the Seven Wonders of the Ancient World, what did they all have in common? Artemision at Ephesus, the Colossus of Rhodes, the Hanging Gardens of Babylon, the Mausoleum at Halicarnassus, Olympian Zeus, the Pyramids of Egypt, the Tower of Pharos—all built by the sweat of slaves. Yesterday's sweatshops.

Which was no excuse for Dewey, the fact that so many of life's splendors came from corruption, except that this was not about Dewey, not for Dewey that Julian had agreed to raise half a million at the casinos; no, it was about being faithful to your own flesh. That, in Julian's eyes, would be the bigger sin, to use your disdain of a single evil man as a hammer of justice against the people.

CHAPTER 16

They had put him up at the palm-treed Four Seasons in Beverly Hills and told him to wait for the phone, a call that didn't come day one or day two or day three. Julian kept getting the voice-mail machine whenever he tried to reach the production office at Sunset Pictures, press one for this, two for that, three if you know the person's number; none of the above for Julian. He tried the main switchboard and when somebody finally answered, she said "Wait. I'll transfer you" and before Julian could stop her he was already back to the machine.

They were paying his expenses, so he ate well. But he wasn't feeling well, which was why he wasn't taking the next plane home. He had gotten on the plane with a cold. On the plane it settled in his ears—he'd always had an ear problem—and got worse by the minute as the result of the cabin pressure.

When he got off, he couldn't hear a thing and it got only slightly better by the time he checked in, and now, three days later, it was still like that, even after a nurse and a doctor had been up to see him, at a cost of $400, not counting medicines, none of these expenses covered by the studio.

So when the call finally came from Clive Edwards, the director, Julian was not exactly chipper and even less so when Clive said: "Where in blazes are you?" Explaining that *they* were in Vegas, shooting, and waiting for him.

So why, asked Julian, did his people check him into Beverly Hills?

"Our mistake," conceded Clive, adding that things do get hectic around production time, and insisting that Julian hop on the next plane to Vegas. "Make that a car," said Julian. "Can't fly. My ears won't take another flight."

A studio limo picked him up and five hours later deposited him at the Hilton, the one off the Strip.

That same day, unshowered, unshaven, he was plunked in the casino, which had been turned into a set at the section where they usually shot craps. In the middle was a craps table surrounded by cameras, lights, actors, extras, production assistants, director, assistant director, crew, numbering maybe 50, plus a crowd of maybe 200 gawkers beyond the ropes and the security people, all waiting for a glimpse of Matt Cain, with but one flick to his credit, already hailed as the second coming of Brando.

Karen Davies, his co-star, was finishing up another picture but was due on the set any day, the same Karen Davies known mainly for her psychic beliefs, psychic prowess, psychic commercials, psychic friends, not to mention her fame as an astral-surfer.

Julian was welcomed onto the set by the gorgeous Lynn Sterling, head of production at Sunset and the most powerful woman in Hollywood after Sherry Lansing. She practically tackled him to the floor with hugs and kisses, gushing, "You're such a dear for coming. We need you so badly."

As he prepared to return her affections, theatrically shutting his eyes and offering his lips, she turned blank, almost sullen, and vanished, lost in the frenzy. People saw. He felt very stupid, as he usually did when he went Hollywood. So why did he keep going back? Vanity. He was not yet so perfect.

He had worked for Lynn Sterling as a technical advisor on one other picture, *Days of Wrath,* which had but one gambling sequence in it, whereas *Scared Money* was all about gambling. Actually all about Matt Cain gambling. He was playing the part of a compulsive, a guy who loses everything, all his money, all his possessions, in one session at the tables. Written, of course, by Donald Oaks, Julian's ex-wife's famous novelist-cum-screenwriter husband, who most certainly must have used Julian as his model, which Donald emphatically denied. Not that Julian cared either way. He kind of liked Donald when Donald used him.

"But the characterization is lacking," Clive Edwards the director was saying at the Hilton's coffee shop, "and I say that, use that word, in lieu of motivation, which has become so overused, were it not for the fact that in Matt's case it's true. He doesn't understand the drive that would make a man risk everything at a craps table. Am I saying it correctly, Matt?"

Matt, the star, the exclamation point for the word *sullen,* maybe 28, shaggy-haired, bleary-eyed, was slouched in his seat Brando-style. He was wearing jeans and a soiled T-shirt and was smoking in the no-smoking section. Clive was wearing what appeared to be a pawn-shop green military jacket, the one with epaulets and other battlefield ornaments, the obvious remains of some old soldier who had faded away without so much as a thank-you. Julian was in his favorite blue jeans and blue polo shirt, his head covered with a Yankees baseball cap. Conversation, without a script, was not Matt's strong suit, Julian recognized right away. But Matt grunted a lot.

Clive was the animated one. British reserve? They never sent that kind over here. "So is there anything you can say to light a bulb in Matt's head? He needs your, shall we say, inspiration?"

Look, putz-face! Quit the smoking, quit the slouching, quit the sour-pussing, quit the routine. It's old. It's tired. It's been done. Every generation brings out a new one. They come and go like fireflies. Come closer. Let me whisper in your ear. *You are not Brando*. Even Brando is Brando no more.

Anyway, that's what Julian was inspired to say. Naturally, he didn't.

"Anticipation," Julian said and leaned back as if he'd said it all.

That lit up no bulb for Matt Cain, but for Clive Edwards it was a moment of clarity.

"But that's exactly it, isn't it?" he said. "What more is there to say? The anticipation that the next roll of the dice could make you king, can answer all your dreams. What do you think, Matt? Does it help?"

Julian winced. He was too familiar with Hollywood effusiveness.

Matt speaks. "Yeah but—the guy. What kind of a guy is he? I mean I just can't picture a guy blowing all his..."

"To be truthful," Clive interrupted, "the script is not too clear on that point."

"I mean, is the guy nuts?"

That remark offended Julian. He took it personal. He could very easily see a man risk it all at one session at the table, even one roll. He had seen it done and there was nothing nuts or pathetic about it, in fact it was quite heroic and glorious to have such faith, such guts. In fact it was the last word on faith, win or lose, even more a testament to faith than the piety of religion.

"Hmm," said Matt, after Julian told him all that, clearly provoked.

"But is there more?" asked Clive. "More to the man?"

"I haven't read the book."

"But you did read the script."

"As you say, lacking in characterization."

"Which we're counting on you to fill in."

"Almost like creating the character from scratch."

"I wouldn't mind," said Clive.

Matt shrugged.

"In that case," said Julian, "I'd forget about making the guy a stereotypical gambler, you know, a degenerate. He's compulsive, but that doesn't make him nuts, it doesn't make him bad. Quite the opposite—that is, if you're looking to create a character with some originality."

"We are," said Clive. "Three-dimensional is what we're after."

To which Julian responded, "What you're really after, I think, given that it's a man who's risking everything on a roll of the dice—what you're after is a man in search of purity, his moment of truth. It's like the surfer who gives his life for the perfect wave. Your man is just like that. That makes him very special. In a way it even makes him holy."

"Isn't that going a bit far?" snarled Matt, slowly unrumpling himself and showing signs of wakefulness.

"Well, depends on what you call 'holy.' I call 'holy' the man who sheds the ordinary to seek transcendence. Like the guy you're playing, he's risking it all so that he can get God to answer the phone."

Clive jumped on that. "That's good. Very good. I think we're getting there don't you think?"

Matt was finally sitting up.

"But how do you show a guy being holy at a craps table?" he wanted to know.

"I'm no actor. But isn't that an attitude you just convey by *being*?"

"Being who? Specifically." Now Matt was sort of into it, showing a glimmer of interest.

"I can only refer you to one of the great books of all time. I even brought it with me. *The Last of the Just.*"

"I've heard of it," said Clive.

"So?"

"Well, you want specific, I'm giving you specific. Read the book."

"Can you summarize it?" asked Matt. "I only read scripts."

"Won't be the same."

"Please," said Clive.

"All right. Think of yourself as the *Lamed-Vov*. You want specific, right?"

Here something happened that changed the chemistry at the Hilton table. Matt chuckled at Julian's use of the term *Lamed-Vov*. That upset Julian terribly. He said something to Matt that one never says to a star, a rising Brando, who could completely shut down a $75 million production by stalking off in a snit if someone, no more than a technical advisor, called him an asshole, Julian's words precisely. But rather than take offense, Matt liked what he heard. "Go on," he said, as student to teacher. "Please."

"Okay. The world exists only on the merits of 36 Just Men, the *Lamed-Vov*. Their righteousness is what keeps us all alive. If one of them were to falter, and here I'll quote, 'the sufferings of mankind would poison even the souls of the newborn, and humanity would suffocate in a single cry.'"

"I love it," said Clive.

"I love it, too. But am I supposed to be one of these Just Men?"

"Sort of. If you're trying to approach your character as someone real, someone original. The thing is, these *Lamed-Vovs,* they live among us and we don't know who they are, and here's the real kicker: Most of the time even *they* don't know who they are. Get it? They're unknown even to themselves. They're holy, they're special, they hold up the world, and they don't even know it."

"That's our man!" said Clive, slapping the table. "He's transcendent and doesn't *know* it! That's it!"

"Not bad," said Matt.

CHAPTER 17

Lynn Sterling had invited Julian to dinner at Caesars on the Strip and he was there on time, six sharp, in the steak-house, or maybe it was supposed to be seven, as that's what time it was when she still hadn't shown up. So he ate alone, and later, when he ran into her back at home base, the Hilton, she emerging from a late meal there with honchos, including Donald Oaks and Clive Edwards, he didn't bother to ask and she didn't bother to explain. She didn't even know she'd stood him up. Never said a word. Just smiled and briskly said hello, then adding, as she brushed past, "We've got to do lunch sometime." Whatever.

But Don, whom Julian referred to as his husband-in-law, Don being married to Julian's ex-wife—Don appeared flustered and wanted a word, if Julian could spare a moment. "Sure," Julian said.

They took the cushioned chairs in the lounge, outside the tobacco and candy shop, the ringing and clanging of slot machines providing background and soundtrack, Don saying he appreciated Julian's input.

"Good," said Julian, well-aware of Hollywood opposite-speak.

Except that Matt, the new Brando, was now taking the character in an entirely different direction, different from what he, Don, had in mind. "Too cerebral. Actually, he's torn and confused."

"Exactly my impression," said Julian, intentionally prompting the next cue.

"No, I mean after his consultation with you."

"Oh!" Julian said innocently.

"I know that Clive meant well, and I sure as hell know you meant well..."

"How's Debra by the way?" Julian asked.

"Terrific. She wishes you the best."

Which was not the thing to say to Julian, a reformed writer whose rejection slips usually signed off that way.

We wish you the best. *Now go fuck yourself.*

"But to get back..."

"So what can I do?" asked Julian. "Debrief him?"

"Frankly, I mean you're the greatest, but I wonder if it was necessary to bring you in. No offense. Right?"

"Absolutely."

"But Clive and Lynn were nuts about my script," he said, eyeballs moving rapidly.

"As, no doubt, they should be."

"They were particularly taken by my characterization. Matt's character."

"I can see why."

"So the whole thing puzzles me."

Julian shrugged. "What can I say."

"I just wanted you to know." Don shook his head. "I mean, what's this about the 36 Wise Men?"

"The 36 *Just* Men."

"Whatever. I mean you've got Matt walking around the set like he's some Old Testament prophet or something. He's not mumbling anymore. We wanted that mumble. He's *sermonizing* for shit's sake."

"That's actors for you," Julian said with a straight face.

"Correct. They're very impressionable. Actors are children."

"Really," said Julian, slightly baffled. "I didn't think he'd take it that far."

"Oh, he thinks he's one of those 36 Just Men."

"Is that so bad for the part he's playing?"

"Hey, I'm talking about for *real*. He thinks he himself, Matt Cain, is one of your Laymed..."

"*Lamed-Vovs.*"

"Right. He thinks he's a *Lamed-Vov*. Clive's tearing his hair out."

"Whose hair?"

"His own hair."

"Must be something we can do," Julian offered.

"You've done enough." Don paused to reflect. "Sorry. I don't mean to be so direct."

"But is it so wrong, for the sake of characterization..."

"Hey, we're talking about a gambler, a compulsive gambler, a degenerate."

"Hmmm," said Julian, reservedly. "But is that really characterization, or passing judgment on a character?"

"Isn't that what characterization is? Passing judgment on a character?"

"Not in my book," said Julian, though it was Donald Oaks who wrote the books, bestsellers to boot. "That's giving a character no inner life, no air to breathe, no chance to develop three-dimensionally."

Don chuckled derisively. "We're still talking about a compulsive."

Julian was getting pissed. "A writer is supposed to love his characters, even the flawed ones."

Don snorted. "You're lecturing *me* on how to be a writer?"

"This might be a good time to end the meeting," Julian suggested.

"I just wanted you to know," Don said, a bit contrite.

"I wish you the best," Julian said, distractedly.

CHAPTER 18

Up in his room on the eighth floor at the Hilton, the red light was blinking on his phone. The message was from Dewey, calling from the Versailles in Atlantic City. Julian was in no rush to make the return call. He had had enough, of everybody. He was feeling exploited and quite useless, and useless was how he generally felt when he hadn't been at a table for a while. Sometimes he was overcome by doubts as to what he was doing with his life. At the tables it all made such sense. Away, he was so utterly lost.

He phoned Monica Travers. He had not seen her in a while. They had not sworn undying love, but it seemed to be heading in the right direction. What he got was her answering machine. He left no message. The 1990s, he shrugged.

He went to the bathroom to shower. When he towelled himself he saw blood on the towel. His investigation revealed a nosebleed. He wondered if it was in any way connected to his ear problem, and grew alarmed.

An hour later—déjà vu all over again—a nurse was up to see him in his hotel room, and she was quite a looker. The doctor was there an hour after the nurse arrived, and he said it was nothing, probably just the nosedrops that Julian had been using. The doctor left, but the nurse stayed behind, for comfort, as Julian seemed quite upset. She offered to rub his back. One thing led to another.

When the phone rang around midnight, the nurse was gone but Dewey was on the phone, saying, with the familiarity of an old buddy, that he'd been after Julian for days, wondering where he'd gone off to, and that if he'd known in the first place that it was Hollywood he could have put Julian in touch with a million contacts—Julian remembering that contacts were what friends used to be.

"I used to pal around with Lynn Sterling," Dewey said, chuckling. "Just ask her."

"First chance I get."

"I used to run horses. We had the same trainer. Ever hear of Buddy Phillips?"

"I know the name," Julian said, holding the man at arm's length, aware that he was keeping tough company.

"Came close to winning the Kentucky Derby that one year. Quite a gal, that Lynn."

More chuckling, followed by some throat-clearing. "Well, listen, Julian, I hope this doesn't change things. I mean, by now I'm sure you've read that thing in the *Times*. Was it as bad for you as it was for me?"

Julian said yes, it did give him pause.

"But we do have a commitment, right?"

Julian said "sort of" and Dewey said that "sort of" and "commitment" were words that did not go together. Julian agreed. He also noted an edge in Dewey's voice and remembered that scene on the yacht when Dewey went bonkers. Deals, said Dewey, are not made in commas. Deals are made in periods. "Funny," said Dewey, "how they splashed all that bad stuff about me on page one and then buried the good stuff at the bottom. They're real busy making me out to be Pharaoh. You still there?"

"I'm here."

"I hope you read what that other girl had to say."

"I did."

"Paints a different picture, don't you think?"

"Not entirely, but it does provide another side to the story. Maybe."

"Exactly. There's the other side to the story that nobody wants to hear. Can I still count on you?"

Julian did not remember making a commitment. He remembered saying that he was *inclined* to help out, nothing firm, except that to some people that was firm enough. In other words, Julian had gotten himself cornered. Not to go through with it would be the same as welching, welching on a bet, something no gambler ever did if he wanted to sustain his integrity, his reputation, maybe even his life. Welching simply was not done. If gamblers had one strict code, that was it—you paid off, you honored your debts, you kept your word.

Responding to Julian's silence, Dewey went on to say that since that article appeared, the noose around his neck was tightening something terrific, let alone from the embarrassment that made him a pariah, but from the crushing tyranny of the authorities, federal and state. Eight of his factories in New Jersey had been shut down overnight, sending his workers scattering. Some, those without the green card, those who could not run fast enough, were being detained to meet up with who-knew-what ungodly fate.

It was only the good offices of some civil-rights motivated congressmen, lawmakers whose districts included large pockets of immigrants, plus immigrant groups that equated the new sweatshop Seizure laws with arbitrary persecution, that was keeping him from complete meltdown. Yes, of course, there were still people in high places who were on his side if only to protect the innocents against the intrusion of Big Government, whose agenda was the casting out—out of the country—of immigrants legal and illegal.

Only these advocates stood between him and absolute ruin—and, in some cases, they needed to be paid.

Dewey made the confession, fuck the bugs and to hell with pussyfootin' with this guy. Anyway, he'd had the room checked.

"I'm being candid," he said. "That half million, much of it is for gifts to the right people."

Julian had suspected as much. He wasn't shocked... shocked. He wasn't born yesterday.

"The need is urgent," Dewey sighed, then getting even more candid by conceding that the girl Sasha Spivak was among those to be receiving a gift for her silence—and this did not shock Julian, either.

"The girl?" he said, only to know more, still suspicious that there was something else in the brew.

"That's something we can discuss later," Dewey said, dismissively.

As Dewey rambled on about the righteousness of his campaign, it occurred to Julian that he doth protest too damned much. Occurred to him that, shit, I am being enlisted to *bribe* people. How good can that be?

"So this is all on the level," Julian said.

"Of course it is. You read the papers. You know the hell I'm in. You know there's people, my people, being sent out into the streets, some nowhere to sleep, some back to where they came from, gettin' tortured. You think conditions are so bad in my factories? So why do I have people begging me to take them back? I swear this is true."

Yes, this was true. People *were* begging to go back, only because there was no other place for them to go. A bad job is better than no job, and sweatshop existence in America is better than random torture in Haiti. America is still the land

of opportunity and no sweatshop worker thinks of her job as
the end but rather, as a beginning, which makes the toil almost bearable, just to know that here, at least, there are possi-
bilities—if not for her, then for her children.

"Something smells," Julian said.

"Like what?"

"That business with the girl."

"She's got a beef. So? Let her get another job. This is a
free country. If everybody who had a beef went to Congress..."

"Apparently it's quite a legitimate beef."

"I say I was perfect? Listen, I can't afford to pay union
wages."

"Yeah, but kidnappings, beatings..."

"All bullshit. Hey, you're not backing out on me now, are
ya? A minute ago you sounded okay."

"I've had time to think," Julian very upset now that he had
gone this far with this guy, regretting the trip to the yacht,
lamenting the meeting at Tony's, repenting the handshake,
drifting into it, into what? But that's how you end up doing
the work of the devil. You don't just wake up one morning
and do something evil, no, you drift into it, one step at a time,
one thing leading to another, so that you're hardly aware that
you've done something *awful,* it being such a gradual thing.
Like this?

My motives were good, thought Julian. *I was thinking of
this as just another charity. I knew what I was getting into.
Or—did I? Did I know this guy was so big that he makes the
papers? Not the funny pages, either. Did I know that the United
States Government was onto him? Did I know that one of his
workers, a 16-year-old girl, no less, has a whopper of a tale
to tell?*

"So this is where I come in," Julian said.

"What are you talking about?"

"To make hush money for you."

"I already told you that," Dewey snapped.

"Pay off the girl to keep her mouth shut."

"Right, so two thousand people can sleep at night with a roof over their heads."

"No harm to the girl, though."

Dewey laughed. "Harm? Giving somebody money, you call that harm? Hey, what's wrong?"

"I'm concerned," said Julian. "Very concerned."

"Still thinking, huh?"

"Afraid so, Mr. Smith."

"Dewey," said Dewey.

"Okay, listen, Dewey, I think I have to say no. Sorry."

Nothing from Dewey. One of those pauses that could mean anything.

"I wish you the best," said Julian.

Again Dewey laughed. "You wish me the best? What the fuck's that supposed to mean?"

"It means..."

"It means you're welching," Dewey said, about to explode, but remembering that he was dealing with an *artist,* a very sensitive person; so taking it down a notch, he lowered his temperature and his voice. He needed this kid, and he didn't need him mad. "Look, there's got to be some way I can convince you that you'd be doing the right thing."

"I've made up my mind," Julian now firm with conviction and indignation and in a hurry to wash himself clean of all this if such a thing is possible once you've stepped in mud.

"What seems to be the problem?" Dewey wanted to know.

"The problem seems to be that you're a bloodsucker."

Okay, he didn't mean to put it so bluntly, but there was no other word for *bloodsucker.*

A long pause before Dewey approached it from a different, more definitive angle: "Let's try this," he said, "and I'm willing to forget what you just said. Suppose," he began, and Julian held his breath, because he knew what was coming. He always knew it would come, sooner or later, and that if it came, it would come from someone like Dewey, someone who asked all the questions and got all the answers. "Suppose," Dewey went on, "I kept my mouth shut about how your baby died."

"Oh, screw you, mister." He thought about hanging up, but couldn't. He was in too deep.

"Debra, your ex-wife, isn't she? I believe so, and I believe you're still nuts about her. People talk. Yeah, and I believe there was some kind of talk about Shaken-Baby Syndrome. You know, where you shake a baby to death, usually a crying baby. Something about her being left alone with the baby and, well, you know the rest."

In fact, Debra had been alone with the baby, and, in fact the autopsy revealed the *symptoms* of Shaken-Baby Syndrome, but it was all inconclusive, and even Dr. Morrow said some infants bring it on themselves by excessive thrashing. He interpreted it as SIDS, Sudden Infant Death Syndrome—for which there was seldom a real explanation.

But, of course, Debra was devastated, took the blame entirely, lived with it every day of her life, since the tragedy happened on her watch, and there was never any doubt in Julian's mind that she was innocent. Debra would never do anything like that; she loved the baby and there wasn't a hateful bone in her body. Never Debra. Not for a minute. But there was gossip, even a police report, which eventually cleared her. Julian, with the help of Dr. Morrow, got it hushed up before the rumors went too far—but secrets like this always come back. There are no secrets, not in this life. People talk.

To bring it all in the open again, even just a whisper of it in the papers, would crush this woman that he still loved so very much, and Dewey—Dewey had something on him now. Not on him, that would be no problem, but on Debra, and that was a problem.

Julian was stunned. Nothing to say.

"But, hey," Dewey went on, switching to good cop after playing his usual game of set-up from worst case to best case. "Let's forget about all that, y'know? Me, I've forgotten about it already. Completely. Out of my mind. Don't even concern yourself about what I just said. I mean you don't think I'm that kind of a guy, do you? Listen, I don't make people do what they don't want to do. Naw. Never gets to that with me. I make suggestions is all.

"Hey, I got scruples. So all I'm asking is you keep your word. I'm appealing to your honor, your reputation, that's all. You got one hell of a reputation, gotta hand you that, and reputation, boy, that's important, so important, yeah, more important than money sometimes. A man like you would never want a stain on himself or his family. So what do you say? We got a deal, right?"

"I'll do what I have to do," Julian said between clenched teeth.

"I knew we'd straighten this out," Dewey said, adding that he expected Julian in action for him soon after he got back to AC, Dewey willing to scrape up $10,000 as a stake, practically the last of his spending money. "You're my man," exulted Dewey. "And listen, I wish you the best."

CHAPTER 19

Julian took a Valium that night to get himself some sleep, but it didn't do the job. He kept thinking how shit usually happened when he left home. Home was where the holy Sinai parchment was, tucked in between the pages of his *siddur,* the prayer book he had bought in Jerusalem, and there it would stay. He once took it with him to New York, and everything went wrong, beginning with the moment he thought he had lost it and was prepared to evacuate the entire city until it was found, and find it he did, still in the same *siddur* but tucked between different pages for some reason, but surely telling him that it was not meant for travel. The Sinai parchment was not portable and apparently neither was the blessing. The way things were going: Ear problems, nosebleeds, humbled by Lynn Sterling, reprimanded by Donald Oaks, the business with Dewey Smith—what's next?

Two in the morning, disgusted, he got back into his clothes, fresh blue jeans and blue polo shirt, and took a cab to Fremont

Street, the *real* Vegas, that vestige of Vegas of frontier days past with the neon-splashed boulevard, where the shimmering lights and the action never stopped, sidewalks teeming with people, the casinos overflowing, cabs, cars, buses spilling out the gambling faithful by the thousands, and here he rallied and felt rejuvenated, and in an instant he realized what it is all about, for himself, for everybody, not about gambling—but the quest for eternal life. There is no day. There is no night. All of it non-stop. Continuous action. Eternity.

Vegas is heaven here on earth.

Julian's destination was Lucky's, a hole-in-the-wall, sawdust casino, around the corner from Binion's Horseshoe, established during the reign of Bugsy Siegel and still going strong. It was a dump, still with swinging doors and poles outside to tether horses, the last of the honky-tonks, but a marvel to behold for the craps pilgrim making his escape from the new synthetic "family-oriented" complexes along the Strip, top-heavy with kids and slots.

Not a slot in the joint, and what a joint it was. A solitary fan made its reluctant rounds overhead in lieu of air conditioning. There were no signs that said "Thank you for not smoking." The floor stuck to your shoes from bubble gum dropped in the '50s. No Muzak, no band, but somewhere overhead came Frankie Laine and *Mule Train*. Clippity-clop. Dark, dank, the smell of armpits, cigars, the women straight out of some Lily Langtry chorus line, the men in pointed boots and ten-gallon hats, the tables brimming with action. This was where craps was meant to be played. Julian had lusted for this. Julian was in his element.

He had come for just that, the action, the purity of it all, which no one but a fellow gambler would understand—would understand that this was where you got lost to find yourself, away from the fraudulence of civilization.

He had pictured it all back in his hotel room, even pictured the table, saw the table, felt the table, imagined his play as only a real craps player could, going by instinct, seeing it all before him.

Julian planted himself at that table in the middle, which was running cold, shooters unable to go beyond three or four tosses without a 7 showing its ugly face, the boys groaning in disgust but playing on, awaiting their messiah, that shooter with the hot hand, Julian just standing there biding his time, even passing the dice the first time around to gather himself, when the tall, thin old man approached him, saying, "You one of them rich Rothschilds?"

Could it be? Yes, it was!

"You one of them rich Belmonts?" Julian said on cue to the running gag, playing back that scene from six years ago, when they first met right here in Vegas, right before Slim Sam Belmont was to become Julian's tutor, the master who taught him all the tricks; namely, the spinner, the shot that sent the dice up—up, up and away, twirling horizontally, helicopter-style, and staying aloft without turning end over end, and coming to a stop softly against the wall, this last touch being the most crucial, since most sharks who used the spin could do no better than make them "stick"—a sure sign that a gimmick was being used.

Not so with Slim Sam's method. He could make those galloping dominoes spin and then come right up against the wall in a soft slide, like Willie Mays, he'd say, diving into second. This skid shot is a storehouse to riches, he told Julian.

Use it wisely, use it sparingly, and practice it every day. Julian finally mastered it and used it so sparingly that it gradually became just something he knew but didn't use—didn't have to, since Sinai. Wouldn't want to. Didn't want to be a *cheat*. But it was good to know, like knowing that somebody loves you; and anyway, was it really cheating or was it skill? The House called it cheating, but then, they also once said the same thing about card-counting, and now card-counting was okay in some casinos. Slim Sam never called it cheating, never called it a gimmick. Called it an *edge,* that little extra we all need to get by in life. He used to say, "Those that ain't born with the silver spoon, we got nothin' but our wits."

So here he was again, and this was a man Julian truly loved. He was an American original.

Even back then, Slim Sam must have been 80 years old. Slim Sam the singing cowboy. A man from the Old West. Lived by his wits all right. Roped horses, shot craps throughout Texas and Wyoming. Rode with Roy Rogers in a number of shoot-'em-ups. Claimed to be the model for Maverick. Remembered Vegas when it was still cactus.

Julian thought he was dead.

"You old sonofagun!"

"Wondered when you'd wise up and come back for the real action. AC's for beginners."

"Just passing the time, Slim."

"Never known you to do that at a table."

"Passing through, Slim. That's all."

"I hear you been doing all right. Just fine."

"The dice have been good to me, Slim. How about you?"

"Oh, you know me. Bit of this, bit of that. Hey, you're some kind of a legend, you know."

"Bull."

"Hottest craps shooter in the land."

"Not so fast."

"Some of them braggin' rights are mine; right, kid?"

"You taught me everything, Slim."

"Yeah, but you got something I could never teach. You got the spirit, the spirit of the Lord."

Slim was only half-mocking. He had been married six times and only twice bothered with the technicality of getting a formal divorce, and he was a drinking man, and a self-described fornicator and all-around sinner, surely a gambling man, but, by golly and above all, he was a God-fearing man (in his own eyes), and it was he, Slim, who back in the beginning had told

Julian that there is something more to dice than just the mechanics.

Yes, there is skill, and yes, there is attitude, that indefinable approach of a winner, and those all work for the sprints, but for the long run, mostly, there is that something that could only come from up above, the angels dancing on your dice. Julian had it, as no other man Slim had ever seen, save for a guy calling himself Jethro, who mysteriously appeared and disappeared in and out of the booming railroad and oil towns of Texas, circa 1930, taking on all comers and beating them without letup while quoting Scriptures.

So far as craps, Julian was Jethro incarnate. Slim saw that six years ago, when Julian had been down-and-out, beaten by a world that had no use for him as a writer and kept reminding him of his inadequacies, a wife deep in her grief after the baby died, too deep to remember a husband, his life riven in shreds, his soul overtaken by despair from a thousand insults— until that moment at the Mirage when Slim saw something, saw something in the kid that he hadn't seen since Jethro.

"I hear you're helpin' 'em make a movie," Slim Sam was now saying.

"It's about guys like us, Slim."

"Nope. Ain't no guys like us, Julian."

"Right you are."

"In the end they always make us look like degenerates. They don't know the truth."

"Beats work."

"Gotta run," said Slim, handing Julian a business card that said "Have Dice, Will Travel," and vanishing into the sunset or wherever the Slim Sam Belmonts of the world ride off to when they're done.

But word spread.

The MAN was here, and the table breathed differently, trembling with expectation. The Jesus Christ of craps was here in their midst. They kept saying "Pass the dice," "pass the dice," "let the man shoot."

The rules of the House would not permit such a thing. Against the rules to keep declining until the dice reached that one designated shooter. "No can do," said the boxman. The table rebelled. Mutiny was in the air. The whole joint picked up a chant: "Let the man shoot, let the man shoot."

"All right," said the exasperated boxman after getting the okay from the pit boss standing behind him, who got the okay from the floorman who got the okay from the shift manager. "But just this once."

Five dice were removed from the box and placed on the layout in front of Julian. He made his choice of two, warming them up by gently soothing them along the green table carpet, introducing himself to them, establishing rapport, making friends.

Urged on by shouts of "Let's see it, kid, let's see it, roll them bones," he sought the angels but felt nothing, no Presence, no seizure of transcendence. Empty. Near panic, he wondered what it was that now made him so damned mortal all of a sudden. His shooting palm, ordinarily cool, was moist from the sweat of anxiety. The dice did not feel like friends; their touch was the touch of strangers. At a time like this he was disinclined to shoot, and wouldn't shoot were it not for the glare of a thousand eyes quickened to his every gesture. To abstain now would be riotous.

So he let loose, and the dealer shouted "Too tall, no roll," as one of the dice had skipped over the ledge of the table, something that rarely happened to Julian; he usually had it all so well weighed and measured.

An omen, he thought. *A bad omen.* The boys took note. Not quite the action of a virtuoso. Worried glances were exchanged. After the errant die was retrieved, calls of encouragement dittoing around the table, Julian grasped the dice again, tossed, and rolled a 7.

That was good. A come-out seven. Pass-line gets paid. But the enthusiasm was muted—because *there were 7s in the dice.* Enough of a red flag to give Julian pause and, in turn, to transfer that doubt and fear to the demons who danced on the dice when the angels demurred. Bad luck (or call it the devil) was attracted to faintheartedness and came calling when fear was about.

Julian sensed the arrival of that particular messenger, the precursor of doubt and fear, announced by a case of the willies—and try as he might to ward off the bad vibrations, he came back to the thought that something was clearly rotten.

He then remembered that only hours before, he had had sex with that nurse. Maybe that was the explanation. But even he wasn't foolish enough to believe in that superstition; when he was playing for real, for a cause, yes, but not when he was playing just for kicks.

If not that, he thought, *then it must be someone at the table,* as his play always went bad, Jonah-like, in the presence of singular evil. Surely, given the surroundings, there must be a murderer among the boys, a thief, a swindler, a rapist, a child molester, a drug dealer, a whore or two, but that still wasn't enough of an answer because the evil had to be of a very special premeditated bent; it had to be a once-in-a-lifetime kind of evil in order for the Presence to forsake him—and it had been years since he felt so abandoned, utterly bereft even of his skill.

Julian saw the wisdom in Pascal's Wager—which held that if you believed in God you might just win, and if you didn't believe you risked damnation—but Julian didn't even need that bet to believe in a Supernal Being, though he was skeptic enough, once in a while, to have his doubts up to a point, the point being that *faith* alone, even without a god, was sufficient to shower charm and blessing.

Practically everything important is in the *believing* anyway, nothing more than an article of faith. Facts do not do the trick. God is not a fact. He is a belief. For that matter, evolution, so far as touching upon humans, is not a fact. It is a belief. The supremacy of Shakespeare and Beethoven and Picasso, none of it is factual, all of it, all literature, all culture, every religion, stands upon the tottering foundation of received wisdom and derives its lifeblood not from fact but from the fact that people accept and believe.

As for me, thought Julian, *I believe, therefore I am. I believe that I am blessed, therefore I am. I believe the Sinai parchment is holy, therefore it is. I believe that I am a Just Man, therefore I am. I believe that (through my dice) I have been commissioned to provide manna for the widow and the orphan, therefore I am obliged. I trust in the dice, therefore they are faithful. None of it can be proven, might even be easier to disprove; all of it may even be bullshit. But there's no choice. A man has to stand for something, and defend it, if he's to be a man, that "singular" man Emerson and Thoreau talked about.*

Me. I stand for the dice. That's my racket. They're good to me when I'm good to them.

Just three weeks earlier, Julian had come across a woman in the coffee shop at Harrah's in AC, mid-40s, mildly attractive, who propositioned him. Funny, she didn't look like a whore and she was no whore, except that she needed the money. Same thing but not quite, since she had a story, as we all do, with this difference: Her entire family, husband, five kids, were killed in a car crash on the Pennsylvania Turnpike—father bringing the kids home to Mount Laurel, New Jersey from camp—and this naturally unraveled her. Couldn't work, couldn't stay home, couldn't do anything, so she haunted the casinos to get lost in the crowds. But now she was broke. "Let's try something else," Julian suggested. He took her last ten dollars, as a token, and brought her back ten thousand.

But that's when he'd been good, good to the dice, which apparently knew a cause when they saw one.

Now?

He was overcome by superstition, the sign of a loser. Everything was wrong. His nose itched, his head itched, his feet itched, he was aware of everything, which never happened when you were focused. When you were focused, you floated and could not be reached by the mundane.

Then there was that broom standing there against a pillar near a blackjack table. Brooms upright were a legendary no-no even to gamblers who shrugged off superstition. Brooms were bad luck from way back. "Can we do something about that broom?" Julian asked the pit boss.

"What broom?"

"That fucking broom over there," Julian explained. "Why is it there?"

"Yeah," the boys around the table wanted to know. "Lose the broom."

The pit boss smiled, smirked actually—he knew why the broom was there—and ordered it removed.

"Okay, shooter, let's go," said the stickman, impatient.

"Roll them bones," said the boys.

Even without the broom, Julian felt no better. He was not using the spinner, didn't think he needed it anymore, was relying absolutely on pure skill, knowing, at least guessing, that the blessing, back home, was too far to reach him, though he'd been here in Vegas other days, other times, and it had been good, very good. Not so far, today. So this was a test. A test of his skill.

Feeling bereft of his powers, damn it all, he tossed. First came a 3, craps, pass-line loses, which included everybody, then came a 12, craps again, and again everybody loses. People were getting pissed. Julian tried to focus, but there was no rhythm to his play, no zip to his movements, no zap to his throw. At last he made a point, 5. The table filled up with mostly greens, a few blacks, voices hollering "Hit that 5," "nail that 5," and he knew, just knew what was coming next.

Outside, three men jumped him and led him to the alley around back and gave him the beating of his life. This was what he heard: "Sonofabitch motherfucker. You come here to seven-out on us? Big man, huh? Greatest craps shooter in the land, right? You're a fuckin' shill for the House is what you are, motherfucker."

CHAPTER 20

A cab drove him to the Harmon Medical Center on Harmon Avenue, a few blocks down the Strip. They stitched him up, patched him up, nothing broken. Two black eyes, though, and a swollen lip, but there was good news, too. His ears came unclogged. The doctor—Julian couldn't believe this—the doctor said, "Where were you? Lucky's?"

Julian was back in his hotel room at the Hilton around six a.m. He felt grimy, quite shitty, and it was even worse when he checked himself in the mirror. *Mistake,* he said to himself, *to expect to look better than you feel.* He showered and felt a bit cleaner, but not much.

Without his golden touch, what was he? Nothing. Without dice, who was he? Nobody. Something even more important than life was at stake. His manhood. The thing to do, he was thinking as he got dressed and clicked on the TV without the sound, is to forget that this ever happened. One of those fluky things, that's all this was.

Or maybe there was a larger message. He took out the book of *Psalms* that he carried with him at all times and read this: "Happy is the man that hath not walked in the counsel of the wicked." Then he read the commentary in his Soncino edition: "To avoid the possibility of being contaminated, the godly man avoids the association of evil-doers."

He knew it by heart, so he was just checking, and quite telling, wasn't it, that that should be the very first line of the very first *Psalm*—the very first thing King David thought of as a guide to the perplexed, down to the generations, now directly admonishing Julian about evil and evil-doers.

Not especially those at Lucky's. No, it was something else. Something more mysterious, more profound, more personal. He had played with evil-doers before, and nothing like this had ever happened.

No, this was different, a direct message delivered to him by E-mail from above.

Dewey?

But he hadn't played for him yet. Only made the commitment.

Come on. He was *blackmailed* into the commitment!

Still, yes, he was *consorting*—and an eye sees, an ear hears.

There's that eye in the sky in the casino, and then there's the real eye in the real sky.

And what had Dewey done that was so bad? Or was it what he was about to do?

How bad could it be?

Maybe it wasn't Dewey. But *something* was wrong, and maybe the worst was yet to come.

The thought chilled Julian. He had always been terrified of having his blessing turn into a curse. This—this thing that happened at Lucky's—was either the end of something bad or merely the beginning.

Since he gave of himself so freely and so frequently, he was often afraid that he might be drawn in unknowingly as an accomplice to some misdeed, and so, soon after Sinai, he had made a personal covenant with God to the effect that he would trust God and God alone to send him the right people—since only He knows what good or evil lurks in the hearts of men. In other words, he struck a deal with the Almighty: "You send me the good people, I'll roll the good dice."

"Surely," Julian said when he proposed the deal, "I do not know one stranger from the next. So don't blame me."

Julian was no religious fanatic. He was religious, as we all are in our fear and deference to a Higher Authority. But he was no adherent to ritual. In fact, he disdained the piety of the pious—those who used God and Bible for personal gain to the point of making a mockery and a derision of those very words *God* and *Bible,* like those healers on TV who sucker the suckers, and like those religious types who are good only on Saturday and Sunday. Julian observed no Sabbath, mixed milk with meat, was seen in temple but once a year, and then only to hear the *shofar,* was affiliated with nothing and nobody, and yet he had a very personal relationship with the Almighty, strictly on a one-on-one basis, with Julian doing most of the talking.

He telephoned Him through prayer, using the 13th gate, as the Cabbalists defined the line, open to everybody about anything, since the first 12 gates, or lines, were reserved for the original 12 tribes. So gate 13 was all-inclusive, available for any petition—even craps. That was the line Julian generally used when approaching a table.

The attribute that had made Julian a man of grace beyond Sinai—at least up to now—was his charity. That was the deed greater than all others—providing for the needy—and it was that *mizvah* that gave Julian the impudence to demand God's intervention. Especially since the charity he gave, through his play at the tables, was near the top of the Seven Levels of Charity.

He gave without thought of reward or public exposure of the recipient. So, to his thinking, he had built up a mountain of heavenly merit. He was *owed*.

He cashed in some of those merits when, ignited by vanity (bad move, Slim Sam would say), and motivated by the indignation that any joint could beat him when he was on display, he of all people, Julian Rothschild, Prince of Dice, well, no choice, no choice but to teach them, hurt them, make them remember, make them pay, make them whisper his name in their sleep. They had seen Elijah, the Prophet of Dice. That's what they'd whisper. The craps table his footstool, he hath come to redeem.

Make way!

So he returned to Lucky's the next night, same time, same place, same table, mostly the same players, including the three thugs, who were too stunned by his show of guts to do anything about him—and this time Julian made the House weep as he made the dice sing. He had the juice. The Presence was with him, though he sensed Its reluctance and disapproval.

A slight case of nausea was the sign. Never mind. "No prisoners!" he declared when he palmed the dice and felt their delicious weight in his right hand. He fisted them the way he'd been taught and flung them spinning, once, twice, three times, then felt no need for the edge and shot them kosher, no matter, they came up 7s for come-outs only and in between those white spots sparkled 5s, 6s, 8s, 9s, 10s, easy way, hardway, any way, any which way that blasted the table full bloom and had the dealers stricken to keep up with the payouts.

In the end, Julian won back all that he had lost the night before and doubled it, for himself, for the boys; the picture of confidence and flair as he tossed winner after winner. He had them awestruck the time he called for a hard 8 and nailed it— even as he knew such recklessness could be damaging, could tip them off that he was scamming, which wasn't the case, after the initial few tosses. No, the rest of it was the exhilaration of conquest in the heat of battle. That's what made him so uninhibited, so bold, so foolish.

The boys wanted to carry him off on their shoulders, but Julian packed it in, cashed it in, with no acknowledgment of the cheers that followed him out the door. He was in no mood for tributes.

He was a bit worried. He wondered how many celestial merits he had used up with this little display of pique at the table. He had played for vanity. There was bound to be a price.

CHAPTER 21

The price was being tallied even as Julian was raking in the chips with both hands at Lucky's. His action had sent the casino circuits crackling all through Vegas, reaching as far as Atlantic City, for up in the Sky there at Lucky's Julian had attracted the attention of Hart Froman, Heartless Hart, as he was known to insiders; top gun at Lucky's and the equal to Roy Stavros in AC in more ways than one.

After Julian made his hasty departure, Froman called for the tapes and had them wound and rewound, watching them hour after hour, focusing mainly on the first three tosses, which was where the joker had to be. The remaining throws couldn't be questioned, but those first three; if they weren't helicopters, then he'd never seen a helicopter. Never seen anything.

Froman knew the guy had a sign on his back and that for one reason or another had yet to be busted. One reason was that he had some kind of juice with the marketing people in practically each and every House, plus the fact that no eye on the floor and no eye in the sky had yet been able to offer conclusive proof that he was using a spinner.

Part of the problem, as Froman had it figured, was that nobody *took the time.* Like he did. He'd stay here all day, all night if he had to, rolling the tape back and forth, forth and back till kingdom come if that's what it took to nail the sharpshooter.

Which was what Froman did, throughout the night, into the day, studying those tapes from all angles, particularly the opening movement, that's where he focused. He was sure that that's where it was, the key, the foundation to it all, now eyeing Julian's right hand, then a freeze on that frame, dissolved to a zoom of Julian's action when he tossed the dice, and Eureka! There it was, a certifiable spinner being *set.* He was *framing* them, using the ol' *lock-grip,* and concealing the action by palming his left hand over the right the instant before he let go, doing it so fast, in a blur, that even the surveillance cameras were too slow, even the slo-mo was too fast.

The guy was sensational, Froman had to give him that; the best. Froman had seen the finest mechanics around, from the sharpies who tossed sliders mid-table and made the blur of speed compensate for the spin, to the sharks who whipped 'em and twisted 'em and Greeked 'em and switched 'em— he'd seen them all and nailed them all.

Come on, was his motto. Come to Papa.

But this guy, hmmm. This guy was special. Very few people could do what he did. The spinner, this was the sign of a true marksman. They were all geniuses of a special sort. You almost had to admire them, and admire them you could if they weren't breaking the rules, which they were. They definitely were. They were *robbing* the House, was what they were doing—and of that entire, exclusive lot, Julian was the best, the finest mechanic Froman had ever seen. From the point of view of his subtlety. Why, throughout the entire session he had used the gaff only three times. How to explain the remainder of his success—that was another story and beside the point.

"We got the goods," Froman told Stavros by telephone. "We got enough to bar him from action across the country."

"Sounds good," said Stavros, nearly doing a jig back at the Versailles in Atlantic City.

"The kid's finished," said Froman. "He's history."

"Sounds real good," said Stavros.

In fact, it sounded positively terrific to Stavros—now that the world of casinos was about to slam its doors on the kid, rendering the Versailles the one and only place for the kid to shoot. NO OTHER PLACE TO GO! Oh yes, definitely, by all means, the Versailles' doors would remain open. The plan was still in operation, very much so, even *more* so, now that the kid would have no choice but to play the game. The private game. The head-to-head. For his life.

First, Lucky's would be finished for him. That was a given. The Network would speak and then they'd all fall in like dominoes. One by one throughout Vegas, spreading to AC and eventually covering even the seafaring and Indian casinos— they'd all get the word, some cooperating officially, according to mandate, as in AC, and others, even the boondockers, freezing him not because they had to but because they wanted to, wanted to keep their Houses from being cursed by cheats.

CHAPTER 22

When Roy Stavros was feeling good, he liked to hit people, and today, the day he got the word from Hart Froman, Stavros was feeling very good, and since Milligan wasn't around and since he'd been warned by Booker about roughing up the boys in Surveillance, he gave his giddy wrath to a punching bag at Smitty's Gym, behind the Taj, there at Virginia Avenue near Baltic.

He did his best thinking when he was hitting something or somebody and now, hitting the heavy bag, he was thinking how much he hated the kid and why he hated the kid. He hated the kid because he was a cheat, yes; and because he was so good even when he wasn't cheating, yes; and because he was champ and therefore an inviting target, yes; and because he showed such disdain for the House and the percentages, yes; but mostly he hated the kid because the kid was so smug, so sure of himself, so humble and yet so arrogant and so... angelic. So fucking angelic. Like he was Jesus Christ or something, the way he carried himself, and drew admiration and applause.

This, the religious thing, irked Stavros above all else, Stavros being an atheist, believing in nothing but the P.C., the percentages, and turning to atheism after his mother had died, in spite of all his prayers. Oh, he had prayed all right, when he was 12, he along with the rest of the family, and the priest, prayed and prayed and prayed, and still she died, in agony. So he stopped praying, at least to the same deity the rest of the people looked up to. Now he believed in nothing, nothing spiritual. Like the game of craps, everything was random, and even if he did believe in a god, he believed in a god contrary to Einstein's—this god *did* play dice with the universe.

The spiritualism, Stavros thought as he pounded the bag, *that's what I've got to take from this Julian fucking Rothschild. That's what the kid cherishes most. That's what makes him tick and that's what makes his dice breathe—he thinks. Destroy the spiritualism and you destroy the kid.*

Destroy the kid and you quash that army of Kreskin types who come in thinking it's a magic show where you can influence the cards and the dice through a force up above or the power of the mind. As a bonus, you also destroy the legion of fans who think it's cute to beat the House by cheating—or by any other means. That's why this kid can't just be taken into the woods. He's got to be beaten, at the table, so that the people may know that this prophet they've been following is a false prophet representing a false god. There is no god in heaven. There is but one god and that is the House.

All right, I'm offering the kid 20 chances. Throws no 7 and he's got a million bucks, plus he's back in good graces at my joint and every other joint. I can work it out with Froman that he made a mistake up there with the tapes.

He beats me fair and square, well, what can I say.

But he throws a 7, and he's a dead man. (How? I got ways.) That's the deal.

But why—why the hell would he take such a deal? He'd take it because otherwise the game of craps is finished for him, nationwide, and craps is all he knows, all he lives for. He'd take it because if he wins he gets a million bucks. Not that he'd use it himself, he'd give it to those stinking charities.

He'd take it because of his *pride,* because he thinks he's champ, can't be beat, and a champ can never turn down the big fight. If he does, he's no champ, he's nothing.

But suppose he says, Fuck craps, I'm joining the French Foreign Legion? Fuck the million bucks and fuck my pride.

No, thought Stavros, *to get the kid into the game to end all games, gotta come up with something bigger. Like testing the kid to put up or shut up about his faith in God Almighty.*

This sounded good to Stavros and he took a breather. This sounded very good.

"Smitty," he said, climbing between the ropes and jumping off the canvas and sparring a soft left-right to Smitty, who was a very old 58-year-old and shadowed back with uppercuts and a left-right roundhouse.

"Yeah," said Smitty, who'd once been a contendah. Coulda been *somebody.*

"You believe in God?"

"Shit, yeah."

"I mean for real."

"Ever met a boxer who didn't? What's the first thing we say after we win? We thank Jesus or Mohammed or Whoever. Me, I never stepped into no ring without first saying a prayer."

"So it's kinda like you test your faith every time you step between them ropes."

"Faith, that's part of it," said Smitty. "Being prepared don't hurt."

"But you got faith."

"Yeah. Why?"

"Ever have your faith tested?"

"Every fucking day."

"I mean *really* tested. Like that guy Abraham, in the Bible. Would you sacrifice your son if your God asked you?"

"What a fucking question."

"Come on. I got reasons."

"How do I know it's God?"

"Say it is. Like a voice from a burning bush or something."

"If I'm sure—yeah. Anybody would."

"You mean anybody would do *anything* to prove his faith in God?"

"Just about."

"Kill a son, kill themselves, anything?"

"We're not talking about them nuts who hear voices."

"No. Legit."

"I can tell you this. Sometimes you step into the ring empty and all ya got is faith."

That was the lightbulb for Stavros. The kid Julian was empty without his faith. Even the spinner was a matter of faith. All ya got is faith and a man of faith would do *anything* to defend and preserve that faith. Those were the words Stavros wanted to hear, and he even heard them again, later on, from George Gardner, formerly a minister.

This guy was defrocked from a church out in the Pinelands, became a degenerate from calling the Bingo and finally graduated to the casinos.

But he was as God-fearing as ever, and Stavros put it to him as he had put it to Smitty. Same answer. For faith, you do anything, Gardner saying, "If a person is true to his or her beliefs, yes, nothing is too much to ask, nothing is too much to give. To be true to yourself and to your God, a person must be prepared to sacrifice."

The only thing left, thought Stavros, *is to put it to Julian fucking Rothschild.*

You got God in them dice? Roll 'em 20 times to prove it, son. Your life on the line.

Your faith in faith against my faith in the House. Your God against my god. That's the deal.

Yeah, like Abraham. You be Isaac.

CHAPTER 23

That same morning Julian visited the set of *Scared Money,* for the last time, he hoped. He was feeling some guilt and thought he owed the project some more of his time, primarily in fine-tuning Matt Cain, who sure enough was walking around like Charlton Heston all of a sudden. No more slouching, no more sullenness. No more Brando. *I did that?* Julian quivered. Matt extended a smile and a handshake, even addressing Julian by name, saying, "You opened my eyes, Julian."

"Maybe we should talk about this," Julian said.

"No, man, everything's cool."

Between takes, the exasperated director Clive Edwards calling for try after try in a futile attempt to get Matt Cain off the pompous diction, Julian spotted Lynn Sterling, forced a smile, which she didn't return, as though she'd never seen Julian before. Either she was upset at him, or it was just Lynn Sterling being Lynn Sterling.

"I've heard all about you," said the co-star Karen Davies, chipper, jumping him from out of nowhere.

"Same here," Julian said, never feeling for a moment that he was in the presence of a STAR. He had been with stars before, and anyway, she wasn't like that, none of them were, not like they used to be back in the days of Rita Hayworth when these people actually glittered. Today their beauty was of a different, more approachable sort. They did not *stun*. They did not take your breath away any more than the girl next door did, or the prettiest girl in high school. That, Julian decided, was more or less it; a high school kind of beauty.

Karen, high-spirited and downright bubbly, said he'd done wonders for Matt Cain.

"Glad *you* think so."

"Fuck 'em," she said, nodding toward the honchos. "So glad you're psychic."

"I'm not," he protested. "Not at all. I don't believe in the stuff."

"We'll keep it our little secret," she winked.

There amid the chaos of lights and sound being tested, voices shouting, people buzzing around like bees serving their Queen, the Queen in this case being the Picture, Karen Davies pigeon-holed Julian with her theory of *oneness,* which proposed that this world would end and a new world of splendor would begin when mankind distilled into one definitive book all the words ever written, distilled further into one definitive sentence, arriving finally at The Last Word. The Last Word, that was the real messiah. Everything written before, Karen gushed, the trillions upon trillions of words, were but stepping-stones to the Last Word. Whatever it was.

Karen belonged to the Oneness Society. "You should join," she urged, eyes wide and sparkling with youthfulness.

Julian wasn't quite sure what to make of this Oneness theory. It was kooky, all right.

But so, once upon a time, was the theory that the earth was *round*.

"Suppose," Julian offered, "that one sentence, or one word, has already been written."

"I'm sure it has," Karen countered. "We simply have to find out who wrote it, where it is."

"What happens to the millions of books that have already been written?"

"Obsolete," she stated firmly, gazing straight into his eyes. "Too bad."

"No. Because when we finally find IT we'll realize that everything that came before was plain gibberish."

"Except the Bible."

"I'll grant you that," she said.

He liked this girl. After the day's filming, which produced only one shot, they met in the coffee shop.

They were in a booth, semiprivate. "You've got to let me read your toes."

"Paw-leeze," he said.

"All right, your face. Toes are better, but I derive almost as much from faces."

She was at it, silently, for nearly 20 minutes with attendant clucking. "Hmmm. Quite a handsome face. Good solid lines. Strong chin. Definitive cheekbones. Clear eyes. But those *lines* around the eyes—telling."

"Of what?"

"You're terrifically romantic," she said delightedly with a bit of a chirp in her voice, still examining him intensely. "Are you a lady-killer or something? I'll bet you are."

He chuckled. "Wrong."

"You're extremely sensual. But you keep your emotions tucked deep inside. They'd call it repressed."

"Maybe so. But we're all repressed, you know, to some extent, thank goodness. Otherwise there'd be chaos."

"We'd be fornicating on the streets, right?" she laughed.

"We already are, if you watch MTV."

Her eyes roamed above his head. He thought maybe some giant was hovering over him.

"You've got a wonderful halo. Best I've ever seen. But it's starting to cloud. Something's wrong, isn't it?"

"Maybe. But it's also true that there's always something wrong with everybody."

"Okay, wise guy. But I see something more. Can't quite put my finger on it yet, but I will."

"I'm sure you will," he said, laughing at her determination and wondering why men, including himself, so often respond to beautiful women as if they, both the men and the women, were children.

"We should have sex, you know."

That startled him, but he *repressed* it.

"Why not?" he shrugged.

"You don't like sex?"

"Love it. It's just a bit overrated, that's all. Like Woody Allen."

"Hmmm," she sort of cooed with a delicious movie-star grin. "We'll see. But some other time, right?"

"Whenever."

"I am very attracted to you."

"Likewise," he said to the truth, for she was more than beautiful, she was adorable.

"So you're the famous gambler," she said, her tone changing the subject.

"I shoot craps."

"For a living?"

"Mostly."

"That's unheard of, but I'm impressed. This is so strange."

"I think so, too."

She laughed. "But it's all so mystical to you, right?"

"People told you?"

"No, I see it in your eyes and above your head."

"Oh," he chided. "My halo."

"Tell me about it, the mysticism and all."

"Some other time."

"I can take a hint."

"I talk too much about it as it is. Some people think there's no such thing."

"But you know there is."

"Some people think I'm nuts."

"Not the people I talk to. They take you very seriously. But I'd give anything if you'd tell me your secrets. You know I'm into these things. I believe in all things celestial."

"You'd give anything?"

"Have you ever fucked a movie star before?"

"Before?"

"Before me."

"Oh. Well, yes."

"Who?"

"Can't tell."

"Good for you." Coyly, she began, "Did you ever fantasize about me, I mean in one of my movies? I know men do."

Actually he had not.

"Not really."

"What about now? In the flesh."

"Hmmm. Yeah."

"Because I'm a so-called movie star, or because..."

"Because you're you."

"Not just some notch on your belt, right."

"I'm done with notches."

"Which tells me you *were* once a rake."

"Once. But I don't know that guy anymore."

"To me," she said in girlish earnestness, "sex is about exchanging secrets. It's about sharing mind, body, and soul. It's about wanting to know *more* about the other person, unlock his mysteries. I guess that's why I'm attracted to you. I want to know more."

"I'm tempted. But what about your reputation?"

"Who's to tell? Anyway, I've already been linked with *everybody*. I'm sure you've read *all* about me."

"No."

"Don't you know they say I fall in love with all my leading men?"

"That disqualifies me."

She chuckled. "No, it doesn't. Oh, hell, let's do it," she said in a single breath. "We've been beating around the bush long enough."

On the way up she asked him matter-of-factly if he carried a pin with him. He asked what for. "The craziest things happen to me," she said, "when having sex. Like the time with this one guy, yes, a big name in the movies but never mind, so this one time he got it in but couldn't get it out."

Julian stilled a laugh.

"I am dead-serious," she said. "Something about the suction effect, which happens maybe once in a billion times. Well, it happened to me. I pushed, he pulled, but nothing. I can't tell you how panicked we were. Can you imagine?"

Now she was practically in hysterics.

"Can you imagine spending the rest of your life like that? Anyway, we rolled over, together, of course, managed to get to the phone at the side of the bed, and dialed 911. *We had to tell them what the problem was.*

"Honest to gawd. An hour later there's a knock at the door. Guy comes in, paramedic or something, doesn't laugh, doesn't smile, just takes a pin out of his pocket and pokes me in the ass. The shock or something—anyway, that did the trick.

"The medic or something, he just leaves. But before he goes, he says to always carry a pin."

"So now," she chuckled, "you know why I ask."

"Too crazy."

"But true. So look out."

She took him up to her room and put on a first-rate show taking off her clothes and revealing a figure that a million men would die for. The sex was blissful and dreamlike, almost movielike, seemingly in slow motion, set in frames, frame by frame. She liked it slow, very slow, only fast, very fast before fade-out.

"Do you like Woody Allen any better now?" she drawled.

They fell asleep soon after and when he awoke, a couple of hours later, he found her studying his face. Then, silently and lovingly, she took the palm of his right hand and clutched it and let go of it as if she'd been holding a hot coal. "There's something there," she said. "Something outworldly."

He was not surprised.

Now she was reading his palm and her body stiffened and her face turned grim.

"What?"

"You're sure you want to know."

"Go on."

"You don't believe in this stuff anyway."

"But go on."

"You're sure."

"I'm sure."

"I don't like what I'm about to say."

"Say it already."

"Okay. There's something very bad waiting for you in Atlantic City. I wouldn't go back there if I were you."

He was a bit stricken by this, knowing that clairvoyants were not to be trusted but also knowing that curses and premonitions likewise had a life of their own, a life in the netherworld, a world once explored by King Solomon. Even Abraham read the stars until he was told that the stars did not control the destiny of his people and their generations, which included Julian. But even the Bible has its seers, the Witch of Endor, consulted by King Saul on the eve of his fatal battle at Gilboa. A certain amount of respect had to be paid.

"Atlantic City's where I live. That's where I play. It's where I do my work. Come on. Let's not get silly."

"Someone's waiting for you there," she said, her youthful countenance dampened of its high spirits.

"What else?"

"Danger," she said. "Your life... oh, never mind. I sound like a carnival Gypsy."

"You can't do that. Come on. What else?"

"Nothing. Really. I'm really an amateur at this, you know."

"Well, I've heard enough."

"I'm sure I'm all wet. Don't you think? I mean what do I know. You're not worried, are you?"

"Me worry?" But he knew there was something else she was keeping from him. He was no face reader, no toe reader, no palm reader, no halo detector, but it was written all over her.

"Let's have another round," she said, jumping on top of him. "Let's fuck."

"I hope that's not the *last word,*" Julian wondered out loud.

CHAPTER 24

Dewey was curious about something, actually something that's been baffling mankind for some time, about a tree, if it topples in a forest far away and nobody hears it, does it make a sound? Big question. Denise would know.

Dewey and Denise were still up there in the golden room at the Versailles in Atlantic City. Dewey's comp, however, was beginning to peter out, as Dewey wasn't showing enough play downstairs in the casino, hardly any play, really, to warrant the remainder of the "Quality" freebie. Dewey had even begun to attract management's cold shoulder, grunts of disapproval, as when he phoned down for more shrimp and caviar.

Denise put down her Kafka and responded with a sigh, "No, Dewey, if nobody hears it, it doesn't make a sound," thus settling the matter once and for all, if not for science, then for Dewey, who liked the answer.

But led to another question, which he asked only of himself: If something happens but doesn't appear on television, does it really happen? Given Denise's response to the first question, the answer must be no to the second question as well, when applying the Socratic method of reasoning—and Dewey had read Socrates through and through, more or less, thanks to the Durants.

Television had his name on its lips practically every single night now, what with the McLellan Hearings just getting started and Sasha Spivak set to testify any day, the network promos showing her in romantic silhouette as the darling about to lead the nation out of its quagmire of sweatshop corruption. All of which meant that he, Dewey, ergo, was happening, and that was pissing him off no end. Terrified to boot at the mere mention of Sasha Spivak's name... a name that never failed to make his skin crawl.

Time to make like that tree, make no sound, do it so that no one will hear when she topples, no one will notice, no Dan Rather to report it, no Peter Jennings to sneer *aboot* it (and when are they going to deport *that* immigrant back to Canada?), no Jim Lehrer to bring in experts from Harvard and Yale to dissect Dewey Smith and the horrors of slave labor in the garment world.

Time to get it done—and it was getting late, later by the minute.

What happened with his offer to Denise to come up with a better plan? Nothing. He kept asking her every day, day after day—give me something, you're so smart, so *educated*. Well?

Nothing. She was stumped. True, she did not know the whole of it and thus the real urgency of it, like the fact, and so sad a fact it was, that his emissaries had failed, flat-out failed, so far, to persuade the child to accept a gift. For her silence.

Difficult as it was to reach her, holed up there in Washington usually in the company of two plainclothes security officers—usually but not always—Dewey's people had managed to make the contact, only to be rebuffed by the girl personally, and even by the shamuses, who could have each pocketed ten thou for their cooperation. Actually it had been one of Dewey's female emissaries who had made the offer to the girl at a Roy Rogers powder room in the Washington D.C. train station, there in the grand food court. Sasha, after so many years of deprivation, had an insatiable appetite for those hamburgers, so it had not been too difficult to catch her alone—hadn't been too difficult before and wouldn't be too difficult again, if it became necessary, and time *was* running out.

Counting on Julian to provide the cash, Dewey had been willing to pay the girl two, three, maybe four, as high as five hundred thousand dollars.

No deal.

All right, be that way, so now the money, once it was won by Julian Rothschild at the tables, once he got back from Vegas, if he *ever* got back from Vegas—the money would have to go elsewhere. To a man with no name. No, not Clint Eastwood, but a real man with no name.

No name, no background, no nothing. Not a thug, either. Just a businessman whose business was doing away with undesirables without the use of weapons, maybe by poisoning or strangulation, nobody knew exactly how, except that the job got done, so Dewey had heard—got done quietly, silently, stealthily, professionally, with no traces back to the man who issued the contract.

About Socrates. Dewey was familiar with the quote that "No man knowingly does evil." Dewey liked that quote because it is so true—if you could forget about Hitler and a few thousand other people—in that he, Dewey, wasn't doing anything knowingly. Not a thing. Other than walking the boards with the man with no name, who did have a moniker, Glass, Mr. Glass, as in nobody can see inside him. He comes and goes like a shadow.

Dewey was six-feet-two or thereabouts, and so he rather dwarfed Mr. Glass, who was no more than about five-six, maybe five-seven, as the two men set a slow pace moving from the Sands on the way to the Hilton, just to be walking, walking and talking, like any other two men with business to discuss, Labor Day approaching.

Aside from the fact that he was smallish, there was nothing to distinguish Mr. Glass. He was, as Dewey framed it in his mind, imposingly ordinary, except for a slight limp, the right leg seemingly the gimpy one. But no mean squint to the eyes, no snarl to the lips, no tattoos, none visible at least, no scars, nothing, nothing but a soft sing-song kind of voice, occasionally accompanied by a kindly chuckle, and a face that wasn't good-looking or bad-looking, just pleasing.

He was also ageless; could be 40, could be 60. On appearances alone, nothing at all to confirm the rumor that Mr. Glass, originally from Argentina, had made some 70 people disappear from there to here—maybe more, counting his years in the Argentine military, back when people there were disappearing left and right during the dictatorship.

Mr. Glass slipped out of the country when the more-or-less good guys took over, effectively erasing his past but continuing the same business once he'd relocated himself in America.

"You seem to object to this weather," Mr. Glass said with a chuckle, noticing the sweat pouring from Dewey's face, his cotton shirt drenched, his breathing heavy, his feet dragging.

"I'm not a summer person," Dewey responded defensively, although he liked the idea of making small talk to take the curse off the real topic at hand, Dewey impressed with the man's capacity to ease into things.

"Pity we haven't found a way to air condition the outdoors as yet," Mr. Glass said, sounding so much like that Swedish actor whose name escaped Dewey for the moment—and sounding so *civilized*.

So ordinary. Which made him the perfect man for the assignment. You do not want someone who looks and talks like Jack Palance. Tough guys in real life seldom look like tough guys in the movies. Central Casting wouldn't give them a second look, the real toughs.

In real life—Dewey always found this a fascinating anomaly—heroes and villains were everyday Joes whom you could not separate from your high school gym teacher; they never came close to resembling your Bogarts, your Gables, your Pecks, your Costners, your Fords, Glenn or Harrison.

Mr. Glass was another without chiseled features.

"Yes, pity," Dewey echoed, and that was something else about Dewey; he usually mimicked another man's way of speaking, involuntarily, but especially so when the other man had a superior-sounding dialect.

"I assume," said Mr. Glass, hands clasped behind his back as he strolled, "that the central parties are in line."

Whatever the dialect, it was understood by both men that it would be a betrayal of etiquette to so much as breathe the word *murder,* and would certainly be an unforgivable breach of form to so much as suggest that the object of their business was a 16-year-old girl. Dewey hadn't been thinking along those lines anyway, so he'd have no trouble defending himself before Denise or *anybody* if ever he were accused of doing something evil *knowingly*. Quite simply, he did not want to *know*.

All he knew was that this guy had a way with people—and that's all he wanted to know. For all he knew, the man never actually killed anybody. He made them disappear, which was a totally different thing. Could even mean that he sent them away to, say, Bermuda, or some such place, an island where they spent the rest of their lives in luxury. Maybe those tens of thousands who disappeared from Argentina were frolicking and living it up someplace where they filmed *South Pacific*. Who is to say otherwise?

"The central parties?"

"Your partner, for one," Mr. Glass said, now rubbing his eyes under a pair of very dark sunglasses.

That was Julian.

"That party is on his way back from Las Vegas." Supposed to be, anyway, according to his last phone call with Julian, Julian starting to get on his nerves, being so evasive and elusive.

"Do I take it that the money is not to be handed over for our enterprise?" Mr. Glass sighed.

Five hundred thousand dollars.

"My credit is good," Dewey said, taking a hard tone.

"Credit?" Still soft-spoken, but with a definite edge.

"As soon as the man arrives..."

"My work is not done on credit, sir. I proceed only upon payment in full, cash. Did they not tell you?"

They had told him. But Dewey had been in a hurry. He had not expected the McLellan Hearings to come upon him so fast, for one thing, and he had hoped against hope that all this would be unnecessary as he kept being told that the girl was open for the money. Responsive, they told him. So actually he'd been opting for the peaceful resolution all along. Anyway, he'd been badly misled, and so had to resort to Plan B, in a hurry, even before Julian made it back from Vegas.

"The money is guaranteed, I assure you. It's as good as my word and my word is as good as done." Dewey tried to sound forceful. That was all he had, bravado, given his weak hand.

"Hmmm," said Mr. Glass, mulling it over and saying nothing for quite some time—but clearly disappointed. Finally, "This is really quite surprising, Mr. Smith. This is not how I do business." Then, "What about the other party?"

Sasha Spivak.

"Everything's in order."

"You mean she's staying at the same place?"

"In Washington." Dewey got reports on her every couple of hours. Like clockwork, she showed up at that Roy Rogers in the train station every evening six-thirty sharp, then around seven visiting the john to brush her teeth—some kind of a fixation about that, her teeth.

"Very well."

"So we have a deal."

"Yes."

"Wonderful."

"As soon as I get paid."

"Now wait a minute..."

"First the money."

"Listen..."

"First, the money, Mr. Smith."

"There must be a way to work this out."

"Yes, there is. The money first."

Dewey sighed. "By then it may be too late."

That's right. She might be stepping up to the Congressional mike, who knew how soon. Fortunately, the hearings were moving along in fits and starts, what with recesses that took up hours and sometimes days, plus the difficulties in summoning certain Ph.D. experts in the field of slave labor, not to mention the reluctant appearances of leading sweatshop operators from around the nation—none of whom, incidentally, had responded to their subpoenas as of yet. Remarkably, Dewey had yet to be so ordered, which was a bad sign. They were saving him for the grand finale, and no doubt setting up Sasha Spivak for the coup de grâce.

"That's not my problem," said Mr. Glass about it getting late. "I'm accustomed to dealing with people professional to professional," he added, words that could be taken as nothing short of an open-faced rebuke.

Now Dewey knew who the guy reminded him of, that actor in all those Bergman movies... what's his name. Claus von Bülow.

Or something. Right. Claus von Bülow.

"Listen, for the kind of money you're asking I think you can cut me some slack." Dewey getting in some backbone.

"Nonsense."

"Would you accept a down payment?"

Mr. Glass almost laughed. "I am not Sears, Mr. Smith. No down payments, no monthly installments."

Dewey was not used to being spoken to like this. He was big-time himself. So he had to keep reminding himself that there is big league, and then there is world-class. This guy is world-class.

The terrible truth was that Dewey had never ordered a killing, before this. Never directly. Indirectly people got killed in transport, mainly that, and occasionally for insubordination once they were here and didn't follow certain rules—but the rough stuff was generally carried out by his men without bothering him with the details. He knew about a hit afterward and sometimes beforehand, but it was all done so obliquely that it barely counted as anything premeditated. As anything that Socrates might term *knowingly*.

This, now, was a bit different, not so much that it was a hit—but a girl. A 16-year-old girl. An orphan. A girl who had known nothing but pain and suffering every minute of her adolescence. Dewey shuddered to think of it all, the meaning of it all, the cruelty of it all, and yet how he hated and feared her, as he would hate and fear anyone who was out to obliterate him. Do unto others, was his motto, but do it first. Dog-eat-dog, that's what the world is all about, certainly and emphatically his world, and if the other dog happens to be a Sweet 16, tough. Survival, that's what it all comes down to. He'd deal with Denise, and his conscience, later.

"I was hoping we could arrive at an understanding," Dewey said, barely able to hide his frustration.

"But we *do* have an understanding. Payment in full."

Like a broken record. Or is it broken CD nowadays?

"I'm in a spot," Dewey was forced to concede, trying to reach him man to man. Find his soft spot. Good luck.

"Yes, that is unfortunate," Mr. Glass said politely.

The politeness was getting on Dewey's nerves. Civilized was okay, up to a point.

"I'm only asking for some time."

Was that me whining? Dewey asked himself.

"Isn't that the cry of all mankind?" Mr. Glass philosophized with a mock sigh of world-weariness.

Dewey was in no mood for philosophy right now or for anything that strayed from the subject at hand. He was not enjoying the mockery at his expense. He did not like him anymore, but he could not afford to lose this man—did not like him because he made him feel so small.

This territory was unfamiliar to Dewey—a guy so used to playing it big, always big, always in charge, being brought low, so very low by some 16-year-old wench, Russian to boot, parents probably old-time Stalinists. Never could trust those Russians. Wasn't life crazy? Go figure. Man runs an empire, all his life afraid of nothing and nobody, along comes some orphan and she has him scampering up the nearest tree in fear for his life.

In his reading of the Great Books—Dewey's never-ending pursuit of culture to gain a foothold into the better circles, and wasn't this a comedown—anyway, in his reading of the dead, white, European males, he'd found his way to Montaigne who spoke of "The Inconstancy of Our Actions," namely that the man you saw yesterday so adventurous and brave, you must not think it strange to see him as a great coward the next.

Exactly Dewey's assessment of himself and Sasha, to an extent of himself and Mr. Glass as well, and on the topic of inconstancy, the contradictory nature of man, it did not escape Dewey that a man of *culture* that he aspired to be was at the same time plotting murder.

"There must be something—some way to get over this hump," Dewey protested, wiping the sweat from his brow.

Ignoring the plea, Mr. Glass said: "By the way, how do you intend to come up with the money?"

Do I tell him? Dewey wondered. *Do I tell him that it all rests on the skill of a mechanic at the craps tables, a me-*

chanic who's somewhere in Vegas diddling with some broad, shooting off his pecker instead of the dice?

Hell, no. The guy'll think I'm nuts. I'm beginning to think so myself. The guy knows I'm using a surrogate. I've told him. Just didn't tell him how.

"That's my business," Dewey said.

"Entirely incorrect," said Mr. Glass, so annoyingly self-assured. "Perhaps if you told me, I might reconsider."

Well, then...

"I intend to win the money." Dewey blurted it out and was sorry the very instant he said it.

"*Win* the money?" Mr. Glass chortled.

"Yes, win the money."

"Not *earn* the money the old-fashioned way?" Mr. Glass now clearly taunting him.

"Win the money."

"How?"

"That's my business," Dewey repeated.

"Is it, now. Here at the casinos?" Now shaking his head in derision. "Hah."

"Maybe."

"I see. What is your game? Blackjack? Poker? Roulette? Craps? Keno? You actually intend to beat the casinos?"

"Actually, it's someone else who beats the casinos."

"Someone else. This is getting most confusing, Mr. Smith. But as you say, it's not my business. Here's a tip for you, though. Just some advice. Nobody beats the casinos. I'm sure you've heard."

"There are exceptions."

"Oh, none at all, Mr. Smith, of that I assure you. Gambling, you see, gambling is a vice, a nasty habit, for this reason... it's a guaranteed loser. Anything that makes a man lose more than he wins is a vice, a sin. Which is why I do not smoke, or drink, or gamble. But that's me."

Just what I need, thought Dewey. *A sermon from an assassin.*

"Well, this is me," Dewey said, unashamedly pointing to the shimmering casinos illuminating the Boardwalk.

Mr. Glass had never heard of anything so ridiculous in all his life. Casinos!

"So be it," he said. "Good luck, as they say. Or should I tell you to break a leg? In any case, you know the price for my services. Personally, I don't care how you get the money, so long as it comes, and when it comes, when you *win* it, or whoever wins it for you, then call me. You know where to reach me."

With that, Mr. Glass turned and got lost amid the crowd of Boardwalk vacationers, indistinguishable except for that limp that made him appear just a bit menacing—and that's when it hit Dewey. Not Claus von Bülow, for crying out loud. Max von Sydow. That's who.

But other than being pleased to have made the connection, Dewey felt that he must be slipping, badly, to let a guy like that get the better of him, a guy like that and a guy like this, this Julian Rothschild—everybody dumping on him, as if he were shit. This was going to stop, he vowed.

CHAPTER 25

Sasha Spivak was an enigma to the two men—both former FBI agents who got dismissed for laxity and incompetence but had set up a successful private security practice—who were charged with guaranteeing the safety of the young lady at the L'Enfant Plaza in Washington, D.C. in advance of her appearance before Congress.

She had them charmed and confounded. Once in a while she was as peppy and carefree as any American teenager, gobbling down pizza and Coke and sending them to near hysterics with her rendition of California-speak in imitation of that girl in *Clueless*—as if!—and then, as though hypnotically induced, turning silent, watching TV, hour after hour, even *after it had been turned off,* just sitting there, seemingly in a prison of her own making, glaring at the screen, her features suddenly gone slack, eyes vacant; sometimes staring at a wall, occasionally staring out the window, as though waiting for some visitor who never showed up.

In fact, she *was* waiting, for Richard Gere.

Sasha loved the movies. At the movies was where she got lost to her dreams even during her halcyon days as a child prodigy, and certainly during the bleak period of her incarceration at the Moscow orphanage where she was dumped after the murder of her parents, when she was shorn of practically everything, first her self-esteem and gradually, through drugs, even her identity.

She was in love with American movie stars for their verve, their glitter, their glamour, their on-screen decency, their magical self-confidence, all of which she associated with America itself; America, the land that would one day welcome her with fanfare and roses, she imagined—she being the dimpled, curly-haired heiress to Shirley Temple, the gifted virtuoso, the violinist without peer from Moscow to New York.

She certainly had not imagined being stripped of family, friends, belongings, even her skill with the violin, to be shipped to America half-lucid for bondage in American sweatshops, toiling 16-hour days and living in a Bowery flophouse, drunks and derelicts keeping her from sleep, invading her dreams, the one possession she still clung to and retained.

Back in Moscow's Elegante Theatre on Peterovsky Street she developed her first crush on William Holden as the anti-Nazi spy in *Counterfeit Traitor,* a movie she never tired of, especially that scene when Holden first meets Lilli Palmer, a sequence absolutely unequalled for its power to convey high romance, to take nothing away from Richard Gere in *An Officer and a Gentleman,* a movie that made her swoon and blush whenever Gere appeared on the screen.

She resumed her love affair with Richard Gere later at the Moscow orphanage, whose one saving grace was movie-night every Tuesday, Thursday, and Saturday, and later still at the sweatshop in New York, where she sought her redemption in Richard Gere, who would carry her off into a world of ineffable bliss, just as he had carried off Debra Winger—also a factory worker toiling away her years in drabness.

Only this. To win over a Richard Gere or to snatch even a lesser man, a girl had to have perfect teeth. American movies were proof of that over and over again in the persons of Winger, Michelle Pfeiffer, Demi Moore, Sandra Bullock, not to mention Julia Roberts.

The orphanage had let Sasha's teeth rot and decay, and now, in America, she carried a toothbrush with her at all times and brushed in all places to banish the stains in her mouth that she associated with the very stain of her entire being. Her rotten teeth were synonyms for the foulness, disgrace, and degradation that had become her lot ever since her parents were slaughtered in Moscow.

Sasha was obsessed. She brushed so hard that her gums bled, and then she wept, as only a 16-year-old girl could weep, when mirror after mirror reflected futility and failure. The tooth stains seemed irreversible, which spoke for her condition as a whole, and plunged her into even deeper sorrow.

Her two guardians, Hank Morrison and Dan Crawford, whose job it was to bring her before Congress in one piece, were constantly fretful about her—about her and their duty to the government.

What the hell was she doing in the john all that time? Slitting her wrists?

It was bad enough in a hotel, in a controlled environment, but even worse when she insisted that they take her out to the movies, where she spent another hour in the john, and still another hour, it seemed, at the Roy Rogers, after wolfing two sometimes three burgers, as if to Americanize herself in one fell swoop by the ingestion of junk food. Damn, the girl could eat, but it was those endless visits to the ladies' room that had them on edge.

They had proposed sending along a female escort to accompany her on her many pit stops, an offer she steadfastly declined, nearly throwing a fit when they grew insistent. Russia had already taken half her sanity, America was closing in on her life; the thing she had, the one thing she had left, was her privacy. That much was hers. Her secrets, her dreams, those were hers, never to be divulged. No, the bathroom was her domain, and on that score she won the day.

That sort of intemperate willfulness, fluctuated with despair, unhinged her two custodians. They were afraid to push her too hard, for she was an angry young lady, on the verge of who-knew-what after all she'd been through and now cooped up like this. They agreed she was like a time bomb waiting to go off. The next word could do it—maybe the next number.

One day, there in the room at the L'Enfant, they found her in another of those trances, counting, mumbling one, two, three... them asking, "Why are you counting?"

"To reach a number," she said.

"What number?"

"I'll know it when I get to it," she said.

Which spooked them.

Given her strange behavior, her two guardians were worried that they'd be delivering damaged goods to the McLellan Hearings, for which they'd be blamed, nobody accounting for the possibility that the girl might be a bit off center even without their help.

For that reason they were hesitant about turning down the ten thousand dollars, each, when approached by emissaries who refused to say who sent them (though it was easy to guess), but did say the money was theirs if they could somehow help buy Sasha's silence. Former FBI though they were, they did give it some thought, reasoning that Sasha might not make the most potent witness for the government, inasmuch as the government was counting on a rather unstable young lady to singlehandedly bring down America's disgraceful sweatshops. But turn down the offer they did (though they did not report it) because they were honorable men, after all.

CHAPTER 26

Sasha had been approached as well by a woman who identified herself as Mary, simply Mary, all this happening on several occasions there in the john at the Roy Rogers, and Mary
had been quick to acknowledge who sent her—Dewey Smith.
Let's not fool around.

"Big money," Mary whispered, "for your silence," Mary
fussing with her hair in front of the mirror as she eyed Sasha
going at it with the toothbrush, wondering what was up with
this girl and her teeth.

This went on eight times over a period of ten weeks, Sasha
always careful to remain noncommittal, for Sasha, despite her
quirks, was a wise young lady, wise enough to know the folly
of drawing the wrath of Great Men, as such men of power
were called in her native Russia. Great Men. A title left over
from the days of the Czar and serfdom.

Dewey Smith had been Sasha's Great Man here in the States,
though she'd never met him and only heard about him once

the government, through their agents, began soliciting for volunteer witnesses against him, targeting her specifically because she was such a classic case, given her decline and fall, and so intelligent and well-spoken despite lingering traces of a Russian accent, which only added to her charm. And she was so pretty, when she covered her mouth. Good for television.

Sasha, of course, was well-aware that she was being used. But she also saw the good in it, the good that might come from exposing the evil round and about. She was likewise well-aware that henceforth, from the moment she took the government's side, her life would forever be in danger. So be it; her life wasn't worth that much now anyway.

At some point it happens, usually to people at an age far more advanced—what happens is that a person wakes up from her dreams, and just like that the realization hits that there will be no Prince Charming. What is, is. No savior, no deliverer, no messiah looming over the horizon. A terrible epiphany that, especially when it comes so early, as it did to Sasha, just at the age when most girls are worrying about a date for the junior prom.

Life happened to Sasha, as the saying goes, while she was making other plans. But while she lost a full measure of innocence, she gained—she did gain a measure of wisdom, seeing most things whole rather than their parts. Seeing things for what they were. Not that she was totally bereft of hopes and dreams. Obviously, she brushed her teeth for a reason, to always be ready, just in case by some miracle she found herself plopped smack-dab in the middle of Beverly Hills with Alicia Silverstone. She already had the slang, Sasha did. She'd seen *Clueless* often enough. *Clueless* had become her beacon. Just to know that somewhere life was about dances, parties, and boyfriends was a measure of some relief.

Braced as she was for the worst, at all times, from all people, toughened as she was against emotion, she still managed to leave some room for tenderness and nostalgia.

Worst of all was bedtime, with no father to tuck her in and croon to her, "Sasha, Sasha, Sasha, my baby Sasha, the world is at your feet."

So, as a young lady without illusions, she played along with Mary. She got to like Mary, a blonde into her 30s and not at all the sort of person you'd expect to be working for Dewey Smith; polite, soft-spoken, sisterly, and on occasion downright motherly, saying things like "You're young, you're beautiful, you've got your whole life ahead of you—think! Half a million dollars. If I were you..."

Sasha was tempted, time and again ready to say yes, and then stopping to think, yes—think—of all the corruption she'd be leaving in the wake of her silence, all the suffering that would simply go on and on by an act of such selfishness. If she took the money and turned mute. Which she wouldn't do, couldn't do.

Then again, half a million bucks and, Beverly Hills here I come! That's what made it so tempting, above and beyond the government's promise to set her up nicely in some strange town, which, she knew, was nothing more than a City of Refuge, sanctuary of the pursued. Nowhere near Rodeo Drive. But they had promised her money and a home far from the reach of any Great Man. Either way, no more sweatshop. Either way she couldn't lose, unless Dewey Smith hunted her down and found her, after she talked—which, she knew, was not out of the question.

Based on materialism alone, Mary's offer was far more generous and glamorous, far more appealing. The temptation to accept kept her vacillating, swaying from one side to the other, until Mary made a final offer.

Mary was used to playing hardball. She'd once been a prostitute. High-class call-girl working her trade from some of Manhattan's finest hotels. Met Dewey on the job, Dewey proposing to take her away from all this. Steady income, no risk of Mr. Goodbar. All she'd have to do is be something like an overseer in one or two of his factories.

Of course, she accepted, and even accepted the role of bitch-on-wheels that came with the job. The girls on her watch tended to be slow and lazy, always eyeing the next break. They needed coaxing, sometimes with a firm hand—and sometimes it wasn't pleasant, for anybody, what went on behind closed doors. Wasn't pleasant for her, either, as if she liked laying down the law and once in a while administering a slap or two, which was sometimes the only way to communicate with those girls who spoke no English.

Such measures would be decidedly out of proportion for a girl like Sasha, particularly now with her being in the hands of the government, their agents no more than a shout away, in a booth, bloating up on Roy Rogers coffee. No, Mary was quite happy to take it slow and easy with this ingénue, prepared to wait her out until she came to her senses and realized that there was no profit in playing the game... very dangerous game of doublecross, as Sasha should very well know—not to bring up what happened to her parents in Russia or anything, when they crossed some Great Men. Not that this was Russia, mind you, but here, too, wrong was wrong and right was right. There were rules.

Here, too (as Mary put it to Sasha), people were held accountable for their actions, their words and their actions, regardless of what they'd seen, been through or imagined, yes even young ladies, pretty young ladies, sad young ladies, *sympathetic* young ladies, even they suffered consequences.

So... what's the big deal? What's the decision? There is no decision. Not really. Except to take the money and run. No one will know. Just say you made a mistake. Had time to think it over.

THEY CAN'T MAKE YOU TALK.

But certain people can shut you up.

This was where Mary began approaching the final offer—
the McLellan Hearings drawing nearer and nearer, Dewey
growing more and more restive, demanding results, results!
All this time she'd been offering Sasha two hands—blessings
from the one, curses from the other.

Neither of which had much impact on the girl.

So, finally it had to be said.

"If you talk, you're dead." In so many words.

Bad move.

"Like I'm supposed to care?" Sasha said in her best Alicia
Silverstone and showing not even a trace of astonishment.
She'd been prepared for this, knowing that if the threat came,
the decision would be made for her. No deal.

She'd sworn off fear. She'd reached the crossroad where
justice was more precious to her than her life.

Mary appealed to her as a friend, as they had developed an
odd sort of friendship.

To which, Sasha responded, "Thanks but no thanks."

"So there's nothing I can say to change your mind?"

"Nothing."

"You're a very foolish young lady, Sasha. You don't know
what you've got yourself into."

"Guess I'll find out."

This was their last meeting, there in the ladies' room at the
Roy Rogers, and it wasn't Sasha who shed a tear at the farewell, but Mary; it was Mary who wept, saying goodbye, plant-
ing a kiss on Sasha's brow and lamenting, with a sigh, "Sasha,
Sasha, Sasha."

The whole world at your feet.

CHAPTER 27

When a man gets on a casino shit-list, his face doesn't appear on the 10 Most Wanted poster at the local post office. The Network swings into action and the grapevine responds, proof of it when the undesirable gets blocked at the door; if he slips past that, they escort him from the table, and if it's somebody who got nailed doing something really bald-faced, like scooting off with someone else's chips, then it becomes a matter for the fuzz; guy gets bagged.

But then there's that fine line between actual crookedness and *assumed* cheating—the very line inhabited by Julian Rothschild, who, by the way, was still very much in the dark about his predicament; namely, that he'd been caught, supposedly, and was on the road to oblivion, so far as craps was concerned, meaning his livelihood, his passion and his life, finis, kaput, doors about to be slammed on him coast to coast.

Not so fast, though, as Roy Stavros was beginning to learn, as Julian had yet to be certifiably identified as a mechanic.

Yes, Heartless Hart Froman out there in Vegas had some pretty strong evidence—but was it really conclusive, and even if so, would it carry to the other casinos?

Seemed simple at first.

The proof would not have to be conclusive for disciplinary action to be taken, but it would help, because, as it turned out, Julian Rothschild had friends, he had a following. He was popular certainly among the players, the boys, most definitely among the charities for which he performed, but he was even well-liked by the brass in some of the casinos he frequented.

Being the corker that he was, he was good for business. His exploits, while costing the casinos cold cash, had the greater benefit of attracting multitudes who would otherwise be staying home, or losing their money elsewhere, at another casino, or at another game altogether, like the race track, or the lotteries, or on football.

As it was, given his reputation, his fame, his ability to dazzle, Julian was a magnet; he brought people in. So? So they lost money when he outlasted the House at the craps table. They could afford the red, the casinos could, because they made up for it so handsomely by the incidental business that came their way merely by his presence. So whatever money they lost to him at the tables was just another write-off, the price of doing business. Julian was their shill, their loss-leader, their bait-and-switch.

That sonofabitch, as Julian was known to Roy Stavros, was not so easy to put down. Hell, yes, came the word from high-ranking execs from casino to casino, as they assured him that they suspected it all along, that the guy was a shark throwing spinners. How else to explain his uncanny successes? But, they went on, they never bothered to stop him because he's an attraction. That's why.

All bullshit to Stavros, now more crazed than ever about crucifying Julian Rothschild, the vindictiveness getting more personal by the hour because in Stavros' estimation, the entire trillion-dollar casino industry was in jeopardy if you let one cheat get away, in this case the top cheat—leading to another and another and another, until finally poof!

No other outcome if cheating became an *attraction*. If cheating brought in business. What business? Even now cheats were doing damage at some casinos and would be doing the same at the Versailles were it not for some unusual defensive tactics. (The frisk room, for one; Lake Calico, for another.)

We're just as vigilant as you are, came the responses from his colleagues, but Julian...

Right. Julian's a *star,* Julian's an *attraction*.

Like Jesse James was an attraction.

Assholes, as Stavros had them pegged, these soft new-fangled casino execs, none over the age of 35, taking their cues from the nerds in marketing, nothing like the rough-and-tumble guys of the past, all business majors these days, coom laudy from the Wharton School, so taken by the bottom line as to be unaware that casinos were nothing about ledgers but about fire and water, blood and guts—their eyes too close to their computer screens to be aware of real danger, the danger of attracting a locust of mechanics if you let one slip by, especially the big one.

An example had to be made. What more perfect candidate than Julian Rothschild, being so popular, so visible?

So adored and adorable, and so stinking famous.

Shut your doors to him, he advised his colleagues, and let me take care of the rest, without informing that *his* doors and his doors alone would remain open to entice Julian into that head-to-head once-and-for-all million-dollar dice duel to the death. Even if it meant holding the game outside in a juice joint.

Stavros, meeting up with shrugs and delays from his colleagues, but who were still listening to him, since he did have a case, lamented the good ol' days in the back rooms of Chicago when slick operators got their lickings right there on the gambling floor. It was all so much more fun then, when it was taboo, when *everything* was illegal, so illegal as to make everything legal, practically. You could do no wrong when everything was wrong. You could do no wrong in Sodom.

These days, as Stavros saw things, it was all so formatted and legalistic, run by accountants and lawyers, a million rules to follow, everything overseen by the State itself, couldn't move a slot machine from here to there without getting an okay from the Casino Control Commission, required the Commission's blessing to blow your fucking nose—and had to beg them to stay open round the clock, here in AC. They finally caved in after what? Almost two decades of pleading, that's what.

How did the business get so soft? Stavros wondered. People so afraid. Which is what happens when government gets into the act and sees all those tax dollars, starts laying down the law because suddenly it's *their* money, so they bring in their people, their bean counters, their lawyers, their experts, all of which amounts to the most shocking, the most incredible thing of all, something the founding fathers and mothers wouldn't have believed in a million years, and must be rolling over in their graves to even think of it now—that state governments all across this great land are serving as *bookies*. Yes, bookies!

Plus—women. Another reason it's gone so soft. That wasn't too hard to figure out, for Stavros. When gambling was a man's game, cigars and spittoons, things were different. Then the women came and made it all pink.

Then, Stavros further reasoned, along came the senior citizens and turned the casinos into a giant nursing home. Home for the aged. They came on crutches. They came in wheelchairs. They came coughing. They came wheezing. They came kvetching. They came by the millions.

(What to do with all these people who were living so much longer and taking up good space? Pack them into the buses and send them into the casinos!)

They spent—but it wasn't the same.

They made the rules happen, for their *protection*. The government wanting to be sure that when the suckers lost their paychecks and Social Security allowances and in many cases their life's savings—they'd lose it all properly.

In accordance with the rules.

All of which took gambling from out of the back rooms and placed it center stage, giving rise to a nation of gamblers, in turn producing a generation of addicts, lured by the promise of quick, easy money and drawn in like the moth to the flame. Ads on radio, TV, newspapers, plus those billboards along the AC Expressway and those two Pikes—Black Horse and White Horse—only glorifying the wins, never the losses; sugarcoating the deception by the gambit of euphemisms, calling it *gaming,* not gambling.

Stavros wasn't one to bite the hand that fed him, but even he occasionally despaired at gambling's power to seduce and beguile, since he himself had once been a degenerate, a compulsive who had to endure five years of GA before he could call himself more or less cured from the "fatal fascination," as it was called during the testimonies.

Except that when he had been smitten, there wasn't so much legit action all around; there hadn't even been lotteries, and casinos only happened in Nevada. So there weren't that many compulsives, unless you counted the stock market, the most insidious form of gambling of all. Now?

Now he could scan any TV monitor up in the Sky and spot known degenerates at every table, like the guy at craps table 1, Norman Blankoff, who sometimes forgot his dentures he was in such a hurry to race down from Yonkers; the guy at table 2, Frank Bellabistrano from the Bronx who gambled away his house, his business *and* his family; the guy at table 3, Horowitz or something, from Jersey City, who had a heart attack on the casino floor after he tapped out at 40 grand.

Rockwell Bluestoner from Jenkintown, there at table 4, he's the guy who crashed his car through his living room after a bad day at the tables; and at table 5 that was Joe Scully who took the $30,000 saved up for his mother's cancer operation and blew it all one fine day right there at the same table.

But he's ba-a-ack. They all come back. Never mind the signs all over the place that say "Bet with your head, not over it," and forget what Steve Wynn said, that the only way to make money at the casinos is to *own* one.

It never ceased to amaze Stavros, man's capacity to endure on false hope, for in all his years in the business, plus, going back to the years when he was a Chicago cop, back further to the years when he'd been a pathological gambler himself (that's one reason he was dumped from the force, forging one lousy check)—in all that time he had never known a single individual to beat the House, on a regular basis that is.

Sure, anyone could get lucky in a burst of good fortune (that's what kept them coming back), but in the long run, no man could say he came out winners, not if he played by the rules. Because the rules were created with one purpose in mind, to favor the House. The rules were in the percentages and the rules were in the limits, those limits set by the House to keep the edge against a high roller getting hot and betting to the sky. It was all fixed, just like life itself. Play all you want, learn all you want, work all you want, the end's gonna be the same. You lose.

But as with any rule, there was always the exception, namely Julian Rothschild, Mr. Invincible. Fuck him. Think you can come to *my* house and beat me at *my* game? No way José.

Stavros was not at all deterred by the resistance he was encountering from his peers on the Rothschild front. He knew all he had to do was keep at it and eventually they'd all fall in, so he could go on singing his Blondie song—one way, or another, I'm gonna find ya, I'm gonna getcha, getcha, getcha....

CHAPTER 28

Julian left Vegas and returned to Margate, happy to be back, now with the leaves beginning to change colors, the ocean turning cold, and the summer faithful beginning their ritualized exodus, back to points north from whence they came, restoring the town to its rightful occupants.

He liked it better this way, now that he was an *old man* in his 30s and no longer the youth to whom summer was a time to flex and romp, though he did miss those days. He did miss being young. Sometimes it was even sadder to have been blessed with a happy childhood, the nostalgia so sweet and yet so bitter for the irretrievable loss.

He had opened all the windows to air out the house, which had been clamped tight in his absence, and did a load of wash in the basement, something that Monica usually did for him. Monica Travers, whom he'd been seeing for nearly 18 months, off and on, mostly off as of late, had been so busy with her job as PR consultant to the Greater Atlantic City Casino Association, and he, well, he'd been pretty much out of reach himself, all of which resulted in placing the romance on hold.

They were left to communicating by voice mail, something like I'll have your answering machine talk to my answering machine. Safe sex, for sure.

Speaking of which, he thought as he went back up and punched in the Brahms *Second Piano Concerto*—yes, the nurse and then of course Karen Davies, his third big-time actress, if anybody was numbering his conquests.

Trouble was, he wasn't counting, and he didn't care. For some reason he did not need sex anymore, and he wasn't even that nuts about love, either, ever since Debra left him. He hated to admit this to himself, but all he really cared for were his dice, the action, the action at the tables.

Otherwise he wanted things simple. Once you got involved, even for a night, things got complicated, as happened there with Karen the actress, who, trifling with the supernatural as she was, managed to throw a good scare into him, the key word being *trifle,* as you do not fool with that stuff; just the believing in it can make it happen, aside Solomon's counsel that faith vanquished omens, futility, and idle chatter.

That's what it was—idle chatter, that business of something bad waiting for him when he got back, and yet he could not help but detect a trend. His trip to Hollywood and Vegas had been a flop; he considered it a flop, aside from the big day at Lucky's the second time around. What about the first time when he got beat up, and what about the ear problems and doctors and nurses tending to him here, there, and everywhere, plus being snubbed and stood up by Lynn Sterling (so what else is new) and turning Matt Cain into Winston Churchill, to the disgust of everyone involved with the picture. Yup, he sure turned that guy around, a hundred and eighty degrees.

Then there was something else that added to the downward trend. That he'd spoken so openly of the 36 Just Men, the *Lamed-Vov*. Julian never used to be so loose-tongued about his mysticism, mindful that some things, like the source of your creativity, became soiled and spoiled when placed out in the open, and there he was shooting off his mouth, to the infidels. There were secrets that were meant to be kept secret. When you spoke of them, they dissolved into thin air. He had cheapened the mystery and cheated himself of something very personal.

Trends worried Julian. Like things happening in threes. Like a table getting hot for no apparent reason. Like a table going cold for no apparent reason. There was always an undertow to things, a netherworld at work beneath the surface, beneath the obvious.

A gambler, even one so steeped in mysticism, especially one so steeped in the spiritual as Julian, had to be guarded against the beyond and the unknown, more so when those were the tools of his trade.

By premonition induced by that Hollywood actress, or merely by the figment of his own imagination, Julian had the sense that he was being pursued. Yes, God seeks the pursued, but so does the devil, and sometimes it's a race as to who gets there first.

So while he itched to get back into full-scale action—his answering machine covered with messages from individuals and organizations petitioning him for his play—he checked the impulse, due to something that had happened the day before, a restraint all too noticeable to Monica Travers who popped in unannounced just as he was beginning to drift off into a trouble-some slumber on the living room couch.

(Since his divorce from Debra he couldn't fall asleep in the bedroom anymore when he was alone.)

"Caughtcha napping again," she said.

"Been a while," he yawned as she smooched his brow and tussled his hair and then kissed him hard on the lips and then brought back some iced tea from the kitchen, mentioning the fridge, how empty it was, proof that this was the home of a bachelor. "A bachelor of craps," she laughed.

She'd never find booze in the fridge or in the cupboards. She could use a scotch and soda now and then, but Julian didn't drink, only because he usually passed high and went straight to hangover.

"Been too long," he said, wakening and tapping her on the fanny.

"Not my fault," she said. "I've been here. Where've you been?"

"I've been there."

"I know. How'd it go?"

"Eh."

"But you always go back," she said as if she'd known him for a lifetime.

"Fool that I am."

"Any stories?" she asked with a touch of caution.

"I only like to tell stories with happy endings."

"That bad."

"Could have been worse."

She went back to the kitchen for more ice for the both of them and when she came back and sat down she was silent, sipping her tea a bit too intently. She was still wearing her two-piece, navy-blue business outfit, the tight skirt part of it riding up to her thighs for a breathtaking display of American legs. Maybe he wasn't so indifferent to sex after all. Her features were still taut from a hard day at the office—the kind of severe look women assume when they have to compete with men from nine to five.

Now she removed the jacket, revealing a see-through white blouse that held in a fine pair of breasts, kicked off her shoes, dramatically shook loose her cascading auburn locks, and the transformation began.

Even her voice began to change from 9-to-5 sharpness to after-hours pleasantness. He could easily fall in love with her.

He met her when a pit boss referred her to him, when he asked why he was never invited to any of the craps tournaments around town. Not that he cared; it was just the principle. They hit it off from the start, though there were no promises, no commitments.

She was divorced and now wanted her freedom as much as he did, to the point where she warned him that now and then she was liable to hit the sack with another guy, if the circumstances were right. She met a lot of men in her line of work, and there were temptations. As far as he knew she had not fallen prey to seduction, otherwise she'd have told him. That was part of the deal, to come clean. He sometimes figured that her defiance of monogamy was only a defensive ploy against his apparent diffidence when it came to declaring his love for her. He was more right than wrong. (She was far more forthcoming in that department.)

"What's up?" he said. "Something's on your mind."

"How did you know?"

"What's wrong?"

"All right. Who's Denise?"

"I give."

"I'm serious. Who's Denise?"

"So am I. Who's Denise? Back to you."

"Someone called me a few days back, saying she needed to talk to you, quite urgently."

"Denise, right?"

"So you do know her."

"No. Just a lucky guess."

"Look, Julian, if there's someone else..."

"Well, it's not Denise."

"So you really don't know who she is."

"Or what she wants."

"Well, she did sound awfully anxious."

"I do have that effect on women, don't I?"

"Oh, shush."

"What'd you tell her?"

"That you were out of town."

"And?"

"That you'd call her when you got back. Except that she wouldn't leave a number. Said she'd get in touch with you."

"So that's the end of Denise."

"Well, then I went and did something bad. She did sound awfully... well, sultry."

"You killed her in a fit of jealousy. Good for you."

"Not quite. I dialed that star-six-nine number, you know, where you can get the party that just called you, and it was the switchboard at the Versailles. I hung up, of course. But strange, don't you think?"

"I wouldn't lose sleep over it," he said.

"Speaking of sleep, *is* there someone else? I mean before, when I asked you..."

Was this where he had to confess?

"There's no one else, but out there in..."

She put her hands to her ears.

"You don't want to hear?"

"Is it anyone you'll be seeing again?"

"I don't think so."

"Is it anyone you'll be thinking about when you're with me?"

"No."

"Then leave it right there."

"Done."

But she did ask him if he'd shot craps out there and he told her what had happened both times, which explained to her the few bruises he had left. "That's what you get for leaving me behind," she pouted.

"Guess I'm finished with Vegas," he said. "Something... something just wasn't right out there."

"Well, we'll always have Atlantic City," she chuckled.

"Hmm."

"What?" she asked.

"Nothing."

"I think something's wrong."

"Nothing. It's just that... I don't know."

"You'll be all right once you hit the tables again. I know you."

"I guess that's what's been missing," he lied, as he did not mention this fact; that he had already been to the tables, zoomed right over to the Palace on the Boardwalk the same day that he got back to AC, which was yesterday. Couldn't get there fast enough, just to get in a game.

He'd been feeling rusty. Needed to get back in shape, back in the groove, here, back where he belonged, home territory. He usually used the Palace as a testing ground, saving the Versailles, and some other casinos, for the really big action, that is, when he played for others. This was for himself, for the fun, for the high, for the *rush,* and to measure himself against the standards that he set for his play.

As always, heads turned when he made his entrance—though Julian wasn't the type to walk into a room big, with pomp, smiling, and waving all around. That wasn't Julian. His entrances were more regally subdued.

Everything seemed normal at first, except that later, when he approached the tables, he didn't seem to be getting the usual reception from the crew, who were admittedly busy but who always in the past found time to offer a wink and a nod, grudging respect for the main man. Not today. If anything, he was being greeted with downcast eyes.

So be it, thought Julian as he stepped up to the middle table, people clearing a path, and plopped down two C-notes for greens and blacks.

Stan, the boxman, looked over his shoulder to Mac the pit boss, as if checking to see if it was all right—something that had never happened before—and Mac gave his assent but kind of reluctantly, Julian noticed, Mac seemingly shy about the transaction.

But Julian got the chips and waited for the dice to make the rounds, which they did in some haste, the boys sevening-out all around—and when he got the dice, he felt it, the surge, the adrenalin. He was pumped. Then it came, that momentary seizure, even paralyzing him for an instant. His face turned blood red.

He felt a wave of muscles creeping up his back and tightening around his shoulders. Then his body froze and he went weak and numb in the arms and legs, there, just like that, in a state of petrification, frightening for the fear that it might last, until it eased and it was over, and he was okay, more than okay—he was superman. The Presence was with him. The dice felt delicious in his hand, those two cubes so hard and perfect inside his palm. Life was good.

Julian had once again entered that celestial dimension usually reserved for the Titans, the likes of Babe Ruth, Jesse Owens, Maurice Richard, Joe Louis, Michelangelo, and Beethoven; and there was no one to dispute his place, for he belonged, he was one of them at his particular craft, and at these precise moments.

But the moment never came. No one stopped him from making his first toss, the crew evidently unaware that Julian was a marked man. As soon as the stickman announced 8 as Julian's point, Guy Stevens, the shift boss, came dashing over from another table he'd been supervising to yell, "Pass 'em!"

"Huh?"

"Sorry, Julian. Can't let you shoot."

"I haven't even started."

"Can't let you start."

"You're kidding."

"Do I look like I'm kidding?"

"This is outrageous."

"I agree."

"They can't do that."

"Yes, they can."

Of course they can. Julian knew this would happen some-day, someplace, where they'd lower the boom on charges that he was using a gimmick. He just didn't know the where or the when or how widespread. One casino, two casinos, three? Four? More? Most likely they wouldn't accuse him directly as that would mean laying out proof, their proof against his proof that he merely had a quirky way of throwing the dice—everybody's got his style, his own idiosyncrasy. Some people blow on them, kiss them, throw them underhanded, over-handed, open-palmed, closed-palmed, so? So he had his own jonah. Merely that he used his own special english.

That didn't make him a mechanic, and he truly believed that, that he wasn't a mechanic, any more than Picasso was less of a painter because he was a cubist. Who decides who's a mechanic and who's an artist?

"What did I do?" Julian persisted.

"I don't know."

"Come on, Guy. What's this all about?"

"Don't ask me," Guy said. "I don't make the rules."

Julian asked for the casino manager, who turned out to be Andy Nichols, a guy Julian knew quite well, so far as know-ing these guys went, meaning that by design they kept up an adversarial (though friendly) relationship with any player. Andy came over and threw up his hands. "Don't know what's going on, Julian. But word's come down to gate you. Sorry. Really sorry. But I sympathize with the way this was handled. It could have been done much more quietly. Privately. We didn't mean to embarrass you. Sorry. But that's the way it is."

That's the way it is, all right. Privately or publicly, he'd been told off firmly, the House had spoken, and it was cur-tains for sure when the stickman ceremoniously removed the dice from Julian's spot and offered them to the next man.

Julian gulped. He had nothing more to say. He'd never been a beefer and he wasn't about to start.

Humbled, he took a walk, promising to take his business elsewhere. In fact, the table, which had filled rapidly when he approached, emptied just as rapidly when he left, and he left pretty much near tears.

He walked the boards, trying to sort things out. Quite a switch. He felt like a loser. First time in a long time. Strange feeling. Like he'd been deposed. Well, momentary setback. But a setback nonetheless. What's next? That's what had him spooked. What's next? Word would get around, that's for sure, and that's what had him worried—losing face. He had lost the first round to the bully, but only the first round, that's how he comforted himself, with that thought; many more rounds to go.

That was not his fix on the Palace alone, but of casinos in general. He thought of them as bullies. People like him, men who had an edge for one reason or another, weren't taking advantage, they were only getting even, cutting the bully down to size.

It was getting dark and a nice breeze was kicking up. The Boardwalk was festive against the dazzling casino lights. The crowds were lively. Near Caesars he stepped down to the beach. There by the piling he saw a homeless guy asleep or dead, face buried in the sand.

Not an unusual sight, except that the homeless were Julian's business, and the man did seem awfully dead. So Julian drew closer, listening for signs of life. But the guy was dead all right.

Cops patrolled the boards mostly by bike, and it took about 20 minutes until the first one appeared, Julian explaining, the cop taking it in stride. "We'll take care of it," he said. Julian didn't wait around. He was feeling a bit nauseous. He looked up at the lights, down at the dead man—it was all too symbolic.

So that was yesterday, and today Julian was still thinking about that, and still licking his wounds from the earlier incident at the Palace. He had not tried any of the other casinos, afraid of what he might find out. He didn't want to know, not just now, not just yet. Sometimes it is better not to know your true circumstances; delusion is useful. We use it to brace ourselves.

"You're just suffering from withdrawal," Monica went on, innocent of the facts. He certainly wasn't going to tell her what had happened at the Palace. That would make it too real; yes, maybe by not talking about it, it would all go away. Like a bad dream. It had better go away. "Withdrawal, that's what it is. I can tell it in your face," Monica said.

Not that, he thought, for it reminded him of Karen Davies, and not the good part.

"Yeah, once I get back..."

"Actually, I thought you'd be there by now. I didn't expect to find you home."

"Thought I'd give it a rest. Gathering my strength."

"You sure you're okay, sweetheart?"

Sweetheart? She'd never used that word before. Didn't sound right to his ears. Like she was weakening. Mushy. They'd both agreed to dispense with mush. He, in particular, found it tasteless. Seemed that the lovey-dovey, kissy-kissy, hand-holding couples were the first to split. Besides, Debra used to call him sweetheart...

"I'm fine."

"Doesn't sound like you. Give it a rest and all that."

"Too much of a good thing; you know how it is."

The sun was going down.

"Would you like me to cook you dinner?"

"No."

"Not hungry?"

"Guess not."

"Do you want me to stay or leave?" she asked harshly.

"Stay."

"I missed you... you don't have to say anything."

He didn't.

She clicked on the TV and they both sat there and watched some sitcom, soundless. Just the pictures. Lately it was disheartening to hear TV people talk, rehearsed or otherwise. Either totally nonsensical or utterly infuriating, take your pick. On CNN here was another famous felon who got a $2.5 million book deal to tell his story, cashing in on his disgrace, except that no longer was there any such thing as disgrace. The murderers, the wife-beaters, the lawyers who defend them, they're all treated as celebrities and signing multi million-dollar book deals. How about this for a book? *When Good Things Happen To Bad People*.

Julian was thinking about that and a thousand other things. But mostly...

"The Versailles?" he said from out of nowhere.

"About Denise?"

"Yeah."

"That's who answered. The Versailles."

"Hmm."

That's where Dewey was staying, Dewey and two thousand other people.

"Does that mean anything?"

"No," he said. "Not necessarily."

He wasn't fooling her. "What does that mean?"

"It means... I don't know what it means."

"So it could mean something."

"Maybe."

Now she showed a trace of alarm. "I guess you know you're in a business with some rough characters."

"Like any business."

"After you tell me what happened in Vegas..."

"That was something else," he shrugged. "You *expect* to get beat up at Lucky's. You haven't paid your dues if you haven't. When it comes to AC, I don't have to tell you, it's all on the square."

"The people I work with," she said, "yes, but then there's that other element, and you'd know more about them than I would. I mean all those people who beg you to make money for them—you're bound to fish up something rotten. In fact, I'm surprised you haven't been approached by the mob or something like that already. Or have you?"

Which did remind him of Dewey Smith, not that he was mob, exactly, and not that Julian needed that much to remind him of Dewey, since there were eight messages from Dewey on his answering machine already, messages that Julian decided to ignore for the time being—until he was ready, ready to play. If anybody would let him play. What a thought!

He kept thinking about that dead guy on the beach.

"Can we talk about something else?"

"Why don't we *do* something else," she whispered as she led him to the bedroom.

CHAPTER 29

Denise Barker had been frantic for a reason, the reason being Plan B (or was it Plan A all along), which came as something of a surprise to her, or maybe not, since Dewey was chock-full of surprises, though this was a bit beyond the pale.

She'd sniffed it out from that one phone call, the man merely asking for Dewey, but the voice—there was something in the man's voice that gave her a case of the willies. Later she caught Skinny alone for a moment, a weak moment for him, and asked him what's going on. He walked away, but not before mumbling, "You don't want to know."

So she knew.

Two and two made five hundred thousand dollars, for an assassination. Now she understood, as if she hadn't from the beginning. He hadn't really fooled her when he was so full of protests against his real intentions, except that she had wanted to be fooled, didn't want to believe he was that low, so low as to order the killing of a 16-year-old child. But that's all it could be, especially after she saw him walking the boards with that man with the sinister limp.

That clinched it for her. She was leaving him, once she put a stop to the madness. To hell what he did to her if he found out that she'd contacted Julian Rothschild and told him the truth.

Exactly how gullible was she expected to be? Well, gullible enough to have stuck with him all these years, through all his deceptions. To think she had tried to *reform* him, change him, love him. Unfortunately she did, she had loved him, strange as it all was, attracted to the danger more than anything, more than to the man. And what a waste it had been to have thrown everything else aside—family, friends, career, all for what? To teach them a lesson. Who? She forgot.

Oh, yes, hypocrisy. That's what drove her from her parents, so upright; and from journalism, so fraudulent as practiced at the *Star*. They thought themselves so superior. They were so quick to find flaws in everybody but themselves. No, they were perfect, her newspaper colleagues were, utterly smug in their political correctness and in their belief that they had the answers.

Never mind their own prejudices, their own agendas, spoken openly in the hallways but concealed between the lines of their reportage.

So she taught them a lesson, taught them all a lesson, by stomping off and embracing a world that was anathema to them, them and their pieties and their self-righteousness. But who's crying now?

She was.

Her first suspicion had been aroused by Dewey's insistence that they stay in AC beyond the summer—and how he'd managed to stretch the comp she didn't know, but guessed that he was cashing in on his good name as a high roller. At present he was not the Versailles' most desirable guest, not quite, his play meager, his reputation taking hits daily over the McLellan Hearings, now in full swing and awaiting the arrival of its star, Sasha Spivak. To the public he was more than notorious, he was villainous. Which surely didn't score big points with Versailles management, but they let him stay. Anyhow, that's what got her to thinking. Of course, she understood that he was in retreat, so this was as good a place as any to keep some distance from the long arm of the law.

He'd be much more vulnerable in New York against the backdrop of his sweatshops. In AC, the gambling, the casinos were a diversion, enough to keep him safe for the time being, before they called him up, before they called *her* up, Sasha.

That's what he was hiding from in AC, ostrich-like, and that's why he was staying, to make that money for a killing.

Once she arrived at that irrefutable conclusion, Denise made the phone call to Julian, by route of Monica Travers when she failed to reach Julian—she certainly wasn't going to leave a message on his machine—with no thought for her own safety, except that she was sick to her stomach to be in this spot in the first place. She was sick of the whole thing, feeling at once like an accomplice *and* a traitor, and beset by the heebie-jeebies when she went downstairs to the lobby of the Versailles to make the calls. She certainly wasn't going to snitch from the suite where she never knew who was bugging whom.

It didn't help that this was Pageant week, the week before the Miss America contest when soon there'd be the parade along the Boardwalk to present America's lovelies before the public. Atlantic City and all of its Boardwalk hotels were festooned with happy faces, the daughters of American chastity, Mom, and apple pie.

Two of them were staying at the Versailles, Miss This and Miss That, Denise never got it straight, maybe because both of them, in fact all 51 of them from across the nation looked so much alike, so many teeth! These two were posing for photos in the lobby at the same moment Denise was furtively using the pay phone. They were preening delightedly and obligingly signing autographs to the fawning multitude.

What a contrast! For so long, feminist that she was, Denise had been contemptuous of the pageant, despite its alleged conversion to education and values over looks and beauty—but in reality it was still about tits and ass.

That was how she felt then, but now, by comparison, she saw herself as lowered to a craven state, cowering, sniveling, sniveling and cowering, crawling on her belly like a snake, while they stood proudly before the world, radiating in their Ivory Soap innocence, so 99 percent pure, so unworldly, so feminine, so fetching, so sexy, so carefree; above all, so *uncorrupted*.

She felt the pangs of envy. Would she trade places with even the least of them? No. This wasn't her kind of life. This wasn't her idea of being a woman, not that the pretty ones were all that pretty and not that the smart ones were all that smart and not that the socially motivated ones were all that socially motivated and not that the wholesome ones were all that wholesome. For sure, there were a million untidy secrets behind those waxy smiles. But just for a moment, this moment, yes, gladly, she'd trade places.

Well, Denise reflected, *that's that and this is this,* and so she dialed, from the lobby pay phone, first Julian's number, and failing there, Monica Travers, as it was no secret that they were a twosome.

Denise had heard about Julian through the grapevine and she imagined him to be rather heroic. In fact, she had a bit of a crush on him, based on his legend. He was usually portrayed as a Davidic sort, the dice his slingshot. Handsome to boot. Of course she had met him that one time on the yacht, but that was all too fleeting.

When she got through to Monica, she was a bag of jitters, declining to give her name, of course, but saying she'd call back and knowing that she'd left Monica in suspense. That was easy to tell by the lady's repeated questioning, "Can I leave him a message? Who's calling?"

After she hung up, she felt better. She'd made the move, a move that had to be made. She felt a sort of triumph long missing since her days in newspapering when just meeting a deadline was a thrill.

She turned—she'd been facing a wall, hiding—and came face-to-face with Dewey.

"Our phone upstairs out of order?"

"No," she laughed, or rather croaked.

"So? What's this?"

"What's what?" stalling for time, to come up with something, anything.

"Why the pay phone?"

"Oh, I came down for a snack and then wondered if you were back up. So I called."

"You were calling me?"

"Yes."

"In the room?"

"I wasn't sure whether you'd be back or not. Thought maybe you'd want me to bring you up something."

"So you were calling me from a pay phone?"

"Yes, because..."

"Not a *house phone?*"

She feigned nonchalance, knowing she was a dead duck. "Exactly why I hung up when I realized my mistake."

He stared her down for maybe ten seconds that seemed like ten hours.

"I see," he said. "I see."

CHAPTER 30

Saturday night, the night of the pageant, Skinny and Fats paid him a visit. Julian had been watching Regis and wondering what happened to Kathy Lee, why she wasn't there co-hosting. He'd never find out probably because most times he watched television with the sound down or completely off, the mute button his best friend.

Skinny and Fats came right in the middle of the swimsuit competition, the best part, the part you weren't supposed to care about, since it was all about family, the environment, education, and good citizenship. It was all about scholarships and caring for the young, the old and the restless. Julian answered the doorbell and let them in, Skinny saying they'd only be a minute and Fats asking if he could have a drink. Iced tea would be fine.

They were both very polite, on their best behavior, as they had been the first time. Except for their swagger there was nothing about them to suggest peril. Julian invited them into the living room, where Fats said, "Where's the sound?"

"You need *sound* for that?" Skinny said, pointing to the parade of tits and ass.

The two of them, though Fats mostly, were quite distracted by the images on the screen. "I'm going for Miss New York," Fats said, swooning. "Or Miss New Jersey. Or Miss Ohio. Wouldn't kick her out of bed."

"You're out of your mind," Skinny said. "Texas always wins."

"Yeah, them southern broads."

"You mean west," Skinny corrected.

"I mean south *and* west is what I mean, all right?"

Skinny turned to Julian, his manner suddenly all business. "We're here on a serious matter, you know that."

Julian knew exactly what he was talking about. "I know that."

"I mean you know about our friend Dewey and about his troubles."

"Yes, of course, and..."

"We didn't come for the ride."

Julian nodded in agreement.

"And you've already made promises to Dewey," Fats chimed in, but eyeing Miss Alabama.

"Yes."

"Which is the purpose of our visit," Skinny said, getting just a bit tough, not too tough, but tough enough to let Julian know that they had not come here to watch the Miss America Pageant, Fats aside. "Meaning as to when you intend to fulfill your commitment."

Julian yawned and it wasn't a fake show of indifference. He really did have trouble taking these guys seriously, though he had to remind himself that the man they represented was serious enough, more serious than ever after mentioning that other thing, the baby thing. So Julian explained that he'd just gotten back from Vegas, was tired, and couldn't simply jump back into action right away. He needed a few days.

"How many days is a few?" Fats wanted to know, now settling on Miss Wyoming as the winner.

Figure a week. Maybe two, Julian offered.

Skinny added it all up. Dewey had guessed that Sasha would be singing to Congress in about ten days. At least that was the speculation in the press. So Dewey's orders had been to get Julian in action for the five hundred thou in no more than five, maybe six, no more than seven days.

Even that was cutting it close. Today, of course, would be best, but Dewey was sensitive enough to know that an ARTEEST like Julian couldn't be pressured too much. So his suggestion to his emissaries had been to take it slow, but firm.

Can't push a man like Julian—though he must always be made aware that he was on the spot. That this was no laughing matter. That life and death depended on him.

Never mind whose life, whose death. But maybe his, too, reputation-wise and otherwise. Never to tell him so in so many words. He was the kind of guy who just might push back when pushed too hard. So play it by innuendos. That's a language he'd understand. The language Dewey himself employed to gain his ends.

"Two weeks is too long," Skinny said, just as Julian pressed the mute button to bring up the sound, just to be contrary, Regis, after some dance number, now talking about all the social concerns—a better America, a better world—that motivated all these contestants.

Fats said, "Y'know, they put padding in their bras."

"Listen," Skinny said, "Mr. Smith, that's Dewey, is very anxious for your play, at your earliest possible convenience, Mr. Rothschild. Meaning, say, within the week. Not that we wish to rush you or anything, but it *is* getting late."

For what?

"Mr. Smith has certain payments to make, certain obligations to meet."

Julian, of course, knew about the hush money and, of course, he did not yet know about Mr. Glass.

Julian shook his head and reminded Skinny that winning at the tables was *not a sure thing*. Even for him.

"Mr. Smith is aware of that," Skinny said. "But there is only one way to find out. Besides, Mr. Smith has the utmost confidence in you, despite what happened the other day at the Palace—oh, yes, he knows."

Oh, yes, thought Julian. *Everybody knows.*

"That was too bad," Fats said mournfully.

"Yes, it was," said Skinny. "But even the Duke struck out once in a while."

"Don't they have to be virgins to get in this thing?" Fats wanted to know during a commercial break.

"Hey, Fats..."

"I just want to know."

"Yo, Fats. We're trying to talk business here."

"Used to be they had to be fucking virgins."

"Fucking virgins, huh?"

"I mean did they used to get inspected?"

"Shut up, Fats."

"I don't think these broads are virgins," Fats opined when the show came back. "Know how you can tell? By the way they walk."

"Like you know," said Skinny.

"Yeah, I know. Virgins walk kind of tight-assed. Broads that've been fucked walk kinda bow-legged."

"You're the expert."

"Yeah, I'm the expert, all right?"

"Thanks for coming," Julian said as a hint.

He got up as if to escort them to the door, but they stayed put. Fats kept eyeing the TV. Skinny, more interested in Julian, finally got up, and motioned for Fats to follow him to the door. "Listen, Mr. Rothschild," Skinny said. "I know you think we're clowns. My friend here especially, right?"

Julian said no, he did not think they were clowns. Indeed he didn't. He knew the score. He also knew that kings often used jesters to send the worst messages. So, no, they were good for a laugh, maybe, Skinny and Fats, Fats and Skinny, but they were not clowns.

"Good," said Skinny, "that we've got that straight, because it would be a mistake to get that idea. We are serious people and we represent a serious man who gave you a serious job to do." Here Skinny extended his hand to Julian. "We are all confident that you are serious, too, about keeping your promises. *Regardless of anything.*"

He paused to let that sink in, meaning that even if there were a change of plans, like the winnings to be used for something else besides hush money, still, Julian was to be kept to his pledge.

Then Skinny continued, "A week would be fine, Julian. Mr. Smith is counting on you."

No threats were made. That made it all the more threatening to Julian.

To Denise, as well. She'd been hiding in the bedroom.

CHAPTER 31

They couldn't agree on a safe place to meet, once Denise got hold of Julian. The whole world seemed to be eyes and ears, for her, and for him, once she'd suggested New York—for him the problem was this; he was claustrophobic, terrified of elevators, and in New York everything was about elevators. New York was too tall.

Margate was flat. No elevators. Denise thought it a rotten idea to be meeting there in Julian's home. Never know who might pop in, and sure enough there they were, Fats and Skinny, Skinny and Fats.

Which hustled her to the bedroom, from where she'd heard the whole thing.

"That was close," she said when she emerged.

She was shaking and asked if he had anything in the house to calm her nerves. He had to apologize about the lack of booze. He offered her a Pepsi, which she took and drank with trembling hands, knuckles white.

"I may have some Valium."

"I'll take one," she said.

She gulped it down and he felt rotten for her. He felt responsible; should have gone with her instinct, met in New York or someplace instead of in here, which was beginning to resemble Grand Central Station. She finally started to collect herself after standing out on the porch and breathing in some ocean air. He joined her out there, and they both studied the ocean together in silence, and there was no mistaking a current running between them. He felt like putting an arm around her and she sensed it, finally hooking him with her eyes, even allowing the trace of a smile. He gave her a non-sexual, non-threatening tug around the shoulders, to which she responded with a sigh.

This was altogether different from the first time, when he met her on the yacht and she was so busy snubbing him. Here and now she was so much softer, so delicate, so vulnerable, and yes, quite attractive. He assumed it must be quite a story between her and Dewey, and he wasn't sure if he wanted to hear it, and he was quite sure she'd be loath to tell it, the details obviously rife with horror, judging from her melancholy eyes.

"I guess you're wondering why I called this meeting," she cracked.

"Not really."

"You mean you know?"

"I'm sure it has something to do with Dewey."

"That's for sure."

The phone rang, and it brought them both back inside. She lit up a cigarette and sat herself down on the couch while he answered the phone in the bedroom and heard a voice that rocked him like a blow to the jaw—that of Debra, his ex-wife. Now here was a call he thought he'd never get, not in this lifetime. He often wondered how he'd react, sometimes practicing it, cool, nonchalant, maybe mixed in with a hint of hostility.

"Hi," she said, and he turned to jelly.

"Well, well," he said, instead of "Look, I'm busy, I'll get back to you when I've got some time." That's the way he had rehearsed it and it sure sounded good there in the shower. "So how the heck are you?" he asked. On the tip of his tongue were the words "I love you, come home." Also thinking but not saying that *I am always here to protect and guard you*, mindful as he was of the bargain he was bound to keep because of Dewey's threat against her. A thing she must never have to relive.

She said she was fine and she sure did sound chipper, calling from her apartment in New York, where she and Donald lived, when he wasn't out in Hollywood. "I thought you'd be out there," he said about Hollywood.

"I don't like to be around Donald when he's working," she said. "He can be such a putz."

"That's good to hear."

She laughed. God, that laugh. How he loved that laugh. How he missed that laugh.

"Don't tell me you miss me," she said softly.

"Me? Are you kidding?"

"You're still a flirt," she chuckled. "Success hasn't changed you."

"Is that good or bad?"

"Oh, it's good. Now down to business."

What she wanted to know was what happened there at the Palace. Word got back to her that he'd been frozen out.

"I thought you'd be calling about what happened in Hollywood."

"You mean about what you did to Matt Cain?" she said, laughing.

"Yeah."

"Donald told me all about that, and he's still crying about it, poor guy. Even blames me. He says I sicced you on him to sabotage the works. But that's Donald. Listen, I called about *you*. I'm worried about you."

Julian said nothing, holding off a stampede of emotions.

"Julian?"

"It's just strange to hear you say that."

"Why? I think about you all the time. Don't you ever think about me?"

Here's where he thought he might play it cool. "Once in a while."

"Really? That's all?"

"All right, twice in a while."

"That's better. So what's going on?"

So he told her what had happened at the Palace and assured her it was just the Palace.

"Well, that's what has me concerned," she said. "I mean what would happen if they all closed you off?"

"Then I don't know."

"Well, *do* you know?"

"No, I haven't bothered to find out."

"Why not?"

"I guess I just don't want to know, as of yet."

"God, Julian, what would you do?"

"If I'm frozen out completely?"

"Perish the thought, but yes."

"I don't know. I really don't know."

Long pause, and then she said something that really touched him: that it would be like chopping the hands off Toscanini, Toscanini being her favorite conductor. This was quite a switch, Julian remembering how mocking she'd been when he began taking craps so seriously.

She'd traveled quite a distance from then to now and he was grateful about it and sad about it all at once.

"This is your life, Julian," she said. "I hope you intend to fight back."

"I sure do, if it comes to that, but I'm not so sure it will."

"Well if it does, will you let me know?"

"Why?" he asked.

"Because I care."

"Okay."

"I really do, Julian. I do care."

"I hear you."

"And because maybe I could help."

"Hmm."

"No, really I could. Donald's got lots of friends in Hollywood and they've got lots of friends in Vegas and Atlantic City..."

"Listen, Debra, if the day comes when I need Donald's help for any fucking thing..."

"Uh-oh, I've made you mad."

"Not a bit."

"Hey, Julian, before I hang up I've got three words for you."

"I'm holding my breath."

"I love you."

He washed his face before rejoining Denise in the living room.

"Everything all right?" she said, now much more self-composed, even offering a full grin.

"Yeah, just an old... an old friend. Sorry to have kept you waiting."

"I really do have to be getting back. So."

"Yes. So."

So she told him. That if Julian went ahead and raised half a million for Dewey, a young lady named Sasha Spivak was as good as dead. The money was slated for a hitman. No questions, no doubt about it, it was fact.

Her own life was likewise now in jeopardy, for giving him the news, which really wasn't such news.

Julian said he wasn't altogether surprised. He'd had his own suspicions.

"I hope you don't intend to go through with it then," she said in appealing to his good character.

"I have to. I gave my word," Julian said matter-of-factly.

This set her back, and her face flushed up hot pink. She was amazed to hear this, from a man so storied for his righteousness. He gave to the poor, and he was handsome. It had always been her cockeyed notion that the more handsome the man, the better the man. Just something she believed in. "You have to?" she said incredulously.

"I have to play," he said. "I didn't say I have to *win.*"

Now she understood. "You mean you'll lose on purpose."

"Exactly."

"You can do that?"

"Most likely. No, I'm sure I can."

"You know the stakes," she said gravely. *Too much so,* she thought. She had hoped to come across more lighthearted, more feminine, despite the solemnity of her mission. "I could never live with myself if..."

"Neither could I, and I admire your guts for coming over."

You don't know the half of it, Denise was thinking, for Dewey had begun giving her the silent treatment, ever since he trapped her there by the pay phone in the lobby. The silent treatment was usually a precursor.

"I'm only worried," Denise said, "that you may just get lucky, I mean that you'll win despite yourself."

Denise was well-aware of his reputation, that of a shark and also that of a mystic.

Before her visit (being the former reporter that she was and knowing the value of research) she had stopped off at the library and skimmed through dozens of books on craps. She learned enough to gain respect for the game. But she also learned that some people believed that the power of the mind could influence the dice. All of which amounted to something supernatural. "Is that you they're talking about?" she asked.

Julian said it was all too scientific for him, these studies of mind over matter, and though he believed in the supernatural, of course he did, for him, it was more about instinct, instinct and faith and practice, practice, practice.

"Well," she said, "whatever you've got, I hope it works. We're talking about the life of a young woman."

"There's nothing to worry about," Julian said. "If I want to lose, I'll lose." He assured her that by hook or by crook he'd never raise the money for Dewey. He'd seven-out all over the place.

At the door she smiled, took a step forward, then backward, and kissed him on the cheek.

"Hmm," she sighed. "To think what could have been."

She stayed there, staring into his eyes, wondering if she should make a play. She was tempted. There was something so gloriously remote and decent about him, and she was in love. But life was complicated enough, so there it would remain, like most dreams, unfulfilled. If there was any justice in the world, this was the man who'd have come along before Dewey, before all the rest of it. *How different,* she was thinking, *it would have all turned out.*

CHAPTER 32

Julian had a pet theory that belonged at the top of anyone's list of political incorrectness, which held that the reason men ran off to war periodically was to get away from women; not from women per se as much as the domesticity imposed by them.

Right or wrong, true or false, he was beginning to feel smothered, mothered and smothered, too many women in his life, new ones, old ones, some good, some bad, none ugly. Not that he had anything against them, bless their hearts, just that too much time around perfume tended to make a man soft, and in his business a man had to serve his tough side, keep himself lean and mean. Shooting craps was like waging war, it *was* waging war, you on this side, the House on the other side, the table in the middle nothing less than a battlefield.

So it was time to get into action and off the funk induced by that session at the Palace, where they wouldn't even let him play.

He had any number of casinos to choose from, to see if his freeze-out was singular or widespread. If it was widespread he'd never be able to play for Dewey, which was the least of it, the most of it being that he'd never be able to play for himself or anybody else—and that was a thought too terrible to ponder.

Which was why he had kept putting it off. But it was time. Up and down the Boardwalk he had the Hilton, Tropicana, Trump Plaza, Bally's, the Claridge, the Taj, the Showboat— plenty more if need be.

One at a time, though. He decided on a relatively new addition to the Boardwalk, the Monaco, which had sprung up only a year ago with European money (some said Monte Carlo money), and it sure had the trappings of a James Bond movie, hush, lush, plush, a casino to end all casinos.

Driving along Ventnor Avenue to AC, he rolled down the windows to whiff the summer-turning-to-fall breeze and turned up the radio on the "Oldies" station to fill up on some youthful vigor and courage. *This is how we did it when we were young,* he thought, *young and crazy, with no one to care for but ourselves.*

Along come the years and suddenly you're no longer number one. But everything'll be all right, he assured himself. Imagine this. She loves me. He had tried not to think of Debra, and it was wrong to think of her now that she was married, again.

But then it had been wrong for her to be calling him, in the first place, and to be telling him she loved him in the second place. But she had said it all right. Wow! He didn't much care for grownups who said wow. But wow!

That old feeling. That old yearning. Speaking of which, he thought, when the AC skyline came into view, the neons sparkling like diamonds against the sun, *There it is. Here it is, and here I come.*

He parked valet and made his entrance. No heads turned. He realized that he was hardly known here, and this was to the good, obviously the reason he had chosen the Monaco. It was new. The people were new. As least so far as he was concerned. He'd only played here once or twice.

He walked around a bit to get the feel of the place, first to the slots where, surprisingly, there wasn't the usual horde of daytrippers, and he remembered that the Monaco allowed no bus traffic and offered no bus freebies. They wanted the high rollers exclusively.

He toured the tables, still no signs of recognition.

The dealers were in tuxes. It was like a wedding.

He stepped up resolutely to a table that was half empty and threw down 5 C-notes; resolutely was his style ever since he saw the way surgeons approach the patient in the operating room. They become fierce. They take charge. They attack. Once you've made up your mind to do something, you do it; you do it without meekness or hesitancy. You do it whole-heartedly and without delay. Delay is a bad sign to yourself and to your opponent. Do it with courage and gusto or do not do it at all, Julian's lesson for craps and everything else; his championship credo. "Greens and blacks," he said.

Placing the chips in his tray he waited for the dreary wails of seven-out, seven-out, seven-out, which came rapidly enough, and when the dice finally arrived he felt the juice and with two greens riding on the pass-line, he whipped 'em hard with english but no spinner. They rolled to a 10.

"Ten is," said the stickman, name-tag Edward Weidemann, a tall man with soft-white skin and wavy light-brown hair, a man who seemed happy in his job, posting a kindly smile as he urged on the boys with words of encouragement.

Julian covered his odds on the 10 with a black chip and tossed two more greens to Weidemann, making his wishes known with a polite command: "Hard 10, my friend," and then completed the routine as he'd done a million times before, by neatly placing another two greens in the come.

A nice, honest bouncing toss to the wall and the stickman grinned and said, "Hard 10 right back, pay 'em boys; we've got ourselves a shooter!"

Indeed, they did.

"What took you so long?" a couple of the players hollered out cheerfully, as meanwhile the table began filling up with new recruits, those boys who were always buzzing around and smelled a hot shooter like bees to honey.

Julian savored the moment, as would any craps player—that pause to enjoy the praise from the boys as the action comes to a momentary halt while the dealers do their job: paying the line. Now it's time to relax and rake in the velvet, bring in those beautiful chips that have a nasty habit of returning to home base.

But not now. Now the chips belonged to the boys.

"Three-fifty," said Weidemann, as he tapped the table in front of Julian with his trusted stick, signaling the dealer to pay Julian for the hard 10. So, three more blacks and two greens end up on Julian's stash along the rail.

Another fifty on the line, and the dice are out.

"Six easy," announced Weidemann, and now, now that he knew his man, certain that another hardway was coming from Julian.

The boys knew it, too, and they scrambled to cover the hard 6.

Sure enough, "One hundred, hard 6," said Julian, knowing that he could make it, either the honest way, or the other way, the Slim Sam Belmont way—set those cubes on a thirty-three leaning left, lift 'em, keep 'em stacked tight, and then spin them to glory.

Of course, he might not hit it on the following toss, or the next... But if he got enough shots at it, he'd nail it sooner or later. That's what made Julian the sharpshooter that he was. Never—like an amateur—going for a one-roll bet, like aces or boxcars. That's too tough for even the best of mechanics.

Hardways, that's what Julian liked best, because, as in this case, he could keep gunning for that sweet 6 of threes, until, of course, he rolled an *easy* 6 (4-2 or 5-1... or a 7), but such worries were not on his mind right now. There was always the spinner to fall back on if he felt his natural powers desert him.

To win honestly, that's what thrilled Julian.

The concentration to call up his mystical powers made him so intense that he sometimes forgot his place.

"Sir, you want odds on your 10, right?" said the dealer.

"Oh, yeah, thanks," said Julian as he flung another black chip to the dealer for odds on his 10. "And bump up my hard 10 another fifty. A hundred coming."

Julian now had two hardways working—the 6 and the 10 for a hundred each. He had the come-bet on 10 with fifty and a hundred odds. He had the pass-line point of 6 for fifty and a hundred odds. He had another hundred sitting in the come.

Down the table they flew, and fly they did those dice, skidding to the wall on thirty-two, not thirty-three, but it was a number, and Julian watched as the dealer moved his come-bet to the 5-box. "Odds," said Julian. "Odds on my five," as another black chip was sent into battle.

Roll after roll, and it's winner after winner for Julian. Still no hardways—yet.

The boys, collecting right along with Julian—the boys were sweating, but it was a good sweat.

Shooters like this do not come along very often.

The boys knew it, and so did Steve Larson, the floorman. Larson, short, tough-looking, dark hair slicked back in the style of Pat Riley, was on the phone, eyeing Julian with a frown. Julian was obviously the topic of discussion.

Julian was too busy to notice.

He took a deep breath before his next toss. He felt it, that very special feeling.

Julian let go, and there it was!

"Ten the hardway," proclaimed Weidemann, offering Julian a smile of admiration, as if sensing that it was just a matter of time, given the quality of this particular shooter.

Now it was time for another break in the action as all the smart boys who had trusted in Julian on his hard 10 from way back got paid again. But for Julian, it was *seven* black chips. Pressing that hard 10 had paid off, all right.

Julian's next tosses drew calls of:

"Three craps."

"Yo-eleven."

"Three craps," again.

Otherwise known as junk.

Julian was after that point of 6. But he wanted it thirty-three. Confident as always when he felt the power, the power that was his and his alone, he knew it was getting close. Meanwhile, he kept throwing more junk and was getting miffed by it all. He decided to let the come-outs hit and just take 'em down, and like any good doobie, they did their job. No reason to get greedy here. After all, it was the 6 that he was pursuing.

"Press the hard 6," Julian said, as he tossed another black chip to Weidemann the stickman.

"Is this gonna bring it out, young man?" said an older player at the other end of the table who had taken a liking to this shooter of all shooters. Why not? He was making the table rich, this kid.

"Yeah, it's out," said the Prince of Dice, and he tossed those babies so fast they sounded like a 30-30 slug whizzing by.

"Winner! Winner 6. Pay the line," said Weidemann. "And he made it the H-A-R-D-W-A-Y, boys. Anyone have any doubts?" Weidemann glanced around the table as he made his call with some literary license. Steve Larson, the floorman, now off the phone, glowered at Weidemann. Larson was not as overjoyed as Weidemann by Julian's performance, and Larson gave his subordinate a cold stare, which read: "Don't get cute, my man. Just call the numbers, okay?"

Julian took the hint, as well. Time to chill. He sevened-out at will.

But he had scored big. This was blood money.

He toked the dealers $100. They said thank you—except, that is, for Steve Larson. But there was nothing he could do. Julian already had the chips, and all he had to do was march over to the cage to collect.

Never mind the money. He'd played, and nobody had stopped him. He was still alive. *Exactly,* he thought, the Palace had just been a fluke. With that in mind he stepped up to the cage and spilled out the chips, ready to collect—already figuring where some of this money was going to, five G-notes for sure to the new wing at AC Hopsital that had opened up to treat compulsive gamblers, and had, ironically, approached him for a donation, considering it only fair, given his line of work.

The bulk of it, though, would go to that home in Cherry Hill for battered women, which he visited about once a month, dropping off a thousand here, five thousand there, since the place subsisted mostly on the generosity of private citizens, people who were as outraged as he was about the whole damned thing, about the way too many men treat too many women, like it was still the Stone Age and we'd made no advancement, even in America, or is it especially in America that we specialize in child molestation and excel in wife-beating? Maybe it just seemed that way from reading the papers but, in any case, he always left the place muttering "What the Hell!" and swearing vengeance on the next husband who dared lift a hand against a spouse, except that the guys who did the damage were never around to admire their handiwork.

Sometimes he took out his anger next door at Garden State Park. He loved the track, this one in particular, which had risen up so gloriously after the fire of '77, and was now peopled by a friendly staff that actually rooted for you to win, so different from the casinos—only here, when he put his money down, usually upstairs at the Currier & Ives, it was the horses who kept getting even.

"Problem?" he said when the Monaco cage lady stepped away and started chatting with a guy at a desk.

The guy, who turned out to be the cage manager, came over and said, "These chips are questionable."

"They're your chips," Julian said with a sick chuckle.

"But they may be no good," the guy said flatly, as flatly as saying *you* may be no good.

"Huh?"

"What I mean is, the authorities may determine your play to be fraudulent."

"Listen..."

"No, you listen. These chips are being confiscated."

Confiscated and placed in escrow in a safe deposit box PENDING FURTHER REVIEW, the guy said.

Julian didn't like it, but he knew they could do that, oh, yes. Chips weren't money. No, they weren't, contrary to the popular perception. They were just chips, until the House paid. But before that, they were exactly what they seemed to be— chips, be they green, black, orange, or gray, very nice, but outside the casino they were worth as much as Monopoly cash.

He was tempted to ask when the decision was made; who had made the decision. Was it the House, just this House, or was it all the Houses put together? He didn't ask because he didn't want to know.

So he just picked himself up by the pants and left.

Pending further review.

Not good.

It was dark now, a full moon out, when he took to the boards and started walking. He was surprised at himself, that he wasn't feeling too rotten. He was feeling rotten, but not too rotten.

Too soon to panic. There was still the rest of Atlantic City, even the rest of Vegas, if not there were the Indian reservations, and if he was frozen out utterly, completely, if the word on him was widespread—then maybe he'd shoot craps in the back alleys, if they still had back alleys. No they didn't. Not anymore. Floating games were out. You want a floating game, go see *Guys 'n Dolls*.

Anyway, what kind of life would that be, relegated to the swamps? Not for a prince, that kind of life.

So who had put the word out? he wondered. Who was behind all this? Or was it a hex, the curse he'd always feared?

When he got to Ventnor, he remembered that he still had his car parked at the Monaco, so he headed back, still wondering if he was jinxed, cursed. He looked up at the sky, the moon and the stars, actually looking for a sign.

Where have I sinned? he asked.

All this time Julian had thought himself so special, as special as David, and Joseph. He had thought himself God's beloved, forever under the canopy of a secret covenant, since Sinai. Somehow, somewhere, it got revoked.

Damn, thought Julian as he approached the Monaco, *I am feeling sorry for myself, and that is bad.*

He got his car and drove home. The house was empty. Very empty. He dialed Monica Travers but got the answering machine again, and again, and again, and again! Technology. No more people. We've surrendered to the machines.

He clicked on the TV and, being starved for company, brought up the sound, then turned it off immediately when he came upon Peter Jennings and Bob Simon. So there was silence again, until he heard a baby crying. But there were no babies around, no more, not among the living. Debra used to say the same thing, about hearing sounds, a baby weeping in the night.

He turned on all the lights. He was scared. He'd never been so frightened, never felt so alone, began asking himself the meaning of life, hated himself whenever he sank to that level.

The meaning of life. Suppose there is no meaning? Suppose it's all a crap game? All about chance. All about randomness. No method to the madness. Except for the pit boss up in heaven just waiting for your number to come up, a 7. You shoot and you shoot and sooner or later you seven-out. *It's the law.* It's all futile. Solomon had it right. All vanity and futility.

Who had put the word out, he asked himself all night. *God himself?*

That's what really had him frightened.

CHAPTER 33

He had spent a sleepless night, even with two pills, and waited until noon to place a call to Slim Sam Belmont in Vegas, where it was nine in the morning. No answer. Which got Julian to thinking maybe the man was dead. That would be tragic, and surely be the end of an era. Somehow the end of Sam Belmont prefigured the end of the American frontier. He was the last of the Singular Men. In this corporate age, a Slim Sam Belmont would never come around again, and that would be a loss, not just for Julian but for everybody; for anybody who still cherished and esteemed the days of rugged individualism, which are no more, regardless, seen to it by the corporations that gobbled up everything in their paths.

Unable to sit still, wild with anxiety, Julian got in the car and drove over to AC, and this time the neons gave him no jolt, no thrill, nothing but a dry mouth, enough to gag, that sinking first-day-of-school jitters.

He didn't know why he was making the trip, except that maybe the car would lead him to his destiny, and, in fact, the car took him behind the casinos, beyond Pacific, beyond Atlantic, beyond the facade, into Arctic, there where the people lived, the real citizens of Atlantic City. No dazzle here, no limos, no doormen, just plain folks, mostly black, trying to get by, and barely doing so.

He parked near a Rite-Aid and got out, and dressed as he was, in tatters, he was not so much different from the rest of the scenery. He was eyed up and down by some of the brothers, but nothing too menacing.

"Lookin' for something?" a guy said.

"Maybe," Julian said. He walked over to the group at the corner of Arctic and Kentucky. Four black guys, two white guys, two black women. All young, tough-looking, waiting for answers. It seemed to be all they did all day long—waiting for answers.

"Name's Mitch," said the biggest black guy.

"Julian."

"Pussy, Julian? That why you're here?"

"No. Thought I might find me some street action."

"What's your game?"

"Craps."

"Got that action at the casinos, man."

"I said street action."

Mitch exchanged knowing glances with the rest of them, who seemed content to let Mitch do the talking.

"That can be arranged. Follow."

He knew he was in trouble and he knew he was being stupid, but he followed. This was his destiny, and whatever it was, was. They ended up in an alley littered with trash cans. They formed a circle.

"Here?" said Julian.

"Let's see your cash."

Julian spread two C-notes.

"That ain't enough."
He spread out two more.
"Make it an even G."
Julian complied with ten hundred dollar bills. The circle
around him grew tighter, and when nobody came up with a
pair of dice and didn't even bother to ask him if he had any,
that's when he knew he was in deep shit, but didn't care all
that much.
"You a hustler, right?"
"No. Like I said, a street game, that's all I'm after."
"Man, you a hustler."
"No..."
"You a slick muthahfuckah.."
"Hey."
"You a shark."
"Hey, come on."
"Yeah," came the chorus. "You a shark."
"Fuck it," he said, preparing to gather up his cash.
"Fuck you. You come to the hood to beat up on some poor
black asses, that your game, man? Fuck dat shit."
Somebody kicked him in the ribs, followed by a blow to the
head, as he was bending down to retrieve the dough. He got
up into a fighting stance, ready to answer—but they were gone,
with the money.
Dazed, he hadn't heard the siren. A cop car zoomed in and
pressed him against the wall. He was frisked and taken to the
station on Martin Luther King Boulevard; detained on suspicion of dealing drugs, until a phone call to Monica Travers
cleared him.
He ran it all back when he got home and it was as though it
never happened, not to him, just some episode that happened
to somebody else. As he had it figured, he had purposely tried
to degrade himself in order to reach rock bottom, and having
gotten there, there'd be no place to go but up. That was how
he figured it, and it calmed him to think that he had not been

motivated by some kind of ridiculous death wish. That wasn't his style, to despair.

Not so soon, anyway.

Not for a moment did he believe that he was so desperate for a game that he'd go anywhere, even down to the streets, where there were no games, only trouble—and he didn't even believe that he'd sunk so low as to get himself bagged, mistaken for a pusher. No, that didn't happen. Placed in a cell with one open toilet and three other prisoners, no room to move, no air to breathe, the claustrophobia causing him to retch—that did not happen, either. It happened to somebody else. Couldn't have happened to him because he was Julian Rothschild, king of the tables.

So none of this happened, and even if it did, nobody saw, nobody in Hollywood, nobody in Vegas, nobody even in AC, nobody that counted. He was still Julian Rothschild, maybe a bit diminished, for the moment, humbled, to be sure, but there'll be other days, he assured himself.

He tried Slim again, and a women answered and he held his breath until she said: "I'll get him for you."

That was good. That was very good. Even better when he heard Slim say:

"Why, you old rattlesnake, what can I do for you?"

Turned out that Slim had information, knew practically everything, in fact, knew more than Julian, as for example, Lucky's. "Word came that Hart Froman put the gate to you after you went back the second time and blew the House away. I knew about it but figured it to be a one-time shot. Didn't know you'd be wearing the mark of Cain all the way back to AC. Shame. Anything I can do to help?"

"No, but thanks. Thanks, Slim. You take care of yourself."

"Also, watch your back at the Versailles."

"Why?"

"Have you been there since…"

"No, haven't tested the waters there yet."

"Well, beware."

"What's that all about?"

"Scuttlebutt has it that Roy Stavros at the Versailles has knives out for you. Any particular reason why?"

"That's home base, Slim."

Slim chuckled. "You mean that's where you take 'em with both hands."

"I guess."

"Seems that he's had enough, this Stavros character. Wants your blood."

"News to me."

"Seems like Stavros and Froman over here, they're pals. Get the picture?"

"It's starting to clear up."

"They've exchanged tapes, supposedly showing you using the spinner."

"The one you taught me."

"It ain't like the old days, Julian. Didn't have tapes back then. Anyhow, now you know."

"Now I know."

"Lay low for a while," Slim advised. "Things can only get better. But stay away from the Versailles."

Easier, reflected Julian—easier said than done.

CHAPTER 34

Dewey kept flipping back and forth among the three networks, all three carrying the same clip of McLellan saying he was satisfied with the sweatshop hearings to date, even though he admitted (under questioning by the reporter, Brian Stern) that nothing really explosive had come from the testimonies so far, inasmuch as the worst offenders had yet to speak, some hiding behind the Fifth, others still to be summoned—but all in all the best, or worst, actually, was yet to come.

That, said Brian Stern, was Sasha Spivak, whose date of appearance was being pushed back because of illness.

"Ha!" said Dewey, talking back to the TV set, waiting to hear more. But that was the end of that, on to commercial.

So she's sick. Good for her.

But details, details. How sick? How long? He needed to know. Sadly, for him, the trail to Sasha had run cold as all his emissaries had lost touch with the girl. She had stopped going to the movies and was no longer a presence at the Roy Rogers, holed up now at the L'Enfant Plaza for days on end.

This had Dewey worried, until now. Now he knew. She was sick, poor thing.

What he did not know was that she was very sick after gulping down a bottle of sleeping pills in an attempt on her life. Her security escorts had found her counting again, and apparently she'd reached the number, the deadly number. Nobody knew what it was, but it was *her* number. At present she was at Roosevelt Hospital, and the prognosis was not good— all this information being withheld from the public. Only McLellan and the rest of the lawmakers on the committee knew that without her, without her testimony, the whole shebang was lost. Sasha was not only their most important witness, she was the only witness willing and able to provide a firsthand account of sweatshop horrors.

But for Dewey this was enough, just to know that something had gone haywire. *Who knows?* he thought. *Maybe she tried to take her life.* It wouldn't surprise him, being the delicate sort that she was.

Anyway, even though he had received a summons, undated, he could relax for a while. Sasha wouldn't be there, at least for a while, and besides, the committee was going into another recess. Thank God for them and their recesses.

None of which let Julian Rothschild off the hook. Not by a long shot. Only this: He had a bit more time. Skinny and Fats had reported back to Dewey that, in their opinion, Julian would fulfill his obligation, if reluctantly. But they had delivered a message. Julian knew what was expected of him, and he knew what would happen if he didn't come through. He *had* to come through. He was a man of principle, a gambler in the best sense of the word.

That's what Dewey had been counting on all along, the man's spleen, the man's character.

He admired the man, he really did, and even said so to Denise, saying:

"I wouldn't blame you if you fell for a guy like that, know what I mean?"

This was several days after he'd caught her downstairs by the pay phone, making a call.

He hadn't spoken to her that same day or the day after, but on the third day, he spoke, and said he wouldn't be surprised if that call she was making was to Julian.

She didn't deny it, that's why he liked her so much, too; she also had character.

"So what are you going to do about it?" she said.

"Depends," he said, on what she was talking to him about.

"About this and that," she said, revealing the in-your-face, spit-in-your-eye contrariness that had been her trademark but missing in her makeup for too long, much too long.

"I hear different," he said.

"Oh? Your spies?"

"Tell me you love the guy and I'll be happy."

"I love the guy. Are you happy?"

"Did you fuck him?"

"Over the phone?"

"No, at his house."

"Who says I was there?"

"They saw your car. Even Skinny and Fats aren't *that stupid*."

No, she thought, *but I sure am.*

"All right, I was there."

"Of course, you were there. Tell me you saw him on the yacht and fell head over heels in love with him."

"I saw him on the yacht and..."

"Just tell me it had nothing to do with *business*."

"It had nothing to do with business."

"QUIT FUCKING ME!"

"I thought we were discussing me fucking him?"

"Was it about business?"

"Why am I answering all the questions? What about you?"

"You have questions? Ask away."

"Who was that man on the phone?"

"What man? What phone?"

"The man you were walking with that day."

"What man? What day?"

"The man with the limp."

"That was business."

"You've deceived me, Dewey."

"I've deceived *you*?"

"That man's an assassin, isn't he?"

"You went running to Julian to tell him that? Say it ain't so."

"I could, but it would be a lie."

"So you told him I had hired an assassin. For what?"

"To kill that girl, Sasha. You're evil, Dewey."

"Don't use that word. I hate that word. Say I'm bad, say I'm rotten. Not evil. I hate evil."

"So do I, Dewey. So do I."

"Never mind the big picture, right?"

"What big picture?"

"What we talked about, if she testifies, how two thousand people end up *on the street*. Because of her."

"That justifies nothing."

"But it doesn't make me evil, for shit's sake. Hitler, he was evil."

He sounded like he was about to cry. That old problem, or rather new problem, kicking up again, and for an instant, just a flicker, she felt sorry for him. She almost understood him. She certainly understood his hatred for Sasha Spivak.

"I never said you were Hitler."

"Does Julian think I'm evil?"

"Not in so many words."

"What exactly did you tell him, in so many words?"

"That when he went gambling for you it would be to raise money for *murder*—in so many words."

"To which he said..."

"He said he was committed to you, no matter what." Denise not telling him the rest, that Julian would be playing all right, but to lose.

"Really?"

"Yes, really."

"Some guy."

"Yes, some guy."

"He really said he was going to keep his word."

"Yes, he really said that."

"Got to hand it to that guy. Class tells."

"Always."

"I get the undercurrent of that remark."

Now he turned his face from her, and when he turned back his eyes were swollen.

Softly, tenderly, he said he admired her spunk in doing what she did, her boldness had been what drew him to her in the first place—but how could he ever forget that she had betrayed him?

"Please tell me," he said. "How do I forget?"

She said she did not see it quite that way, as betrayal. She saw it as performing a moral duty.

"I was hoping to keep you from shedding blood."

"That makes sense," he said. "It does. It makes sense. It's almost something you'd do for someone you love."

"I don't love you anymore, Dewey."

"I know that, and it makes me very sad. Very sad. Does this mean you're leaving."

"Yes."

"When?"

"Now. Today."

"Let me make a suggestion."

"Oh, please."

"Stay with me until the hearings are over."

"Why?"

"Because I can't let you leave now, Denise. Don't you see?"

"You mean you'd harm me."

"I didn't say that. Did I say that?"

"No, but the threat's always been right around the corner."

"That's your opinion. Anyway, if you stay until this all blows over, I'll know I can trust you. Otherwise..."

So she was expected to stay while he planned the assassination and tried to carry it out. She was expected to stay while Julian played craps for his half a million, to pay the hitman. Didn't sound like an attractive invitation, except that he had a point. If she left now, it would be absolute, irreversible betrayal, and she'd really leave him no choice but to detain her, forcibly—or worse. She did owe him some loyalty; after all, there was some kind of an investment involved here, and besides, there'd be no half million, Julian would see to that, so there'd be no assassination. Period.

So she agreed to stay.

"You hear that?" he now said, days later. "Your girl Sasha Spivak is sick."

She'd been in the bedroom, reading the latest Puzo.

No, she hadn't heard.

"I ain't dead yet," he said.

Only he was a bit worried how Mr. Glass would reach her when she got well again, since she wasn't going out so much anymore. Well, that was for Mr. Glass to figure out. He was being paid enough, the bastard.

"I'm going down to shoot some craps," he said.

He'd been losing. In fact, he was into the casino for close to ten grand. He was playing on credit and upstairs in the eye in the sky Roy Stavros had begun counting. Stavros knew he had a delinquent guest on his hands, except that the man ran with fast company. He was good.

Stavros did wonder, though, what was keeping him so long. He knew the man was wanted by the government. The man was under some kind of indictment, to do with his sweatshops.

But what was the purpose of hanging around? Past the summer. He should be in New York. Tending to his business. What was he up to? What was he waiting for?

CHAPTER 35

Roy Stavros was in a waiting mode, and he liked the word *mode,* sounded so corporate. It was a word that his boss, Hayden Booker, used frequently, that and "challenge," challenge being another PR word for things being rotten in Denmark. Stavros was no big fan of the corpies, especially here at his own *venue*—now there was another word. They were soft here as well, creampuffs, though Booker was smart enough to have given Stavros a free hand, seeing how the place had begun to get run over by con-artists. Not anymore, except that there was one shark to go, the biggest catch of them all: Julian Rothschild.

That damn Julian Rothschild—as if he were the first man to believe in the supernatural so far as craps. That went way back, that belief that a higher power controls the outcome of a toss. It was bullshit then, back in the Stone Age, and it is bullshit now, other than the fact that it worked for Julian Rothschild. *Something* was working for him. Like maybe the spinner, the english he used. That helped. That sure helped the supernatural.

So Stavros was in a waiting mode, waiting for Julian to run himself out, run out the string, the string of casinos up and down the Boardwalk and along the bay. Until finally, no more action. Except for the Big Game.

If Stavros liked what happened to Julian at Lucky's in Vegas, he *loved* what happened here at the Monaco. Because what better way to rub it in, rub his nose in it, than to let him play, and then stone him at the cage.

No tickee, no laundry.

Give the man a towel. Stavros loved the story about how Julian stood there, stunned, raising a beef, and then turning tail. He loved that story. Even more than the story about his arrest. But that was just a taste, and it wasn't enough.

No, the works, this was going to be played to the hilt; he wins, he lives and collects one million and most important for him, gets back his playing credentials here and everywhere— loses, he dies. That's the game. The only game. Only trouble was, the rest of the casinos had not fallen in with the freeze-out, officially. The usual. You couldn't get the whole lot of them to agree on anything.

All kinds of politics, petty jealousies and vendettas. Each casino protecting its own turf.

But unofficially it seemed to be happening. They'd told him they'd think about it and act in their own best interests. There was still a residue of affection for that sharpie, ARTEEST, excuse, since he was such a draw. Still reluctant to let go of their shill. But they were coming around.

Stavros had a hunch that the Monaco was just a foretaste, especially since Phil Black at the Monaco had seemed to be the most reluctant to ice Julian—and then ice him he did. So the others ought to be even more of a sure thing.

Which was why, Stavros guessed, this Julian was so afraid to try, afraid to know the truth, the facts, that he was being stoned up and down, east and west, north and south.

Afraid to know but desperate for the action, any action, taking him to the streets. Like a bum, a degenerate.

"One thing worries me," he was saying to Mike Milligan, VP of casino operations.

They were up in the Sky.

"I know what you're gonna say."

"All right. What am I gonna say?"

"Suppose he actually beats us."

"Correct," Stavros said with a pained expression. This was something he had not even considered, the chance that the corker might sail through 20 tosses without bumping into a 7.

"You wouldn't be thinking of loading 'em," Milligan said.

"Been years since I've even seen a pair of loaded dice."

Back in Chicago, of course. Back in the old days, naturally. Loaded dice, shaved dice. Dice known as "passers," loaded to favor anything but a 7, and then of course, the good old "missouts," dice loaded to favor the 7; in other words, favor the House.

"That would be going too far," said Milligan.

This after Stavros said that there used to be a catalog gambling supply house that used to *advertise* those balonies. If they were still around, he might be interested in seeing about those missouts, those dice loaded for 7s. Just out of curiosity.

"The man's no chump," Milligan said about Julian, further reminding Stavros that there was always the water test. Which tipped you off that deception was in the works if the same spots kept coming up no matter which way you dropped them in.

"You think he'd resort to that?"

"If you were playing for your life, wouldn't you?"

That was another thing. Would the man be willing to play for his life, even with a million bucks dangling as bait? Of course, he would. That business out on the street, Julian down on his knees with the brothers on Arctic, that was just a sample of what dice meant to the guy, a sample of what happened when you took away his candy. No, the man was hooked. That was no problem.

The problem was that he might just get hot, hit one of those streaks, those streaks he was so famous for. Hell, he'd hit a streak just like that at the Monaco, using the spinner of course— which emphatically he'd be prevented from using when it came to the head-to-head. They'd be watching him up and down, frontways and sideways to make sure he was on the level. That's for sure.

No more edge, unless you believed the stuff about his being a puppet to a power on high. Which Stavros didn't. No, the edge this time would be with the House, and if that wasn't enough, maybe, just maybe...

"Just curious," Stavros was saying, "if that mail order joint is still open. I think it was in Reno."

"Y'know, Roy, we get nabbed using a gimmick and it's the end of the Versailles. Please, not another word."

"Anything you say, Mike," the sarcasm dripping.

"Don't even think about it," said Milligan.

That'll be the day, thought Stavros, *when people tell me what to think.*

"Oh," said Milligan. "Have you cleared this with Booker?"

No, he hadn't. He'd only tell Booker that he was raising the limit for a special game, nothing about the real risks.

"I'll get to it," Stavros said.

"Hmm," said Milligan.

CHAPTER 36

Monica Travers babied Julian for several days, playing mother, a role she didn't mind when it came to Julian. He didn't want to talk about it, and neither did she, about his arrest, though she was beginning to think it was funny, almost. Almost funny, her man Julian winding up in the slammer, taken for a pusher, after escaping with his life from Arctic.

She did ask what drove him there; he said, his car. Very funny.

She had taken off from work—she had days coming—in her job as PR consultant to the AC Casino Association, just to be with him and bring him back to life. He was a mess, though putting up a good front—like none of it was bothering him.

He still carried himself like a prince, like royalty, but she knew he was hurting, not only for himself but for all the people who counted on him. There was one drug rehab center on Indiana Avenue whose sole means of survival was Julian, practically, and there were plenty more cases just like that all over AC and the rest of South Jersey.

So she was staying with him, and she was determined to stay for as long as it took, to put him back together again. Mostly now, they took long walks on the beach. At night they made love on the beach, under the stars. Together they watched the sun rise and the sun set. All quite powerful. The sex was especially good; the pent-up frustrations had turned him into a bit of a dynamo.

She left him alone when he blasted Brahms and Beethoven, knowing that he needed his privacy then, the music charging him up with currents of heroism. The *Psalms* on his lap, sometimes *Ecclesiastes,* sometimes the entire Soncino edition of the *Pentateuch,* he'd drift off and be gone to his kingdom. All very mysterious and mystical to her, but it was Julian—Julian and nobody else. She'd never known such a man.

She was falling in love with him more and more, even as she knew that he was still smitten by Debra. She knew. There was no way she couldn't know. He had told her about the phone call from Debra, even about her saying she loved him. He said it meant nothing to him.

"Really," Monica had said. "Give me a break."

All right, he had confessed. Maybe it means something.

But not too much.

Then, on top of that, there were those calls and those messages on the machine from Vegas, from the set of *Scared Money*. Karen Davies. The famous Karen Davies saying she missed him and when was he coming back. One message laughingly referring to a pin, which made no sense, except to suggest that more had gone on there than she wanted to know. She didn't want to know.

Well, he had his secrets, and she had hers, Monica did, and she was in no hurry to confide.

From her pulse on the business, she knew; she knew that he'd been frozen out. Completely. Except for the Versailles.

Where there was a game waiting for him. A game to end all games.

She'd have to tell him, sooner or later, the later the better, she figured.

On the fifth day of his recuperation, over dinner, he quoted something to her, out of nowhere, of course.

Sometimes he'd bring up things as though they'd been a topic of discussion, when, in fact, he'd only been talking to himself. He was frequently out of context, which she found charming.

And David was old, and stricken in age, and he could get no heat—that was the quotation from the Book of Kings.

"What do you think?" he said.

"Wonderful. Beautiful."

"Nobody writes like that anymore. Never did."

"What about Shakespeare?"

"He's bull. Great writer, yes, but he never wrote where people lived, never brought it home."

They had quarreled about this before, and usually she nipped it before it went too far. But this was a sign, a sign that he was getting revved up. So she took him on about Shakespeare, just to keep him going, get him good-and-riled, which was easy enough to do on the subject of Shakespeare versus the world.

"He's just a monument, admire but don't touch. Give me one *Death of a Salesman*—attention must be paid!—one *Catcher in the Rye*—and you can toss all your Shakespeare in the can. That's what I think. Or am I not being politically correct?"

"Oh, but you are. Dead, white males are out."

"That's too bad."

"What is?"

"That I'm being politically correct. I was hoping I'd be different."

"Oh, but you are different."

"You're sweet. What's wrong?"

"Wrong?"

"Something's on your mind."

This was as good a moment as any. So she told him. Choosing her words carefully. But it didn't help. He left the table unfinished and walked off to the beach. She gave him some time, and then joined him.

"Only the Versailles?" he said, clearly rattled.

"That's it," she said.

Slim had prepared him for this, but not all of it, not the head-to-head game. Stavros had let it be known, through her, that his place and his place alone would take Julian's action, but first he'd have to play head-to-head—details still to come. In other words, this much he had kept back; what the stakes really were.

"So it's the Versailles or nothing."

"He's waiting for your call."

Which reminded him of what Karen Davies had said: "There's something waiting for you in Atlantic City."

Spooky. So it all started with Lucky's in Vegas and wound its way back to the Versailles in AC—and there was even another guy waiting in the wings, Dewey Smith, as if he needed that complication, to boot.

"Any idea what this head-to-head game is about?"

"No, just that it'll be a private game, you against the House."

"I wonder what they've got in mind."

"You'll find out soon enough. Of course I couldn't dissuade you from checking it out, could I?"

"Well, look, if the Versailles is all that's left, what choice do I have?"

"No choice, I guess. Unless you gave up craps."

"Which you know is impossible."

"Except that I don't know what this guy Stavros has in mind—but I'm concerned."

"Why? Worst they can do is try to tap me out. That's probably it, bleed me dry. Should be fun."

"I'm not so sure. Roy Stavros is a man with some reputation."

"Me, too. I've also got a reputation, remember?"

"I suppose he'd be wanting to make an example of you."

"Works both ways. I could end up making an example of him."

"I must say, you're taking it well."

"You mean about me being frozen out?"

"That, and the Versailles."

"If that's the only game in town for me, well, it's a game. It's still a game. I'll still be able to play."

"So what's this all about? I mean a head-to-head game."

"That's not so unusual. It's done all the time. Maybe not all the time, all right, but when high rollers come in, say from Arabia, or the Orient, it's done; tables get roped off and let the best man win. I know I can beat them, head-to-head, foot-to-foot, toe-to-toe, any way they want it, it's my game. The dice are *mine.*"

"You're assuming that if you win, they'll let you keep on playing."

"Why not?"

"Suppose you lose?"

"I guess those are the stakes. If I lose, then they've got me. Meaning I'll have to scrounge for action."

"Like you did the other day?"

"That was plain stupid. I'll never do that again. No, hell, I don't know what I'll do. Hey, who's talking about losing? I can't lose." The moment he said that he remembered; he can't win. Winning would mean winning for Dewey.

Can't win. Can't lose.

He'd have to figure some way out. Maybe one game for himself, to win, to win his rights to continue to play at the Versailles, and maybe the others would eventually open their doors for him as well, and one game for Dewey, to lose. Or something like that, he was thinking, but finding himself growing irritable and confounded.

That night he didn't want to make love, not on the beach and not in bed, and it gnawed on him, that it had all come to this, they'd finally ganged up, a day he thought would never come, because he was blessed, because of Sinai. Because he played selflessly and righteously. Because he didn't cheat, no matter what they said, what they called it; it wasn't cheating what he did, it was skill, a talent, a gift. All of it too much for them, because there was money involved and they weren't in the business of doling it out; they were in the business of raking it in; no room for an artist.

So they finally got together and said "Here, there's one door open for you. Take it or leave it," knowing that he had to take it—what else? Tell Peter Serkin there's only one piano left in the world and what's he gonna say—no?

In one sense, Julian was grateful, all things considered, considering that there'd been the possibility he'd be out in the cold completely. So he was grateful for that, grateful for the Versailles, even grateful for Roy Stavros, who was at least giving him a chance, never mind what he may have up his sleeve. Stavros may be a gorilla—but he is *my* gorilla.

Only thing was, Julian reflected one sleepless night after another, can't win, can't lose. There had to be a way. *Funny,* he was thinking, *how it all started going downhill after I'd committed myself to Dewey.* As if there really was an eye that saw, an ear that heard. If he didn't believe it before, he believed it now.

There'd been evil about it from the start. He should have known better. Must never play for evil. That was part of the covenant, and once you played for evil, or committed yourself to evil, you lost the covenant. You were alone, and that's precisely how Julian felt, alone. No more self-pity, no more despairing, no more panic, but alone.

It had come down to him against the House. Not that the thought was without a thrill, to think that he'd be given an opportunity to really topple Goliath.

Or, more to the point, the House represented the Throne of Judgment, and Judgment Day was fast approaching.

CHAPTER 37

Judgment Day first came from Dewey who, without the company of Skinny and Fats, paid Julian a visit, personally. Quite an honor, Dewey saying the time was now, Dewey not saying that he'd been given a date to appear before McLellan, which was six days away, and also not saying that Sasha Spivak was set to talk *five* days away.

That, at least, was the report in the press but only a ploy on the part of McLellan to put the rest of the witnesses on notice that the committee meant business; that the committee had the goods. So they'd better come clean, before Sasha did it for them, which would only make it all the worse for their cause.

McLellan was gambling, being privy to the fact that Sasha Spivak had been not only sick all this time but in a coma.

Now she was dead.

This was news to be kept secret until McLellan got the most out of his challenge to America's sweatshop owners that if they talked before she did, it might go easier for them. He was counting on the ruse that Sasha was about sing, to frighten them into talking.

But Sasha was dead.

She'd been admitted to Roosevelt Hospital under an assumed name, so there was small chance of the press getting a whiff. Shirlene Templeton was the name that was used to effect the concealment. Shirlene Templeton because Shirley Temple was the star that Sasha had been identified with in Russia, in Sasha's golden years as a violin virtuoso. Her two security escorts, who'd grown quite fond of Sasha, despite her quirks, came to know her as Shirlene Templeton, at Sasha's insistence. The name Shirlene Templeton raised no eyebrows in hospital admittance since the clerks there were awfully young and had never heard of the famous child star, neither Shirley nor Shirlene.

Except for her bodyguards, Sasha left without mourners.

Though who knew what tears would be shed in Russia?

When word got out, as it eventually would have to.

For now, though, it was hush-hush, even Dewey in the dark. Dewey, in fact, under the impression that she was about to flail him to shreds in a matter of days. So he was in something of a panic when he got to Julian to collect his marker.

Julian played along, assuring Dewey that within the next couple of days he'd do right by him. "I'll be ready," he said, still confused, knowing he'd have to be ready to lose for Dewey, win for himself. Very confusing.

Dewey, as promised, offered to bankroll Julian to the tune of $10,000. Julian said it wasn't necessary, but Dewey insisted that a deal was a deal, and put that way, on the honor code, Julian was compelled to accept, guiltily.

"You the man," Dewey said, adopting street lingo, so fitting. "Say hello to Debra," he added with a wink.

Dewey left, his palms itching from the $500,000 he was about to inherit. Or rather, pass on to Mr. Glass. For a killing that was academic on its face.

The second Day of Judgment was Julian's visit to the Versailles for a formal discussion with Roy Stavros about the head-to-head competition, whatever that was all about. The meeting had been set up between Julian and Stavros' secretary, after Julian, with some trepidation, had decided to put off the inevitable no longer. This was a big move for Julian; he had no idea what to expect, and he approached the hour of his appointment with a bad case of the jitters.

The worst part for him was the elevator ride up to the 16th floor. Then, once in the office, recovering from the ordeal, he was kept waiting for nearly an hour. Until finally Roy Stavros came out and extended a firm handshake, while sizing up the man he'd come to revile.

Despite the charm and bonhomie, Julian felt the pulse of an adversary. Thick hairy fingers, bull neck, gruff voice. Heavyset but fit. Could have been a prizefighter in his younger days. The man was a billboard for pure brute force. He walked with the shouldered swagger of a thug or a corrupt police officer. In the office he leaned back and lit a cigarette with a hand-grenade lighter. He coughed, bringing up a thousand nights of backroom gin and smoke.

"So you're Julian Rothschild?" he laughed. "You've been giving us fits. Over the years."

"I take that as a compliment," said Julian.

"Oh, you do," his manner swiftly dropping from cordial to scorn. Quizzically, "Do you know what this is about?"

"About a match race, one-on-one. I guess. You tell me."

Stavros nodded, as if happy to be dealing with a sharp character. Wouldn't need to start from scratch.

"You know, of course, that you're the victim of an all-around freeze."

"Yes. It's come to my attention." Saying so with some sarcasm.

"Which is too bad." Stavros shook his head and stared off into the distance, bracing himself to share Julian's distress.

"Very regrettable. The whole business. Me, I tried to stop them. But these new boys, they've got their own agendas. You know how it is, these bean counters from Wharton, always the bottom line. No consideration for an artist. Such as yourself. You do consider yourself an artist."

"I shoot craps, that's all."

"But very successfully," Stavros said with a polite chuckle.

"Lucky, I guess."

"Very lucky."

"Some people have it, some don't." The set-up was altogether too transparent.

"So what is it you think you've got?"

"You're losing me."

"Word is you've got the supernatural on your side."

Julian responded with a shrug and, "So who doesn't? We all got to believe in something. Don't you?"

"Yeah, I believe in something, but I don't believe the supernatural's got anything to do with dice."

"If it's good enough for you, it's good enough for me," Julian not about to offer any rope.

"Me," said Stavros, holding up his hands as if in surrender, "I got no gripe against a man whose success becomes suspect. More power to him. Supernatural, whatever. Whatever it takes. These other guys, though, at the other casinos, they take a dim view. Which is why they took these drastic measures." A cough and a chuckle. "Hell, you know what they think? They think you're a shark."

"Obviously."

"They don't like sharks. Neither do I, if I thought I was being clipped. You haven't been clipping me, have you?"

"I've been beating the House. Is there a law against that?"

"No-o-o-o," slowly, leaning back, then forward, close-up. "But there is a law against shooting spinners."

"So that's what they call skill these days."

"No, that's what we call cheating."

"That's too bad. Too bad some people can't tell the difference. There are no spinners in my game."

Mostly true.

"There's tapes upstairs that tell a different story. Would you like to see them?"

"No matter."

Stavros got up, turned to look out the window, then wheeled back. "But you're in a pickle, you grant that much."

"Okay."

"We agree you're on the outs everywhere."

"Agreed."

"Which leaves you with me, right?"

"Exactly how?"

"Well, that's why you're here, for me to explain."

"So explain."

"No need to get nasty, specially since I'm the good fairy."

"Hmmm."

"Since I'm your only recourse, I thought I'd put you up to a challenge. I mean if you want to keep on playing here at my House, the only House left to you, not to rub it in or anything, I want to make sure it's all on the up and up, fair and square. Sound all right?"

"So far," Julian's heart thumping.

"Which brings us to the head-to-head. You have no objections to that, do you?"

"Might be fun."

"Ever play against the House, alone?"

"A Proposition Game? Nope."

"No distractions. Just you and the House. Might be fun, as you say. Why, a man with your skill!"

"The stakes?"

"Oh, yeah. The stakes. One game, and one game only. No second chances. Still sound fair?"

"I guess."

"But you're with me."

"So far."

"I mean, you'd be doing this of your own free will."

"Considering."

"Considering what?"

"That your House is my only House."

"I'm glad you understand. Really, I am. I thought you might be skittish about the whole thing. I mean one man against the House, could be a bit intimidating. But you—you trust your, shall we say, skill."

"Always have."

"So you'd be confident."

"Gambling is gambling. You can only be so confident."

"Same goes for the House. We're also taking a chance. Especially with a guy like you."

"You're very flattering, Mr. Stavros. When do we go beyond the bullshit?"

"Right about now. Like I said. One game, one shot. But different rules. Still with me?"

"You've got my full attention."

"The rules being that you never toss a 7 before 20 throws."

"That's an awful lot of tosses."

"You've done it a thousand times, right here in my casino."

"Too much."

"All right," abruptly, "what's fair?"

"Ten."

"Ten throws?"

"That might be fair."

"For a genius like you? Come on, give yourself more credit than that."

"Twenty's too much to ask."

"But do you have a choice? Remember, I'm the only man offering you any kind of break."

"All right, suppose I say yes?"

"Then we play. Let the games begin."

"Play for what? You still haven't told me."

"Oh, I keep forgetting. First we play for your future. You beat us, the House is yours. You like that?"

"I like that."

"Considering how the rest of them so unceremoniously dumped you. Left you to me."

Beginning to sound sinister to Julian.

"I see," Julian said.

"But, as with everything in life, there's a catch. You beat us..."

"I don't seven-out before 10."

"Twenty. Remember, the House makes the rules. Twenty, right?"

Julian was cornered. He was up against it and there was no squirming out. This was it, all right, if he ever wanted to play again, anywhere. There was only *here*. "Okay, twenty."

"So, you beat us, you continue to play, here at the Versailles, and you win a million dollars."

This should have stunned Julian with delight. Instead it terrified him.

"What's the catch?"

"The catch is, you're playing for your life, don't you know?" Stavros fixing him with a devilish gaze.

"Don't I know?"

"What do you expect? One million bucks. Your future. Look what we're offering. What are *you* offering?"

"My life, huh?"

"You can't tell me that's not fair. Gambler like you."

"I don't get it," Julian said, as it was all beginning to sink in.

"What's not to get?"

"You mean you're going to *kill* me if I seven-out?"

"It's what I would call the ultimate game. I would think that'd be very attractive to a gambler like you. I mean, just think, this is gambling at its purest, at its highest. This is the

Mount Everest of shooting craps. Takes balls, but if I know anything about you, it's that you've got the cojónes. My money's on you, that you'll take the bet. Fact is, you have no choice."

Fact is, thought Julian, *I have no choice.* He could not have put it better himself. No choice. Precisely. Exactly. Totally. Absolutely. Perfectly. What a fix to be in! Straight into the hands of a gorilla.

"How do you intend to... do away with me." Wasn't that, he thought, the strangest thing he'd ever said. The words sounded so off-key, so crazy. For a moment he had the sensation that he was hallucinating. Any minute, he thought, he might wake up from this, were it not so real, so utterly, desperately real.

"That's not your worry."

"Not my worry?"

"Wrong choice of words. Sorry. But let us take care of the details."

"You've done this before."

"That's what makes this so charming. This is a first. You ought to consider yourself very special."

"Oh, but I do."

"No, really, Julian. Ask yourself this. Are you up to the biggest crap game of all time? Your life."

Started to sound good, almost.

"You're putting your money on me, did you say?"

"Yes, that you'd take the offer. For one reason. Your pride. Your pride as a gambler, a craps shooter par excellence. You beat us, never mind the million bucks, you've got bragging rights as top dog. And, once word gets around, I can assure you the doors will open again, everywhere. So you see the stakes, quite a bit in your favor."

Except that if I lose, thought Julian, *I die. If I win, Sasha dies.*

He remembered that with a pang (unaware, of course, that she was already a goner).

Something had to give, and at present he was too confused to settle the conflict. Right now he had to deal with one thing at a time. His future in craps, meaning his future, period. He had no other life.

"I'd like to give it some thought," was all he could come up with at the moment.

"Think about this," said Stavros, "you wouldn't be playing just for yourself."

"Oh?"

"I mean you being so spiritual and all. What I'm talking about is this: You'd be playing for God! You'd be playing for all the people who believe in God!" That was really rubbing it in. Stavros smiled a scoffing smile. He was enjoying the moment, the moment he put the kid's faith into play. He had cornered the kid into believing that he was shooting the dice to defend the celestial throne, rather than the celestial throne's defending him; turning his spiritualism upside down, inside out, a true test of faith if ever there was one, a test of Stavros' faith in the House, the Almighty Percentages, against the kid's faith in the Almighty, period, the God up in heaven that Stavros had forsaken years ago.

Julian understood, and he also understood that no man could count on favors or miracles.

The dice were still random. Like everything else. No matter what.

"I'll need some time," he said.

"It's now or never. Sorry. This is a one-time offer. Take it or leave it."

"How soon?"

"How soon for the game? Today's Wednesday. How about Friday?"

"You're on."

CHAPTER 38

Those two words came out involuntarily, from the voice of Julian's subconscious. He just blurted them out and the decision was made. He heard himself saying it, as if from a distance, though his conviction was firm enough, urged on by his own sense of justice, to do unto them tit for tat, meet them spite for spite, answer them vengeance for vengeance.

A duel to the finish. There was a certain beauty in the arrangement, Julian had to admit. If ever he was going to live up to his Biblical heroes, namely, David, this was the time. David and Goliath.

Finally, Julian's chance to match David, if by a much smaller measure, but still, there'd be a kinship with his hero of heroes, win or lose. There was something wonderfully Biblical about the whole thing, so in a very real sense Julian began approaching his destiny with the heartbeat of exhilaration. To a degree. But this, after all, was something he'd always dreamed about, the chance to prove himself against a Biblical test—and this was a Biblical test nonpareil, apt for the pages of *Samuel* and *Kings*.

More likely, though, it wasn't David he'd he playing but rather Isaac.

Plainly then, this was the flip side of the blessing from Sinai. It came with a price, a demand for sacrifice.

He had the rest of Wednesday, all of Thursday and part of Friday to think things through and wasn't sure whether to inform Monica or not; Monica and what about Debra, and Slim, and the friends he had all over Margate and AC and elsewhere, plus relatives here and abroad, a sister in Montreal with whom he'd been out of touch for years for no particular reason except that that's the way it goes, and another sister in Cincinnati that he spoke to occasionally, though he loved them both, an uncle in England, two aunts in Minnesota, and he loved them all, everybody.

Suddenly he loved everybody, as if he'd never be seeing them again. Which would be the case if he sevened-out to spare Sasha. But he still wasn't sure how he'd be handling that; he was only sure he'd come up with something. He'd listen, and be told. *But what is this I am doing,* he asked himself, *putting my house in order? If so, time to pay off all the bills, get the shirts out of the cleaners and ask for forgiveness from mine enemies.*

Well, bullshit to all that. Nobody's going anywhere, not just yet.

Still Wednesday, alone in the house, listening to Brahms, he wondered, almost mirthfully, just how they were going to execute him, if it came to that; probably snatch him one day on the way to the bakery. What day? Could be the next day, next week, a month, a year. The waiting itself would be murder. Suppose he lost and *still* refused to give up his life—went to the cops? Well, obviously Stavros was counting on the honor code among gamblers, specifically Julian's honor, and then, too, tell the cops what? The cops would say, What proof?

And even if they went so far as to question Stavros, he'd only laugh.

Then, what manner of execution? By gun, by knife, by strangulation, by hanging, by drowning? He didn't want to think about that, but it couldn't be helped. He forgot to ask. Oh, but he did ask, Stavros saying it was none of his business. Right. As if he, Julian, were an innocent bystander in all this.

The phone rang just when Brahms was getting especially good, so he let it ring and it was Karen Davies on the machine imploring him to call her back.

He hadn't been too attentive to her, ignoring past phone messages—he didn't know why exactly, or maybe he did—but this time he ran to catch her before she hung up.

She was too hip to complain, she was marquee after all, and she called only to say that the filming in Vegas was coming along fine, except that Matt Cain blew up after 16 takes of that crucial scene where he's supposed to lose it all, all his money, the reason for the title, *Scared Money*.

"Clive thought he should be more expressive," she said. "Show more emotion. Matt said no, no doubt on account of your influence, Julian. Anyway, Matt thought his character shouldn't be showing any emotion *at all*. What do you think?"

"I think Matt's right."

"Really."

"Absolutely. That's the sign of a real gambler, as opposed to a greenie."

"Just be stoic about it, right?"

"Clive wants him to remonstrate?"

"Yes."

"I'm surprised."

"Why?"

"Because I thought we agreed that the character was to be the consummate pro, something special."

Like a Just Man, Julian was thinking. But there they go again, seeking his advice, then doing just the opposite.

Figured.

"But the man's playing for everything he's got," she said. "He's sacrificing..."

"All the more reason to be stoic."

"I'll pass the word along to Clive."

"Better not. He's the director."

"But he respects your opinion."

"As you wish."

"Julian?"

"Yes."

"Wish you were here."

"Likewise," he lied.

"I'm curious to know," she chuckled, "you know, about my silly fortune-telling. I was wrong, wasn't I?"

"Everything's fine."

"Good. You know I was worried that maybe I'd put a bug in your head."

"I'm okay."

"It's just that I can't help what I foresee."

"Nothing happened."

"I must be losing my touch," she laughed. "Good thing, too. You're not mad at me, are you?"

"For that?"

"For saying there's a boogieman waiting for you when you get back home. I should have kept my mouth shut."

"Don't worry about it, Karen, I took it all in fun."

"So you think Matt's doing the right thing?"

"Yes."

"He thinks you're the greatest, by the way."

"I'm looking forward to seeing the picture."

"It ought to be in the can in about another couple of months. I think Clive's shooting for a summer release."

"Can't wait."

"Will I be seeing you before then?"

"You never know."

"Love and kisses."

The rest of Wednesday wasn't so bad, but Thursday was a long day, until Monica dropped in late evening. She arrived bearing French bread, his favorite delicacy; nothing beat plain old bread and butter if the bread was French.

She had expected a minor display of appreciation, not the works! Still by the door and still clutching the shopping bag, she was being ripped out of her clothes, carried to the bedroom, all practically in one motion, thrown to the bed, where she was fucked senseless.

"Wow," she said quite a while later. "What have you been smoking? But don't let me stop you."

Later still, down on the beach, she asked how the meeting went with Stavros. He said, "Fine, just fine. No surprises."

"You're sure."

He said sure he was sure. Just as expected, the man was challenging him to a one-on-one. If he, Julian, wins, he gets to come back for more, any time. If he loses, no harm done, except that he loses his privileges.

"Which means you won't be able to play anywhere."

"I guess," he said.

"Nothing more," she said, suspiciously.

"Isn't that bad enough?"

"Yes, that's why I'm wondering why you're not taking it too hard."

"Because I'm gonna win."

Still suspicious—"Awfully generous of Stavros to be extending himself like this to you, when all the others..."

"What a guy."

"You're joking but I'm serious. This isn't the Stavros that I've heard about."

"You never know about people."

"Why do I sense that you're not telling me the whole story?"

He walked to the water's edge and pretended not to hear her. He thought if anybody should know it was... who? The rights belonged to Monica. Debra was yesterday, Monica is today.

"All right," he said. "If I win, I get a million bucks."

"You're joking," she gulped.

He faked a deep voice. "Stavros doesn't joke."

"That's if you win."

"Oh, sure. If I lose, I'm dead."

He looked at her and laughed, but she didn't laugh back, because she was a smart lady.

She knew it had to be true. She worked with these people, the casinos' top echelon. Among them there was the good, the bad, and the ugly, and Stavros was the ugly. Practically the only one. The rest were mainly suits. Stavros was a holdover from the wicked days of gangsters, when the mob ruled. Gambling had become a business, like IBM. Only now and then there was still the pungency of the past.

But now it all made sense to her, why Stavros, of all people, was being so *generous*.

"Something tells me you're going ahead with this."

"I am."

She asked him if he knew whom he was dealing with, and he said, yes, he did.

"I've never heard of such a thing."

"That's the charm," he said, unaware that he was quoting Stavros himself. But aware that perhaps he'd made a mistake by telling her. He'd hoped she'd take it like a man. Nowadays they were supposed to be men, weren't they? Obviously they still had a ways to go, fortunately.

"Well..."

"I really don't think we should discuss this anymore."

"I was going to say if that's what it takes to turn you into Rudolph Valentino..."

"That's my girl," he said, finally holding her, and hearing her laughing in his arms, her head snuggled deep in the cleft of his shoulder, until she pulled back and he found that she'd been bawling.

Some things, he was thinking, *never change.*

CHAPTER 39

Friday he rose up early and took a long hot shower, and then a bath, and he tarried in the bathroom to cleanse himself, like a high priest, from all imperfections before entering the tabernacle.

He dressed himself in whites—white shirt, white pants, even white shoes, the white bucks he'd saved from his youth. He combed his hair several times, not sure whether to go sideways or up back. He'd always had crazy hair, sometimes waking straight, sometimes all curled up, sometimes tending upward, sometimes tending sideways. Like most people, he did not like the hair on his head, though who was he to complain? He had hair, after all. Today he settled on sideways, but was not completely satisfied with his appearance as he checked himself over and over again in the mirror. He wanted to be perfect for this day, this day of days, this Biblical day. He imagined himself being observed and chronicled from on high, being measured and judged, his actions to be inscribed in some holy writ, like his fathers before him, who'd been tested repeatedly.

Which is, he reflected, what life is all about, each day another test, usually small ones, but then once in a while, and sometimes but once in a lifetime, the BIG one... Take thee now thy son, thine only son...

Not that he was anything in that league, but it was all right to pretend, it was *necessary* to pretend, to aspire, or else what was there to compensate for the mundane reality of existence?

He spent most of the day alone with Beethoven, as opposed to Brahms, since this preparation called for sublimity, and he had no trouble drifting with the music, drifting *into* the music until he was one with the music and Beethoven, soaring high beyond the clouds and into the heavens.

He was more than relaxed. He was sedated by the knowledge of what he must do. There was no more question about it, about whom he was to play for, himself or Sasha Spivak. The answer was always straight before him. If this was to really be a test, then so he would be tested, against the moral standards established by the Akeda, the Binding of Isaac.

He was not perturbed, vexed, nor troubled by his decision, since his code of honor prescribed but one choice—to lose and save the girl! So there was nothing to fret about, nothing to second-guess, nothing to fear; it was written. It was already written.

The phone rang all day and the messages were piling up but he heard nothing, not even Monica's prayers and best wishes, not even Debra's inquiring about a rumor she had heard, the grapevine telling her of something momentous in his life; same as with Slim, who phoned to ask if it was true, word having spread all the way back to Vegas.

He did not even respond to Denise, who said she had something very important to tell him—about another rumor, concerning Sasha Spivak, so would he please call her back immediately.

But he didn't.

She called him five times, leaving five messages, saying it was urgent, very urgent, and she even drove over to his home in Margate, just as he had pulled out and driven off, missing him by a matter of seconds.

In one of her messages she had come out with it, about the rumor that Sasha Spivak was dead. So there was no longer any reason for him to die for her. (She, too, had gotten wind of the worst-kept secret in the world, about Julian's head-to-head for his own future, while unaware of the full jeopardy.) Just a rumor, she said, and Dewey doesn't believe it, not 100 percent, thinking it may be a trick—but if true, Denise went on, play for *yourself.*

None of which Julian heard, over the Beethoven.

CHAPTER 40

He got to the Versailles quarter to eight, 15 minutes before game time, and was met in the lobby by a large guy named Frank Busher who identified himself as an associate of Roy Stavros and said there'd been a change of plans. The game wouldn't be held here at the Versailles.

"Why not?" said Julian.

"Can't find an open table."

Which was a lie, the truth being that Booker smelled a rat and wouldn't permit Stavros to raise *any* game to a million-dollar limit, which was in and of itself suspicious, too hot to handle. (Booker beginning to regret the day he had let Stavros in the door. Never figured the guy to be such a heavy. Knew the guy was strong-arm, but, being a former cop, trusting him to show reserve now and then.) Leaving Stavros no option but to steer his prey to the juice joint on Morris Avenue, down from the Trop. A better deal all around for Stavros, except that now the million bucks would have to come from elsewhere, and Stavros knew just where; "certain people," he called them. Certain people who hated it when you called them *mob*.

Stavros had done certain favors for these certain people, and he figured they owed him. The million bucks was good anyway. Not a chance the kid could throw 20 times without a 7—especially with loaded dice. Not that Stavros had an easy time making his case to a man simply known as Hector, who kept asking if the kid was worth the risk, Stavros insisting that he was, yes he was, and anyway, there was no risk, not really. Hector grudgingly said okay, which came with a look that said there's always a risk. Stavros got the message.

Not so, Julian. Not so fast.

"You're taking me where?" he asked Frank Busher, who had begun to lead the way toward his car, parked right in front.

"There's a joint on Morris. Everybody goes there, y'know, it's for insiders," now grabbing Julian by the arm.

"Let go, please."

"You gonna hurt me?" Frank laughed, and stopped laughing when Julian took him by a police hold and straightened him up against a wall and held him there with the simple maneuver of applied pressure against the Adam's apple, the guy flailing and fighting for breath and then, after coughing and retching, saying, "Okay, okay, all right. Now what?"

"Now we go," Julian said, aware of a set-up, but no difference.

Either way, it was still craps, and anyway, he was playing to lose.

The place was in back of Sammy's Candy Shop and to Julian it was a world revealed. He'd never heard of the joint, one reason being that it had no name. It was just there, the flip side of all the Boardwalk action. The boys that played here were the boys who couldn't get into the legit joints because they had police records. They were underworld.

So they discovered their own America.

But it had neither the feel nor the smell of a steer joint. No, it was all done to conform to the best any legit casino had to offer. Blue carpet as thick as Montana snow. Chandeliers aglow end to end, from room to room; one room for blackjack, another for roulette, another for baccarat, and finally, way in the back, craps.

Here there were rich drapes covering all the windows, which was more than could be said for the women, who were walking around half-naked, offering drinks or standing side by side with the boys along the rails—but practically all of them stunning to behold.

One thing about these guys, Julian reflected, they know women.

The crew was ready and in-station when Julian stepped up. The pit boss looked familiar to Julian, very familiar. Now he remembered—and if it wasn't Louis Freed, from the Versailles, though no longer, after he'd been caught skimming. Freed had always been a thorn. A wise-ass and a confrontational sonofabitch, always with a smirk. Pit boss? More like a pit *bull*.

Julian took second base and waited. Eight-thirty sharp Roy Stavros entered, alone and grim and businesslike. Stavros placed himself behind the boxman and alongside Freed—Julian and Stavros making fleeting eye contact the same moment that the stickman withdrew five dice from the box and caned them over to Julian, who rolled them against the felt, and chose two, feeling their weight in his palm, and knowing instantly that they were rigged, that they were loaded, that they were balonies, guaranteed for 7s.

There could be no doubt. Julian's palm was sensitive to the slightest shift in weight. He wasn't a corker, the prince of dice for nothing. He gave Stavros a hard stare, and then a soft, wicked smile, Stavros blanching and shifting nervously from leg to leg.

"Anything wrong?" he asked.

"These are fine," Julian said.

For Julian's purposes, they were perfect. He had already appealed to the 13th gate of prayer, to lose, he had made love within the past 48 hours, to lose, never imagining that it would all be unneccesary. The fix was in.

Ready to shoot, Julian gazed up at Stavros with a twinkle in his eye: "Ten, right?"

Stavros, at the threshold of going bonkers: "Twenty, Mr. Rothschild," addressing him formally, to fit the occasion. "The game is for 20 tosses. Should you throw a 7 before then, you lose. Should you succeed..."

"My mistake," Julian smiled coolly.

"We agreed," Stavros persisted.

"Yes, we did. No need to get into an uproar."

"Nobody's getting in an uproar," said Freed, mocking. "We're just here to see what you got."

"Well, fuck you, too," said Julian.

"No, fuck you," said Freed.

"Enough," said Stavros. "This is no back alley game."

Freed kept on smiling and glaring at Julian, enjoying the side action.

Julian paused to gather himself. He felt good. Too good.

So good that it was all wrong, dead wrong, dead wrong for Sasha, the party he was playing for, since he felt an attack coming on, the seizure that flashed through his body like a bolt of lightning and announced the arrival of the Presence—which Julian had not called for.

Wait a minute, he thought as he felt his body stiffen to a pillar of salt, his arms and legs going numb, the spasm beginning its climb up his back, to his shoulders, up to and around his neck, until he could hardly breathe—*I did not ask for this! I do not want this. Thank you, very much. But I am playing to lose, remember? I want those 7s!* he thought as he slowly began to recover and regain the use of his limbs.

Only this, he reflected with a glint of mischief—can even God beat a pair of loaded dice?

"Let's see how good you are," said Freed, keeping up his tactics. Freed, like Stavros, like any good casino operator, took it personal, as if it were his money. It once was. He used to own a joint in Vegas and he used to fire entire crews on the spot when they ran into a streak of bad luck.

"Oh, I'm good," cracked Julian, almost wanting to win just to show this guy—but knowing that he couldn't.

He couldn't and he shouldn't.

"Yeah, but this is for blood."

He knows? Sounded like he did. No difference.

The room went still as Julian swiftly let go and it came up 10, easy.

"That's one," said the stickman, Stavros blinking and rocking back as if the dice had exploded in his ears.

Next roll came up 5.

"That's two," said the stickman, Stavros' eyes going wide in disbelief.

The 5 was followed by a 4, then a 6, then a 12 boxcars, then a yo 11, then a 10 again, then 3 craps, a 9, a 5 again, and where the hell are the 7s? Julian asked himself. I thought these dice were rigged.

Stavros, in the throes of alarm, asked himself the same question.

Not only that, but Julian, being the peerless mechanic that he was, was doing everything right, to lose, not taking any chances; he had lock-gripped the dice as artfully as only he could and spun them up into helicopters, cheating, yes, but to save a life. This was one of those times when crookedness was in the right. The spinner worked for him 90 times out of a hundred when he went after a specific number; this time the 7, 6-1, which wasn't happening for some reason, a reason Julian did not want to consider; namely, the possibility that whatever supernatural forces were at work were sparing him and dooming Sasha.

Was it really true then that all along he had not been merely good but lucky, and not just lucky but blessed? All that was true? The spasms were real? Sinai was real? You mean there really is a God, whose countenance shines down upon him? He'd had his doubts, being a man not totally bereft of skepticism. He used to wonder if it was all true or just imaginary, a whim of his romantic Sinai-induced fantasies.

He had always been a believer before, with just a hint of suspicion. Now, though...

Another reason for the spinner's failure was this: The boxman called "no roll" each time he suspected the gimmick. That Julian was trying to employ the good old spinner was no secret to Stavros, nor to the crew—but so what?

The dice were fixed.

Or so Stavros had thought—Stavros beginning to sweat when Julian was still in the game with ten tosses to go. When he should have been done already, if the dice were true, truly false, that is. What the fuck is going on? The man ought to be dead by now.

That thought was clearly not on Julian's mind—the thought of dying, of being executed, a notion entirely too chilling and too ridiculous to entertain. His approach had been to notch it up as just another game, never mind the consequences, that his life was on the line.

On Julian's 11th roll the first die came up 6, the second die showed 1, making 7, finally, finally for Julian, finally for Stavros, finally for Sasha Spivak, and, just as Stavros was about to cheer and do a dance, it rolled over a second time and tipped up to a 2.

"Eighter from Decatur," said the stickman as the breath went out of the room.

We had him, thought Stavros. *We had him! How the hell did that die tip over like that, like it had a mind of its own, as if it were alive, responding to a pull of gravity not of this world?* I'll be damned if I believe this, this crap about the supernatural. No such thing. The House—WE ARE GOD. We're the supernatural. We set the rules. We know the odds, and the odds are supposed to be 7 *at least* once out of every six throws, and once out of every *three* rolls when the dice are loaded as these are.

I'll be damned if I believe there's a God up there shooting for this shark, this spin artist. If I start believing that, he was thinking, *everything's* out the window, everything I've trusted in, namely the percentages. The percentages—that's god! In The Percentages We Trust. "Let's take a break," he suggested.

"Why?" Julian wanted to know.

"Ten minutes," said Stavros.

"Not interested," said Julian.

"My dice, my game, my rules," said Stavros.

Dry-mouthed and practically staggering from the intensity of life-and-death combat, Julian decided that if he ever needed a drink, now was the time. So he wandered over to the Chelsea Pub nearby, right where Denise stopped him.

"What are you doing here?" he asked.

"I just hope I'm not too late," she said frantically.

"For what?"

"To tell you the news. Sasha Spivak is dead."

"That's impossible. I haven't even..."

"You had nothing to do with it, Julian. She took her own life."

She was 16, Denise explained to a horrified Julian, but a very old 16, her life vexed from misery upon misery, with no end in sight. Apparently she saw only the past, no future, so she did herself in, took the early train. Who could blame her, after all she'd been through, after all she'd seen, after all that had been done to her from continent to continent?

"This means..."

"This means that you're too late to play for her safety. It's *your* safety you have to worry about now."

"What a development."

"I just hope I'm not too late. Am I?"

"We're only halfway through."

"You mean it's started?"

"So far, so good. Does Dewey know this?"

"Yes, but he wouldn't tell you. He's still expecting his half a million, now for himself."

"Well, I did promise."

"Makes no difference now, does it—except that you have to win."

"Why do I have to win?"

"To save your skin."

"Just curious, but how do you know this?"

"Oh, come on, word gets around."

"I thought it was all a big secret."

"In this business?"

"My ten minutes are up. Got to get back."

"Please..."

"I will."

I will what, he thought as he turned back. I will play to win. That's good. Bad for Sasha, good for me. So this is what it's come to—mortality, for some earlier than later, and what a waste, what a damned waste about her, that young girl, she never had a chance, and as for me, my mortality? Nine, nine tosses, nine tosses to go. Then this: If the word's really gotten around, even Hayden Booker must know, and if he knows, won't he stop it if somehow I manage to seven-out? No, he'd never believe it, that this kind of a duel was in the works, a dice duel to the death, and even if he did, even if he confronted Stavros, Stavros would deny and probably put off my execution until it was convenient, made to look like a thousand other accidents. Accidents happen.

Almost as bad, though, to Julian's way of reasoning, was to live your days knowing that another man held the marker to your life, so that the execution itself might not even be necessary; there'd be terror enough in having to constantly look over your shoulder, assuming every stranger to be an assassin. Maybe that was Stavros' game all along; gotcha either way, coming and going, dead or alive.

But aren't I the lucky one? Julian reflected without bitterness. All our days are numbered, but today mine are reckoned by nine more flings of the dice. That's something. That's an edge in itself, to know that to some extent you are the master of your own destiny, if your luck holds. There's the rub.

There's the rub, all right. Now wouldn't that be perverse, he was thinking, if I should lose now that I must win? If I should seven-out now that I shouldn't, now that I mustn't? If I'd been set-up from above by a power with a *sense of humor?* Not out of the question, not at all, since so much of life is a joke, Sasha Spivak's, for one.

If her life meant nothing, why should mine mean more? Who am I that He should be mindful of me, and even if He is, surely it's not to answer my dreams but rather, to fulfill His own schemes, whatever they may be. Mortality, that's the lesson He may choose to teach, even to the Prince of Dice. The dice, after all, are in His hands.

You throw them, yes, you throw them, but He decides, He separates the light from the darkness, the heavens from the earth, the earth from the seas—the 11s from the 7s.

So, with mortality on his mind, his *smallness* evident to him against the firmament, it was a much-humbled Julian Rothschild who approached the craps table behind Sammy's Candy Shop for the second and final round of the head-to-head, every man at his station, all eyes expectantly on their quarry, Stavros significantly peering at him with a mixture of contempt and deference.

"Nine to go," said the stickman, Freed, the pit boss, back to his smirk but bouncing anxiously on his toes.

"Ready?" Freed said as Julian weighed out two new dice, still loaded. For 7s.

"Ready," said Julian, cupping them, arranging them between his fingers, this time for snake eyes, as far away as possible from any 7; never mind the fix, he could overcome the fix with his skill, his genius, and then...

"Hold it," said Freed. "What's that you're doing?"

"What?"

"No more spinners," said Stavros. "Forget the english. We're on to it, okay?"

Must have been a little confab during the recess.

"Oh," said Julian, faking innocence. "In that case, how about a glass of water."

To test the dice.

"You had your break," said Freed.

"Not for me," Julian chuckled. "I'm not thirsty. But the dice sure need a drink."

Stavros' face went ashen. "You accusing *us* of a gimmick?"

"I sure as hell am. I wasn't born yesterday."

Stavros turned to Freed in a theatrical show of exasperation. "You hear that? Can you believe this guy?"

"You welching out on us?" said Freed.

Julian, still smiling—"Just asking for a glass of water. Why's that a problem?"

"Tell you what," Stavros jumped in. "How's about we give you a fresh pair?"

"They're all the same," Julian said. "Aren't they?"

"Try these," said Stavros.

"No good," said Julian, sensing their false weight in his fist. "Get me a pair from that other table."

Another pair was brought over from another table—and these were clean.

"Now do we play?" said Freed, sarcastic, impatient.

"Now we play," said Julian—and he rolled. No spinner, but hard, so that they bounced up high and came back down in a twisting whirlwind. "Three craps," said the stickman. "Eight to go."

Three craps, thought Julian. *I was shooting for* two *craps.* He knew that if he could get those aces, that 1-1, those snake eyes, it would mean he was on his game even without the spinner. Aces would be the sign.

Next roll, the seventh to go, came up 4, the hardway, followed by a 9, then an easy 6, after that an 11, then another hard 4, and another 9, and finally—one shot to go.

One shot to determine whose life was it, anyway—his or Stavros'.

"This is it," said Freed, plainly stricken, as was Stavros, by Julian's virtuosity, his contempt for the odds, even without his spinner; spinner or no spinner, this is some guy. He *is* an artist! Beautiful to behold, yes, beautiful.

Stavros, stunned to his toes, was becoming a believer, almost, in whatever the hell it was out there that was EVEN BIGGER THAN THE HOUSE. He wasn't ready to believe in the supernatural just yet, but something was out there, something even more awesome than the percentages!

Maybe. Maybe not.

But the next toss would tell all. One last, final shot for everything. The works. Make him mine, Stavros prayed, but still worshipping his god, his only god, the Almighty Percentages, which had always been true, since the beginning of time—the god praised by the Trumps, the Wynns, the Hiltons, the Harrahs, the Ballys, the Caesars, the Trops, the Luxors, the Showboats, the Golden Nuggets, the Excaliburs... praised be the Percentages, which hath showered us with your bounty from generation to generation.

Never mind the God of Moses and Jesus, and this Julian Rothschild. Their God is faith. Our god is *fact!* That's what this is all about. Faith over fact. Casinos were *built,* sustained

and nourished by the power of that god, the god of Percentages.

He has never let us down, thought Stavros.

Until now. For Julian had rolled aces.

CHAPTER 41

Stavros had been correct. In the days and weeks that followed Julian's triumph, doors opened for him again and he was welcomed into casino after casino, except that Stavros would never know the full extent of it, as it seems he had come up a million short. The man named Hector—the same Hector who was often referred to in the press by the term *mob boss,* the man who had bankrolled Stavros and had warned Stavros about the risk—this Hector was none too pleased to be left holding the bag.

On a cool, brisk Sunday evening, the sun just going down and the ocean nice and calm, Roy Stavros left the Hard Rock Cafe at the Taj Mahal where he'd had his favorite sirloin, walked to the Claridge to share a cozy drink with some buddies upstairs in that cozy bar, then went downstairs to shoot some craps—since he wasn't allowed to do it in his own casino, the Versailles—and was feeling none too good, despite some winnings because he knew he still had a big debt to pay.

He'd been given time, Hector was being reasonable, and the time was up, but tomorrow, Monday, he had another meeting with Hector, to come up with another plan, a delay, in fact.

He left the Claridge and, strolling up to the Boardwalk, two men approached him and asked him if he'd like a ride.

One of the men kept poking something in his ribs.

Three days later, his body washed up in Lake Calico.

CHAPTER 42

As for Julian, his legend spread. All that was to the good, except that Julian was having none of it, preferring to spend his celebrity in isolation, turning his attention inward, partly in mourning, for Slim Sam Belmont died nine days after Julian's big win.

So Julian grieved, saddened by the loss of his mentor, the man who had given him the skill and taught him the conduct of a champion. Sinai had been the inspiration, Slim Sam had been the means, and with that life extinguished, the spark departed from Julian as well. He was left with an emptiness, a restlessness, an aimlessness, a loathing for the schemes devised by men, to which he'd been a partner, unwittingly perhaps, but he had been a player, even in the big game, the game that had stamped him, defined him but also left him with a sense of futility. He had been to the top, so where does a man go after he's reached the summit?

Now that he had played for his life, would he ever get that old rush playing for mere *money?* Unlikely. But that was not entirely the reason behind his reclusiveness. There was also the disquietude that he had trifled with fate, call it God, call it fate, call it the supernatural, either way, he had trifled, so there had to be a tax. You do not win something so big as your life without paying the devil. You do not throw 20 times successfully, partly with *loaded* dice, dice loaded against you, without depleting your merits. You had to have used up a good part of your blessing.

Proof of which happened the very night Julian returned home from his conquest at the big game. Just as a test, he took his dice, the pair he used at home for practice, and tossed them, tossed them with the spinner, tossed them without the spinner, and they kept coming up 7s as they would for an *ordinary* shooter—number, number, 7; again, number, number, 7. Seldom could he go beyond two throws without a 7 rearing its ugly face. Those 7s that never showed up (thankfully) for the big game now came in torrents.

Simply, the dice had turned on him. The percentages were happening after all, with a vengeance, and this terrified Julian, and kept him secluded because life itself, he feared, had turned on him.

That Stavros himself had paid a tax for trifling did not comfort Julian. He finished up exactly as he had tried to finish up Julian. Perfect vengeance, poetic justice, but it was no gain for Julian. There was nothing in it for him and he was not one to wallow in bitterness.

Fear was another story, fear that no matter what he attempted in life, inside or outside craps, he'd come up a loser for all the merits he'd used up, for all the nasty 7s that still had to be played out—and the 7s kept on coming. He tossed those dice day after day and those 7s kept on showing up, maybe with less frequency now, but enough to persuade Julian that he had lost it—lost his touch, his power, his *everything*.

For certain—certain to Julian—something demonic was at work. He'd been handed over.

He kept tossing them, hoping to one day balance the percentages, regain the equilibrium, achieve the norm, meaning his norm, the norm of a champion; on that day, perhaps, he'd feel safe again, safe to venture out, maybe even play again.

Only Monica understood his terror. That he was rich with half a million dollars, the other half bound for Dewey—and good riddance to Dewey when that day would come—was no tonic to Julian, and Monica understood that as well.

There'd be no reconciliation with Debra. That she also knew, as Julian, motivated by his quest to regain a semblance of purity, the purity he'd always sought, had made the break complete by assuring Debra that her future remained with Donald Oaks, and Donald Oaks alone (Debra having begun to wage a campaign of pursuit to win back Julian, for one reason or another). So she'd made her choice, and that's what we live with—our choices. That had been Julian's farewell address to her, though it did break his heart, not for the loss of Debra, but for the loss of his youth, of which she'd been so much a part.

Monica kept urging him to pick himself up and get out of the house. She urged him to try the casinos, assuming that once he got back in action everything would return to normal. He finally hearkened to her and made the Taj his first stop and they remembered him and greeted him with reverential nods and whispers, the main man was back, but he surprised them by starting, and finishing, at a $10 table, where he sevened-out almost immediately. Same as at Bally's, the Claridge, Trump Plaza, the Trop, the Hilton—different day, different place, same shit, same 7.

Back in Margate he checked his den for the *siddur,* the *siddur* that contained the holy Sinai parchment. No *siddur,* no parchment. In fact, an entire bookcase was missing. Baffled and stricken, he asked Monica about it and she reminded him that weeks ago he had asked her to donate 100 books to the Margate library.

So that's what she did.

"Including the Hebrew book?" he said.

"Whatever was there," she said. "Did I do something wrong?"

He was ready to tell her, tell her, rage in his heart, that she had given away the most important thing in his life, the thing that made him tick, but the fury left him when he realized that firstly it was not her fault, and secondly, maybe it was time for somebody else, someone else to have it, and isn't that what charity is all about, the highest form of it, to give what you value most—and wasn't it odd that this particular act of benevolence had not come from him, was none of his doing? Something else made it happen.

"You did fine," he assured Monica, who had turned ashen from fright.

"You're sure?"

"I'm sure," he said, holding her.

"Maybe we can still get it back, whatever it was..."

No, he said, there was no getting it back.

That's for sure, he thought. *No getting it back.* He was on his own. Pretty much the way it was with everybody. Unlike merchandise, life does not come with a written money-back guarantee from the maker. No, we have our moment, and then we wear and tear and use it all up.

Julian had become reconciled, to everything, practically, except Dewey. Julian had his money but kept postponing payday, Dewey livid with threats, the usual, and Julian not caring all that much, sending both Fats and Skinny, Skinny and Fats— sending them both away emptyhanded time and again. They had tried to work him over but saw soon enough that he had moves of his own.

Then Dewey showed up, demanding his money. Julian took him outside to the beach, near the water's edge, and reminded

him that if money was his due, so was this, for Sasha. For
Sasha and all the rest of them; this then, was also payment,
and he took the man by the hair and dragged him out into the
deep and dunked him up and in, up and in, now keeping him
down in the water, lifting him up again, gasping, down and
up, gasping, sobbing to be saved from drowning, pleading for
his life, the way Sasha Spivak had once pleaded for hers.

Convinced that the man had had enough, only then did Julian
make out a check, sending him off soaked and wobbly, but
still Dewey, same Dewey muttering vengeance. Nothing was
changed. Julian knew that the man would go on and if it wasn't
Dewey, it would be someone else. They could be stopped for
a while, but they couldn't be beat. A Moses and a Jesus, they
come along once every two to five thousand years. Pharaohs
and Hitlers are with us every minute, every generation. What
the hell!

"Good," said Monica when she saw how he had paid off
Dewey.

But Monica was alarmed by what she noted as Julian's growing sense of defeat. He seemed to have given up, on himself
and on everybody else. He kept tossing those dice and they
still kept turning up 7 all too frequently. He kept mumbling
that the devil had gotten into them, and he sometimes woke up
screaming in the night.

Monica held him and comforted him. She was his only refuge. She cooked for him, did the laundry, made the beds,
stayed over night after night, watching him, unkempt, unshaven, tossing the dice into infinity. Hoping, once again, to
be touched by grace.

He would prevail, of that she was sure. One day the 7s
would be gone, and he'd be back, because he was Julian
Rothschild, prince, Prince of Dice, and no fair-minded God
would deprive a prince of his kingdom forever.